Fisher of Souls

Fisher of Souls

Published by The Conrad Press in the United Kingdom 2020

Tel: +44(0)1227 472 874
www.theconradpress.com
info@theconradpress.com

ISBN 978-1-913567-29-3

Typesetting and Cover Design by:
Charlotte Mouncey, www.bookstyle.co.uk

The Conrad Press logo was designed by Maria Priestley.

Printed and bound in Great Britain by Clays Ltd, Elcograf S.p.A.

Fisher of Souls

Chris Cantor

Author's note

Torminster Hospital, its patients and staff are entirely fictional, but the Plymouth region used to have a hospital dating from Victorian times situated on the south west side of Dartmoor, near where Torminster is set. I worked for a year in psychiatric units in and around Exeter, to the south east of Dartmoor, including at Exminster Hospital, which is briefly mentioned and inspired some of my descriptions of 'bricks and mortar,' but not its inhabitants—neither patients nor staff.

PART I

... the pursuit of demonology empowers Satan, delivering the terror he so desires. I call on you to exercise moderation, to practice the loving acceptance preached by our Lord and to love thine enemy, for he is still your neighbour.

Abbot Stephen, 1357 AD

1

Out of darkness (1347 AD)

Friends, it is with pleasure that I start my reading from 'A Medieval History of Torminster Abbey.' My story relies primarily on the meticulous journal keeping of Brother Frederick. His original, written in Latin, was concise and employed a devoutly conservative viewpoint. Forgive me if in my translation I have used artistic licence to make the story more intelligible and engaging. Chapter one...

Priests ought to know what to say when Death calls. Stephen sat at his father's bedside, bewildered, staring at the floor, wondering what to say. His father, once so strong, now lay withered, with sunken cheeks, yellow eyes and flaking skin as his sickness consumed him. He awaited the end that comes for us all in one form or another.

Stephen's father, Isiah Wylinton, gazed up at the turf roof above his bed. 'Your mother needs you,' he said, coughing, choking and becoming red in the face. Feeling duty bound Stephen stood up looking around as if there was something useful he might do to assist, but recalling his father's resentment of help he sat down again and waited for his coughing to subside. He asked himself where had his compassion flown? After all, he had not seen his father in many years.

His father's breath smelt foul and his bedclothes were filthy, though their odours were masked by those of the animals beyond the wall, tethered in the lower end of the longhouse, through which the sound of the old carthorse defecating resonated.

'I haven't long. Then she'll be alone.' His father paused to take a few more breaths. 'You must come home, care for her; manage the farm. The Lord will understand.' Stephen had been his parents' only child and his mother needed care, so to who else could his father turn?

His home lay near the remote hamlet of Torminster on the south west aspect of Dartmoor. The farm stretched for many miles and provided for grazing cattle, sheep, pigs, turkeys and chickens, though a few vegetable crops managed to survive the severe weather of the moor. Water dripped from the neglected reed roof and trickled down the granite walls to the floor's rushes. Stephen, looking up, noted a large expanse of the roof needed attention. His father's sleeping quarters were shielded from the rest of the house by newly installed wooden screens. The house appeared smaller than Stephen remembered it, yet it was much larger than his meagre cell at St Madern's Charterhouse, a Carthusian monastery, across the border in Cornwall.

His father's room smelt of sickness, it was smoky and lacked air, despite the strong autumn westerly winds. Struggling to find a reply to his father, Stephen put his hands on his knees as if he were about to leave. He wanted to say something but his words seemed to have taken flight and he looked to the doorway as if to escape.

Stephen had devoted his life to the monastic pursuit of virtue and spiritual perfection in the service of God; but a dutiful son does not desert a loving mother in her time of need. He would do his best to help her, but he could not abandon his spiritual quest after so many years. 'I will see mother is well cared for, Father.' His words sounded hollow, deceitful even, but it was not worth openly disagreeing, it never had been, only ever enraging his father, so it was better to keep quiet.

'It's time you came home,' his father repeated. A spasm of pain crossed his face. 'Now leave me, I must rest.'

Stephen stood up, relieved to have been dismissed. He found his mother outside washing clothing in the water trough. Chickens scurried out of his way as he walked over to her and kissed her hair that blew in the wind. It smelled of smoke and cooking—of home. Her eyes were moist; she smiled uneasily then looked away.

'How long have you known?' Stephen asked his mother, knowing she had always done her utmost to protect him.

Drying her hands on her apron, she said, 'Your father became too weak to continue working the farm six months back.' She hesitated, as if to speak of Death commanded its appearance. 'Dr Englefield from Exeter said there's a large growth in his belly. Nothing can be done save prayer.' Tears started flowing down her cheeks. How helpless she looked.

Over the following days Stephen spent more time at his father's bedside, but his father said little, having said what was needed. All these years and still as remote. All those beatings, yet Stephen never shed a tear, better not to feel when feelings were unwelcome. Small of stature, Stephen had taken his punishments as if immune to them. The only time he cried was the day his father struck him on his left shoulder. It wasn't just the pain; it was the realization he could not move his arm. He was afraid, not knowing what was wrong. Instead of striking him again his father said with contempt, 'Go to your mother!' His arm had never been the same—to the present day. It surprised him that he now felt so little for his father. Was he, the son, as cold as the father?

His father's death would present a host of problems, but otherwise it appeared devoid of meaning. As his father's communication focused on practicalities and persuasion, so Stephen's thoughts responded likewise. Should he abandon his mother only to return to his self-made disillusionment? While he still believed in his life's mission, he was losing his way at St Madern's. How he wished his week's leave of absence could be a year, but he could never abandon God.

Near the end of the week he sat alongside his father listening to his snoring, intermittently interrupted by gasps for air. Stephen acknowledged Death's presence. Death, why did it exist? Why did God the Benevolent allow such an evil? Not only did it exist, Death dwelt in perfect balance with birth—no one died who had not been born and all those born would die. God the Creator. The struggles of theologian Thomas Aquinas rang through his head. The word 'God' implied infinite goodness, therefore, if God existed Aquinas argued, there would be no evil discoverable. Yet there was evil in the world, implying God did not exist. Stephen found it easier to settle on the doctrine of St Augustine of Hippo who deemed God was not the parent of evil.

As the end of the week arrived Stephen said his farewells, telling his father, 'I will care for Mother and see to the farm,' carefully avoiding specifics. His father flinched and grunted in response, before turning away. Stephen knew he would never see his father again. Without looking back, he walked out of the house with his mother, who buried the side of her face in his arm. 'Mother, I promise I'll care for you, just give me time to work out how best to do so. For now, I have to return to St Madern's, but I'll write soon.' The doorway faced southeast affording them some shelter from the eternal westerly winds. They walked through the mud to the doorway of the cattle shed, where Stephen loaded up his pony with water and provisions. He kissed his mother farewell, mounted his pony, turned, waved, and set off along the trail crossing the south west edge of the moor, travelling from the Devon bleakness of Dartmoor to St Madern's on the even bleaker Bodmin Moor of Cornwall.

The rain lashed his face and the wind blew directly at him from the west, preventing his hood from staying up for long. He rode alongside a babbling stream and despite the weather could see half a mile ahead. He hoped the rain would keep the robbers away. Robbers were a hazard on the roads, often setting upon travelers, sometimes even killing them and monks were by no means immune, but Stephen did not worry, such was his trust in God. Today as usual he preferred his own company, avoiding seeking protection by hiring a local guide. He might meet fellow travelers by staying the night in an inn, but mostly he preferred to be alone with his Lord.

His path took him into dense woodland, yet he remained confident he would be safe despite the shelter and more hiding places it provided for robbers. The tree limbs wound in mysterious shapes, as if a higher force had plaited them. Riding onwards, granite boulders were strewn all around as if arranged by giants to prevent travelers from straying from the path and were increasingly covered in moss as the forest grew darker.

As he approached the river, Erme, his young but usually reliable pony took fright, jerking sideways to avoid crossing the ancient stone bridge. Stephen spoke soothingly, urging it onwards but as it reached the bridge it reared up all but throwing him. The bridge was narrow, merely a few massive granite slabs laid on top of stone uprights standing in the water, with no parapets to prevent falling. Dismounting, he stroked the beast's nose before leading it onto the bridge. 'Hush, He protects us.' He stroked the pony's nose again but it appeared reluctant to accept his assurances. As they crossed the bridge the pony whinnied preparing to rear again, but this time it responded to Stephen's firm but gentle handling. As they crossed the bridge he stared down at the water surging over the rocks beneath; the shallow water raced over large boulders. How cold it would be. 'Is that what you're afraid of?' He looked into the animal's eyes and saw not fear, but terror—a look from a simple beast that would return to haunt him in his final days.

Relieved that they were safely across the bridge, he frowned, patting his pony's sodden flank, puzzled by the usually docile beast's reaction to the river. A few miles further on he found an emaciated horse tethered to a post. Dismounting, he saw it was blind in both eyes. With sadness and shame on behalf of mankind, he realised it must have been stolen and blinded so it would be unable to find its way home or to recognise its true master. He patted it, fed it handfuls of lush grass beyond its reach and let it nuzzle him. 'Farewell my poor friend,' he said.

Riding onwards, the blowing rain stung his face and saturated his garments. Cold drips trickled down his chest and back as he sat braced into the wind, yet he felt invigorated, free from his family troubles and those of St Madern's. The harsh elements were a blessed relief, helping him forget uncertainty, indecision and dread, his main companions of late.

The long journey gave him time for reflection and he was in no hurry. During his youth his mother and the benevolence of his Lord had made up for his father's distance. He had always been content, until recently. He had never been interested in farming, but how could he, a youngster, say so to a father used to having his own way? His aspirations to pursue a higher purpose, that of divine service, were formed by the age of fourteen, though from where they came he did not know. Even as a youngster he felt his life was different, as if he had been selected for a special purpose. He dreamt of a perfect relationship with God, the creator of all things. For years he pretended to be following his father's plans for him, and when he finally stood his ground his father, a devout Christian, had struggled. To this day his choosing God over the farm was his one show of defiance. His father told him he would tire of the monastic lifestyle and return to the land. After all these years of service was his father about to be proved correct?

Prior Paul was performing his me miseram again. Stephen, sat with his brothers in the chapel of St Madern's, watching their esteemed prior, stripped to the waist, whip himself crying out, 'Your humble sinner repents, Lord.' Stephen squirmed. Self-flagellation was absurd, an embarrassment resulting in more evil than good, yet Prior Paul promoted it to his brothers for the atonement of their sins. He led by example and seemed to have no shortage of them.

St Madern's Charterhouse, being a Carthusian monastery, followed an austere devotion to God. Silence, discipline and prayers sat comfortably with Stephen, but not harshness. He wished he was free to look away, but his prior would interpret this as disrespectful. On the few times Stephen had tried the whip on himself, he felt it was wrong; would that evil was such a feeble foe.

To suggest his prior was wrong would be akin to suggesting God was wrong. Yet, while his prior saw sin everywhere, Stephen saw beauty, the good in humanity and he craved sharing this with others. But how? Was he blind to evil standing before him? Complacent? If Satan lurked within him Satan's approach must be subtle. His mind went around in circles pondering such questions, all the time hankering for a better approach to serving God. Never faltering in his devotion to God, he knew at St Madern's he was wandering down the path of disillusionment.

In the weeks following his farewells to his mother and father his prayers remained unanswered, leaving him torn between serving God, in one way or another, and helping his mother, but at a loss as how to do both.

One gloomy, grey morning in November when the sun appeared to have overslept, Brother Simon brought him a letter from his mother, written in Latin by a local priest. Even before he read it, he knew his father was dead. He felt a brief sense of relief, quickly correcting himself, recognising the sorrow his mother must be feeling. Prior Paul declined him permission for another absence, condemning her to stand alone at his father's grave.

In January he received another letter explaining his father's will. As he feared his mother proposed to transfer to him the burden of the estate left to her, irrespective of what he chose to do with it.

Stephen's personal dilemmas coincided with a crisis at St Madern's involving Brother Hubert. Hubert was a tall lanky individual, with a hard, sunken skeletal face, in contrast to Stephen who wore more flesh, having been well fed as a child. While Stephen by nature was easy going and tended to radiate peace and goodwill Hubert was dour, particularly pious and often pedantic, but the two shared their devotion to God. Stephen admired Hubert's self-discipline, which he himself lacked. Most of the other brothers distanced themselves from Hubert, as he who strives hardest may embarrass others. Partly because of this Stephen embraced him, becoming close to him—as close as Hubert and his Prior permitted.

Stephen was in the fields working apart from his brothers, weeding and planting seed, when he looked up and saw Hubert approaching. Hubert's eyes flitted first one way, then another, then to the ground. He appeared flustered, so Stephen walked him aside and sat him down on the trunk of a fallen tree to calm him, well away from listening ears and questioning looks. Stephen said with the formality Hubert needed, 'Brother Hubert when you are ready pray tell me what troubles you.'

Hubert made a guttural noise preparing to speak, while Stephen remained silent, not rushing his brother. Eventually, clearing his throat, Hubert asked, 'How does a priest chose between serving God and serving his prior?'

Stephen shot a glance at Hubert as if Hubert was accusing him, the question resonating so loudly with his own recent deliberations. Did Hubert know? His eyes suggested not, but Stephen was taken aback. 'I do not see the problem Brother Hubert; by serving our prior we serve God, we all know that.'

Hubert looked towards the charterhouse buildings as if he might leave, but he lingered, fidgeting on the tree trunk. 'What if one's prior strayed from the path of virtue?' Hubert's facial expression appeared one of confession, not accusation, but Stephen wore the crown of doubt. 'You, brother know as well as any of us, we do not challenge the wisdom of our prior. We may not always understand his decisions, we do not have to, we obey.'

Hubert flinched with the reprimand he so wanted. Had Stephen been softer he would have felt contempt. 'Yes, I know that well. You know I know that and that I have never been inclined to rise above my station, or to treat my superiors with anything other than the full respect due to them.' Hubert paused.

'Are you suggesting on this occasion you know God's will better than does our prior?'

'I regret that appears my position.'

Stephen drew a deep breath; 'I have heard enough brother.' He put his hands on his knees and stood up preparing to leave. 'I suggest you pray to our Lord for forgiveness and direction on this matter.'

Hubert reached out and grasped Stephen's forearm. His hold was light, Stephen might easily have shrugged it off, but this was the first time to his recollection that Hubert had ever touched him. 'I have prayed to our Lord almost every hour of every day for many weeks and He has yet to answer my prayers. I cannot turn to my prior. If I cannot turn to you, who…' the rest of Hubert's plea was voiced by his eyes. Stephen turned and walked away, struggling to contain his sense of panic.

Weeks, then months went by without further mention of

their discussion. They prayed to God the Creator of all things but received no answers. Even though Hubert never explained the nature of his problems with their prior they were now shared, he was no longer alone. Little did Hubert know his mentor was floundering in unison with himself.

The revelation, if that is the right word, came one frigid day when at a chapel meeting with all the ordained brothers the prior spoke further about their sinfulness, once again stripped to the waist demonstrating on himself the value of the whip. Stephen glanced in Hubert's direction, their eyes met, each seemed to understand the other, before they looked down. Stephen's left arm twitched as it tended to do when he was agitated, ever since being struck by his father as a child. Seeing the hairs on his prior's chest an image of his prior fully naked entered his head causing him to raise a hand to his mouth as if he might vomit.

Prior Paul declined Stephen's further requests to visit his mother, about whom he fretted daily, knowing she could not manage the family estate, which he had no desire to manage himself. Worse, he had lost respect for his prior. How could he now pretend otherwise? Losing respect for his prior was not far short of losing respect for God. God was divine, perfect, but might some of his human representatives be fallible?

Stephen's brothers, Hubert excepted, seemed as one with their prior. If Satan inhabited their souls as they believed, they seemed none the better for recognising this, nor for following Prior Paul's lead. Now more than ever, Stephen heard the calling of his youth—to help good flourish and to eliminate evil. How? It was God who presented him with this question.

One blustery cold day he was working in the monastery's

fields, digging up vegetables for the kitchen, feeling lost. He wiped sodden earth from a cabbage, then put it in a box, when he saw a black and white cat approaching him—a scruffy individual, with matted fur and a kink in its tail. Curiously, instead of keeping its distance, the cat ran up to him and nestled against his legs. Stephen, grateful to receive this unusual display of affection, wiped a muddy hand on his habit and bent to stroke the animal. It purred in response, before running off, stopping about twenty yards away and looking back to Stephen as if to ask, 'Are you coming?' And that's what he did. Stephen abandoned his duties and left St Madern's without telling anyone—accepting his calling from a cat.

Stephen saw smoke rising from the chimney of his home in the distance. As he drew closer his mother appeared outside and bent down to the stack of firewood, but as if she heard his call she turned and looked his way. Joy, suppressed and downtrodden, for so long leapt within his chest demanding to see the light of day, to be reborn.

Minutes later Stephen dismounted and his mother hugged him like the prodigal son, tears cascading down her cheeks. He embraced her, free of the restraints from his father's prying eyes and from his usual monastic reserve.

'You've lost your hair at the front,' his mother said with a grin.

Stephen passed his hand over his forehead. 'Given time, boys become men,' he said smiling. Today he allowed himself to luxuriate in the joy of being as one with his mother, his other plans could wait until the morrow.

Stephen had known for some time that sooner or later

he would leave St Madern's. He had planned that he would approach the abbot of Torminster Abbey, a few miles from his family's estate, which being a Benedictine monastery would be more compassionate than St Madern's.

Only a week later he was ushered into Torminster's chapter-house where he met with the elderly Abbot Justice, who looked searchingly at Stephen. Stephen maintained respectful silence until the abbot spoke. He invited Stephen to explain himself and he did so, avoiding all but a hint of criticism of Prior Paul.

After several minutes of Stephen talking—the abbot encouraging him by way of nods—Abbot Justice came straight to the point. 'You have considerable self-doubts despite your years as a priest. You appear not to have respected your former prior. You have defected from St Madern's. How would you respond if our roles were reversed?'

Stephen had anticipated such a question and prepared himself for it. His heart raced faster, but controlling his trembling he looked the abbot in the eyes and said, 'Blessed are the poor in spirit, for theirs is the kingdom of heaven. Blessed are those who hunger and thirst for righteousness, for they will be filled.' He let Christ's words linger, hoping his reply would not be interpreted as arrogance. He stared at his feet, not wishing to prematurely end the silence needed for Abbot Justice to digest his retort.

After a long pause the Abbot said, 'You wish to start afresh in our monastery. I will consider your proposition further and notify you when I have decided. You may go now.'

A few months later the plague of 1348, 'The Black Death,' intervened. Death called everywhere without discriminating between the young and the old, the rich and the poor.

Endeavouring to defy Death Torminster barred its doors to the world outside, with a notice saying, 'To preserve purity and keep the pestilence at bay the monastery is closed.' Reading the notice Stephen believed God rebuked him—he had misread God's will.

He worked thereafter as an independent itinerant priest, a friar, visiting the overwhelming numbers of those approaching Death and tending needy children bereft of their parents. The villagers and townsfolk were panicking. In the early days, individuals struck by the plague invariably died within three days of feeling unwell, some within hours. They developed fevers, before finding themselves spitting blood. As time went on the plague changed in nature with the development of large pussy abscesses—buboes—in the groin and armpits. Death thereafter arrived at a more leisurely pace, but just as reliably.

No one of that time knew about germs, let alone bacteria or viruses. Disease was thought to be caused by sinfulness and divine judgement. The people believed God had abandoned them because of their sins, leaving them to die this foul death. Worse, they might die in agony from the plague, only to face God's or Satan's wrath in the life beyond. Those associating with the sinful might share in their fate—infection by association—so even family members were readily abandoned. 'Love thy neighbour' was a long-forgotten commandment.

While others fled, Stephen stayed to comfort the dying and their grieving, frightened families. The sights of carts loaded with corpses being driven away and of crows pecking at bodies were parts of his daily travails. Once he stepped over a body in a narrow laneway startling a feasting crow, which then attacked him, trying to peck his eyes. Another time he entered the dwelling of a family he visited two days earlier and found them all dead, with their dog and pigs devouring them. He turned away and vomited. The stench of Death dwelt everywhere.

Despite such horrors, his work with the sick and needy brought him a sense of relief. He believed he had earlier misinterpreted God's call to come home. It was to God's home, not his mother's, that he was called. Stephen expected to die from the plague, this was God's will, but he vowed he would help as many of the needy as possible in his remaining days. Amidst the chaos he felt a surprising sense of tranquility and purpose from helping the sick and needy. Prior Paul would have interpreted the pestilence as the price God demanded of man for his sins. The God Stephen worshipped was not so harsh.

Only once did he falter. He heard a whimpering so entered a home to find a small child sitting alone between her parents who lay in filthy straw, dead but her mother was still warm. The child looked healthy but was covered in excrement. He gently bent to pick her up, to which she responded with silent inertia, as if healthy though she was, she had given up on life. Why should such a little one suffer? Death was all around. Was it free to make its own decisions? Was Death commanded by his Lord or by Satan? It was not for him to ask such questions. He would find a home for the child.

One day, on a weekly visit to his mother, he found her still in bed. Her face was ashen grey and a large red swelling in her neck, beneath her right ear told him the rest of the story. 'It cannot be,' he cried aloud, but his mother had not the strength to contradict him. He tended to her every bodily need over her two remaining days of life. Then he dug a grave facing east from the longhouse and said his farewells. He prayed his own end would come quickly, that he might leave hell on earth to dwell with his Lord, but Death proved oblivious to his entreaties.

In the autumn of 1350, the plague abated having killed almost forty percent of the country, including most of the monks at Torminster, but not one of St Madern's, and not Stephen. Might Stephen's service of the sick have been met with a further rebuke from God? He remained alive in a world he wished to leave, having lost his mother, the one person he loved, and his hopes of joining Torminster Abbey appeared over, as the monastery bereft of many of its brethren had closed.

Stephen's dismay that God had not taken him soon gave way to the conviction that God had another plan for him. Alone in Ildiscombe church, not far from Torminster, he knelt praying to his Lord to give him direction and this time God appeared to deliver an answer. Stephen's thoughts took on a life of their own. He found himself being led as if in a dream back to St Madern's, back to a day which was one of his lowest at the charterhouse. He had been alone and it had been raining incessantly for days, but now in his dream, he sat in the cloisters watching rainwater draining from gargoyles when he heard a voice, 'What beyond drainage are the functions of gargoyles and other grotesques?' Turning he saw no brother and with growing realization he submitted to the voice of God. Although his quest, the containment of human failings so good might flourish was in disarray, God this day seemed to take him by the hand. But what did His words mean?

He awoke finding himself back in Ildiscombe church, still bent in prayer. He looked up at the altar and expressed his gratitude before rising with an unusual sense of tranquility. Nevertheless, his Lord's question remained a puzzle. In the days and weeks following he deliberated further the question which struck him like an appeal. What was the function of grotesques? Apart from gargoyles' functions of drainage what was the deeper purpose of these hideous stone figures? A drain could be discrete and many grotesques sat apart from drainage systems, with no drainage chores to perform. The people believed gargoyles and other grotesques protected those below them from evil and warned them of the hell they faced if they sinned. Most parishioners, even the very few who could read, could not read the Bible because it was written in Latin, but staring up at these stone demons they could read their tortured expressions and did not want to share their fates. St Augustine, the font of ecclesiastical wisdom, stipulated that everyone was born sinful, only the Church could deliver salvation, so parishioners had better come to church or risk damnation. Stephen accepted that grotesques promoted church attendance, but there must be something more.

One night at home, he was on his knees praying that the grotesques might speak to him. A faint glow arose around him and he heard a voice, clear and authoritative, 'Grotesques provide contrast with the divine to help mankind.' This was an epiphany for Stephen and from there his central plan developed: grotesques might be used as repositories of evil, their tortured expressions might reflect not just the sins of mankind, but more specifically those of his brothers, who could transfer their sinfulness to the stones where it could do no harm. Grotesques would alleviate their burdens of sin, purifying them, enhancing virtue without any need for the whip.

The image of the black and white cat that led him away from St Madern's returned to him. White is never whiter than when contrasted with black. In his mind he bent to stroke the cat, only to find it was cold and as hard as stone.

Subsequent folklore has depicted the black and white cat that led Stephen away from St Madern's as the Devil, but most medieval associations of cats with the Devil have involved pure black cats.

2

Torminster Hospital (1983)

Patient care must improve. How many years had she stood here witnessing the consequences of neglect? Human beings for goodness' sake. If things don't change soon, Matilda told herself, she'd follow the long list of medical staff who had left, even though this would involve abandoning those who needed her most.

Head throbbing, she stood on the top steps of the entrance to the administration block of Torminster Hospital surveying the grey landscape. Two patients wandered aimlessly in the rain. They'll be getting wet through, she thought. Brian's ladder remained up against the wall. She had reminded him yesterday to put it away. A bus driver? Might she enjoy driving school kids? Anything seemed better than growing old working as a cleaner in such a dump. 'Don't you bloody laugh,' she called out to the Monkeys perched on the decaying west façade of what once, long ago, had been an abbey. 'And it's about time you buggers looked after yourselves,' she called to the grotesques above, before taking another drag on her cigarette. God her head hurt. She'd let herself down yet again, though in fairness it was almost a year since her last alcoholic binge. Thank goodness Fergus had dragged her home from the Torturer's when he did. Who knows what she might have done?

But what about the patients? she asked herself for the umpteenth time. What would they do without Brian and her? And Horace of course. Always the patients, her life sentence, yet they had done her good, she needed them as much as they needed her, they'd kept her on a level—mostly.

Three crows flew across the driveway. 'G'mornin' Alfred. Out with the family, are we?' Would the new senior psychiatrist coming today be any better than the others? Senior psychiatrists had come and gone over the years, almost all of them pretty hopeless. Might this new one deliver to the patients the modern state of the art treatments they desperately needed, dragging the hospital into the twentieth century before the next one began? Pigs may fly. Old Horace had once described Torminster's long-term residents as 'the discarded, the forgotten, those erased from the canvas of society,' and he should know as he was one of them. Inhaling again, she asked herself, who wants to live to be a hundred? Gazing down the hospital driveway, she blinked, 'Christ, is that a Porsche—here? It'll be the Queen next.'

Dr Douglas Wright had farewelled the swarming mass of humanity in London for the desolation of Torminster, one of Dartmoor's remotest outposts, its isolated hospital a legacy of the asylum era when removal of the insane from public scrutiny was the priority. This must change; he would see that it did. He drove through the rusty wrought iron main gates, one of which was at an angle, having broken away from its hinges. 'Abandon all hope, ye who enter here,' he said aloud before stopping one hundred yards or so from the main hospital entrance. Struggling to see through the wet windscreen, he turned up the wipers of his Porsche, freshly decorated with rich Devon manure—Jersey or Friesian, who could tell?

That must have been the original main entrance over there in the ornate west end with its two small towers. There is the old abbey's main tower, over the top of the main block where the monastic buildings must have been. A hollow tower—I've never seen anything like it. There, standing out from the tower's alcoves against the grey sky are some of the famous grotesques. Absurdly ornamented for a hospital, but many are terribly decayed. God's even slacker with his household maintenance than I am.

Over to one side he saw several smaller buildings of recent, banal but utilitarian design. How ever did they receive planning permission? 1960s boxes alongside a medieval marvel, albeit a decayed one.

He drove on to the front entrance to find no red carpet laid out for him. Getting out of his low Porsche he groaned as he stretched his back. It had been a long drive. Mounting the front steps, he noticed an athletically built middle-aged woman, smoking a cigarette. Disgusting habit.

Matilda looked him up and down, this bold pin-stripe suited doctor with a well-preserved head of thick but grey hair. He was tall, in his fifties and slightly overweight. Under her breath she said to herself, 'Goodness, what have we here?'

Might she have uttered her thoughts louder than intended? for he replied, 'I am Dr Wright. I believe I am expected.'

'Expectin' are yer? How many months gone are yer? Sorry, my hearing's none too good. Na! Don't you worry, I'ze only joking. I won't eat you. Mind you, in that fine suit, I dunno. Come in a bit closer or you'll get all wet,' she said taking him by the elbow. She enjoyed playing on her Devon heritage, which ranged from natural to full on comic according to her audience.

Wright was a lady's man, but there are ladies and ladies, he thought. This one had nicotine stained fingers and looked worse for wear, though her well-toned physique suggested this might not be her habitual state. Nevertheless, the briefer his exchanges with her were the better for both of them.

'I'm glad to make your acquaintance Doctor. You coming to join us is a rare privilege; I was only talking about you this morning.' Matilda knew how to manage the male species, identifying Wright as one who might thrive on flattery. 'I be Matilda, Director of Sanitary Services, otherwise known as Tilly the head bloody cleaner.' She took a final drag, before knocking the tip off her cigarette, pinching it and putting the stub in her pocket. 'How can I help you, my lover? I expect you want to meet the manager, Mr Castle, the king of hospitality,' Matilda said, 'I'll help you find him. I'm sure he's itching to meet you; itching anyway. Not my type he isn't. I like the more refined types.' She gave Wright a lecherous look.

The doctor had nothing against lechery, but he was accustomed to having the privilege of leading the way. Noting the twinkle in her eye, he thought that if they were both still youngsters and he was not a happily married man, a stroll through the fields might have been an enjoyable introduction to rural Devon customs.

Matilda led him along the former abbey's cloisters, now dreary corridors. Brickwork filled in the lower parts of the original archways to above waist height with glass panes above the new ledges. Through the arches he saw the garth, the open quadrangle surrounded by the cloisters with its pointed arches.

Oh, to see it in its original state, but then again, the abbey had come to an unfortunate end.

They came to a door bearing the sign 'Manager.' 'Sit yerself down Doc, I'll see if he's in.' Without knocking, Matilda entered the manager's office. Several minutes lapsed before she emerged. 'He said he'll be out to see you quick as a jiffy. I'll be getting along now, leaving you to him as I got work to do, unlike some of them round here.' She'd enjoyed her rustic act. The daft bugger thinks it's for real, she thought. He must be wondering what he's come to. What'll he make of the Castle?

As he waited outside manager Castle's office, Wright looked about him, without taking anything in. A strong scent of disinfectant assailed his nostrils, reminding him of his school days. Suddenly he felt overwhelmingly tired. He hoped his decision to accept the appointment as Torminster Hospital's medical director would give him opportunities for creative reforms but right now he had a sinking feeling. He was an advocate of 'Better to be a big fish in a small pond,' and if that pond happens to be a stagnant one a good clear out and reform should be easier to achieve. But stagnant ponds tend to stink.

After what seemed an eternity a small thin wizened figure in a grubby suit with a stained off-white collar emerged. No words of greeting came forth, just an icy look as a hand was extended. Wright gratefully held out his hand in return, only to find it grasped in a vice, which his host progressively tightened. Might his hand disintegrate if the vice underwent a couple more turns? When he was finally released Wright asked himself what was that ridiculous greeting about? Is that alcohol I smell? In the absence of any utterings from his glaring host, Wright volunteered with a pretence of mutual hospitality, 'I am most happy to meet you Mr Castle, and to have the privilege of working at Torminster.'

'Well, you'd better be getting on with it then. How long was you planning on staying?' Castle turned his back on the doctor, returned to his office and closed the door.

Disbelieving, Wright looked around for someone to give him directions, but saw no one. It was just after a quarter past twelve. Perhaps they'd gone for an early lunch. What am I going to do now? he asked himself. I don't know where my office is, or my wards. Perhaps I should just seek the exit, but coming in was like a maze. If only that cleaner woman was still at hand, she was preferable to this cold little twit. Such a manager could become a thorn in his side. Little did he know of Castle's expertise in that respect.

Retracing his steps, he peered through the former cloisters' windows up at the grotesques. They are damned well laughing at me and I have only just arrived, he thought. All around gargoyles vomited cascades of water.

3

Comes light

*W*é*ll continue our story of the Abbey with its second key figure, Baron De Juniac. Stephen may have had the basic ideas, but it was De Juniac who was the creator of our grotesques. But the chapter begins with Stephen.*

Village after village it is the same, Stephen thought, approaching Little Peniton on his pony. So many abandoned homes, especially on the villages' outskirts where the poor used to dwell. The plague has left its mark everywhere. Abbot Thomas, with whom he had stayed the previous night had warned him Little Peniton had been devastated by the plague. It used to be such a quaint little village. He had travelled through it a number of times on his way to Exeter, fifteen miles further on. His fingers hurt they were so frozen. He let go of his reins and wrapped his arms around his chest burying his hands in his armpits.

Six crows flew into view from the west. Stephen clasped his elbows and shuddered. He was not superstitious and was determined not to allow six crows, a portent of Death, to bother him. However, despite knowing he was alone, he looked over his shoulder checking for others.

All settlements smelt but this stench was different to those of other villages he had passed. It was deserted except for a few dogs, pigs and hens roaming wild; no villagers tending their fields or talking to their neighbours; no traders selling their wares; no one at all, only animals and crows scavenging all around. Many houses had no roofs and were in various states of collapse having been stripped of their valuable timber and their cob walls. The crows had warned him.

Saddle sore, he dismounted to ease his loins and give his pony a rest. Standing alongside his pony he steadied himself against it as an unusual attack of giddiness overtook him. It lasted only a matter of seconds. I'm tired, he conceded, it had already been a long journey. A half-starved dog ran up to him growling. Looking with authority at the dog only appeared to make it more aggressive. It circled him and his pony, where-upon his pony kicked out its back legs and though they did not connect, the dog took the hint and ran off. Stephen patted the pony, 'Thank you my loyal friend.'

Walking on, Stephen noted that the scavenging animals looked curiously thin. In previous villages the scavengers had appeared well fed, a result of the availability of so many corpses and rats. Even where villagers received proper Christian burials the rats, dogs and pigs sooner or later dug them up and feasted; as a result, the living became less dedicated to their burial tasks. Most of the corpses here seemed long gone but many rats were scurrying about.

He tied his pony to the low branch of a tree and called out before entering a small house. He needn't have bothered as its occupants could not hear. All around were bones scattered haphazardly and some had obviously been gnawed. It was the same in the other homes he entered; not one living soul remained in the entire village. Death had been busy. Why does the Lord allow it? Benevolent and omnipotent, so why? Were all these people sinners, or might they have been condemned because of the sins of others? Humanity one way or another must do better.

He remounted his pony with a heavy heart and was relieved when two hours later he reached the city of Exeter. Riding under the main Exeter gatehouse he looked up at its two round towers standing over fifty feet high on either side of the pointed arch, above which stood a painted statue of the King. He grimaced and made the sign of the cross to the usual array of decomposing heads and limbs of felons, hanging like washing from a line.

The city seemed to seethe with travelers and traders after Little Peniton, but it was much quieter than on his previous visits. Riding up South Street he felt relieved to have returned to a place where he was no longer alone, despite the usual stench. Here he could see some of the wealthiest of Exeter's homes, but looking down a side alley between the tiny chaotically angled houses he saw entrails, hopefully animal not human ones, and other rotting meat. That combined with plentiful human faeces gave the city its pungent aroma. The lords' servants were cleaning the impressive main street, shoveling up horse manure, its perfume mild compared with those wafting in from the lesser neighbourhoods.

Today's the day, Stephen told himself, I won't take no for an answer, I have to succeed.

At ten o'clock he was due to meet the Bishop of Exeter, John Grandisson. He entered through Palace Gate and was struck by the palace's size and opulence, even though he knew it was the largest building in Exeter, save the cathedral. The palace attracted his gaze in all directions. He walked through the courtyard with the Bishop's private garden to his left, noting the heavy frost. He entered the palace through the monumental south porch leading to a wide cross passage with more archways. Welcome kitchen smells and the smell of ale being brewed assailed his senses. A young brother told him to be seated and whilst waiting he saw a hive of activity with workers building the new west wing and working on the chapel's timber roof with its ornate guilt bosses. He had never met Bishop Grandisson but had heard of his interests in the arts. Finally summoned, he was led up a spiral staircase to 'the Bishop's camera,' his private chamber.

Grandisson was seated at his desk alongside a large fireplace endeavouring to keep the cold at bay, but the room's high ceiling added to the challenge. After the usual introductions he said, 'I hear you wish to assume the role of abbot at, where is it? Ah, Torminster. Tragic that it closed, like so many others. What makes you think you can resurrect it from the dead?'

Stephen stood with hands clasped in front of him, looking down until he was expected to address the Bishop. Looking up he said, 'Your Excellency, I believe I have been called…'

'Haven't we all?' interrupted His Excellency.

'Called specifically to Torminster. It adjoins my former family's farm, which I have inherited, but what use is a large estate to a humble priest?'

'What use indeed?'

'If I had the honour of becoming Torminster's abbot I would sell my land to fund the abbey's restoration. It was run down before the plague and it has since been looted.'

'The depths of depravity to which some people sink. Even so an abbot is a senior position and I must ask how you might be qualified for such responsibilities?'

'It is not for a humble servant of the Lord to have airs, but my calling tells me I can undertake such responsibilities. My dream is to build a monastery that stands on the foundations of virtue as an aid to serving Our Lord.'

'Noble words, but words they are.'

Stephen had hoped his virtuous intentions would win the day but he saw that he must be more mercenary. 'If you have other applicants under consideration, I would ask how many have volunteered their own funds for the restoration? Not only will I fund the restoration of Torminster Abbey, I would also like to upgrade it so that it can better serve Our Lord.'

Stephen was small fry but that day he knew he held persuasive advantages and Torminster would be of little interest to the Bishop, who had far more pressing responsibilities. He probably had no other applicants and was unlikely to have any for many years for a semi-derelict backwater, when so many senior clergy had died in the plague. Even if applicants were to step forward, they would be asking for funds, not supplying them themselves.

Looking around at the stained-glass windows, Stephen added, 'I note the magnificent work you have underway in the Palace and the Cathedral. I do not wish to appear presumptuous, but it would be a privilege if I were permitted to make a donation to such worthy endeavours.'

Abbot Stephen it would be.

Stephen left the palace with a smile of satisfaction and walked towards the cathedral. First challenge accomplished, but he was less than optimistic about the next one. His smile changed to a look of uncertain resolve. He shuddered and waved his arms around him to ward of the cold.

Within the cathedral precincts he awaited his meeting with another potential master builder. He had already interviewed three others, two of whom appeared clueless and the third looked like he might not survive the winter. Today's applicant was different—he was French. Strange, that someone from France would apply, the two nations still being officially at war, though hostilities had been interrupted by the plague devastating both their countries. He was wary about foreigners, especially French ones, but he had read that French cathedrals were magnificent, especially those influenced by Abbot Suger of St-Denis who had spearheaded the modern architectural style he sought.

It was a fine day with a blue sky and a sharp frost. He stamped his cold feet to improve the circulation. The cathedral's courtyard in front of the western entrance appeared almost deserted. Instead of the usual bustling throng were only a dozen or so wanderers. Scaffolding of alder and ash still stood against sections of the cathedral, but there were no signs of the hectic building activity he had witnessed on his previous visit. Exeter Cathedral's features were impressive, much grander than Torminster could ever be. He had seen it several times before, but he never left without learning more. The dazzling beauty of the cathedral contrasted with his recent memories of the dead strewn all around as if discarded by some ravenous giant who had found them unpalatable. He recalled Death's insatiable appetite during the plague; had he been spared or merely found unpalatable?

Wiping a drip from his cold nose, he espied a handsome, strongly built man similarly aged to himself in his forties, dressed in a heavy grey full-length gown with a jaunty red cap. He was looking around with expectancy. This must be the French master builder he was due to meet.

'Excuse me sir, but might you be Baron De Juniac?'

'I am indeed, Father, it is a veritable honour to meet you,' said the other removing his hat and bowing. After the usual polite exchanges, the two of them strolled around the cathedral, the baron pointing out some of its features from the perspective of a master builder. 'It is no longer sufficient to be a master builder. Today's cathedrals need architects. Mathematics, geometry and science have replaced some of the earlier dominance of craft. Precision is required if you want cathedrals to reach up to heaven. This new style is not just ornate, it is practical.' Pointing, the Frenchman said, 'Flying buttresses, those massive ornate external arms, support the cathedral's walls, providing additional strength, enabling the walls to rise higher without bowing out and collapsing under the weight of the roof.'

Once inside the cathedral De Juniac said, 'Perhaps you are aware, Father, the arches above the doorways and windows here differ from the traditional rounded arch. These pointed arches provide additional strength permitting doorways and windows to rise to greater heights. Also, larger windows and higher ceilings better display the light of God to those looking up to heaven.' Holding their hands behind them the two men gazed upwards in awe, De Juniac confidently extolling his design imperative. 'Light emerging from darkness is the essence of what a well-designed cathedral delivers to its congregation.

The light of Exeter is unique, for Exeter has one of the longest uninterrupted vaulted roofs in the world.'

'I didn't know that,' Stephen said smiling and nodding with a sense of local pride.

They went outside to be greeted by a blast of icy wind. De Juniac looked at the sculptured saints and to the stone babewyns beyond. 'Come,' said Stephen, 'the sun is struggling in its battle with the cold, let's seek sanctuary indoors.'

Entering the nearest ale house, the frost from their boots left damp patches on the freshly laid rushes. The ale house keeper's talbot barked a warning, before his master ordered 'Quiet!' The large hound, determined to have the last word, uttered a quiet growl before returning to his master and lying down.

Now they could talk in comfort about Torminster's redesign and Stephen could better assess De Juniac's credentials. Stephen ushered De Juniac to a table near the fire. The landlord's wife hurried over to welcome them, seat them and to take their orders.

'I should have asked if you prefer wine before bringing you here,' said Stephen.

'Ale is fine, wine these days leaves a sour taste.' De Juniac's face appeared strained as if he was drinking sour wine, but Stephen noticed his lingering expression of anguish. His brow was perspiring despite little heat coming from the fire. Stephen recognised a troubled expression when he saw one; he gave the baron breathing space before exchanging further pleasantries. 'Since coming to England I have developed a preference for ale,' De Juniac added having realised Stephen was looking at him.

Sipping their ales, Stephen noted the ale was sour and herbs and spices had been added to disguise this. Their lack of customers must be difficult for them. De Juniac had regained his composure so Stephen decided it was time for the unpleasant exercise of determining the Frenchman's suitability, or otherwise, for the job.

'Tell me Baron about yourself. Why might I consider your services?'

De Juniac set his mug down on the table. 'My work is driven by God, to whose service my life is devoted. I serve Him by creating the Divine.' He looked down with a look of humility. Stephen was impressed by the apparent sincerity of his answer.

De Juniac continued, 'At Chartres, where I have worked, the bishops value the works of natural philosophers. Some of them, the philosophers I mean, live on until eternity in the stone carvings on the exterior of the cathedral, where they continue their endeavours. The clergy at Chartres are progressive. They believe reasoning may shed light on the world, that God made a comprehensible universe. I share this belief.'

Stephen's curiosity was aroused. De Juniac continued, 'But building churches also requires mathematical expertise; mathematics is beautiful, it is precision, it is perfection. Perfection is divine. Divinity is God. God is infinite. And infinity is to be found at the end of mathematics.'

Stephen was taken aback but listened with curiosity. Was the Frenchman a crank or might he be enlightened?

De Juniac appeared to wake as if from a reverie. 'My work brings me closer to Him—but only if I am building.' With an imploring look he added, 'I have not done any building in more than a year.'

Stephen nodded. Embracing either reason or mathematics would not have been tolerated at St Madern's, but maybe that was a plus. Stephen was inclined to agree with the clergy of Chartres, scientific and abstract spiritual ideas did not have to stand in opposition, one might compliment the other. He also believed that even the Church did not have all the answers, it never would; it should strive ever harder to discover ultimate truths. He cleared his throat, 'France, I believe suffered as much from the pestilence as did England, if my information is correct. That leaves both countries short of cathedral architects. Why did you come to England, instead of continuing your work in France?'

De Juniac stared at the table. 'I have relatives from my mother's family who live in Winchester where I hoped to work on its magnificent cathedral for which they sought a new master builder. Our countries' years of fighting have been a disadvantage to me, despite French cathedrals leading the world.'

No doubt this was the case but it was strange that a Frenchman of the baron's stature was now interested in a modest abbey in Devon. Stephen said, 'It has been a blessing the war between our two nations has subsided since the pestilence, but does it not concern you Baron that our countries may yet resume the war?'

'It concerns me greatly, Father, but both sides are guilty. Did Christ not say "Thou shalt not kill"? Did he not also command, "Love they neighbor"? Yet we slaughter each other with the blessings of our churches.'

Stephen was again taken aback. His question was pitched at the level of the baron's personal welfare and like most English, he believed the French needed to be put in their place, if not by war how else? But his gentle side felt unease about the practice of war, so he conceded the Frenchman's point.

Stephen noted that the fierce looking talbot was on the prowl and was cocking its leg against a bench. At least the rushes are fresh and they are using lavender to cover the smells, he thought. Changing the subject, he continued, 'I have to explain my project's uniqueness.' He paused, 'This is to be no ordinary abbey. I have unusual aspirations for it. No, not on that scale,' he said, noting De Juniac staring out of the window at the cathedral.

'You like my ugly stone friends,' said De Juniac with a knowledgeable smile.

Stephen's mouth fell open; he looked askance at his guest. The Frenchman couldn't have heard about his plan as he had told no one.

'How did you know?'

'How did I know? The French are less than welcome in England these days, yet you are granting me consideration. My skills are with the modern design. So...'

'Yes, but how did you know about the grotesques—your 'ugly friends'?'

De Juniac stared into Stephen's eyes. 'That I did not know before meeting you today. If you want grotesques—babewyns—you may be my saviour, we may be well paired.' Stephen felt ill at ease; it was meant to be him assessing the applicant, but was the reverse occurring—and something more?

'Please Father, I seek your forgiveness, I have been impolite. Before we met it was obvious you sought an architect experienced with the new design skills. You wouldn't be wasting your time on a Frenchman if that was not your intention.' They were interrupted by a maid refilling their wooden mugs. 'Babewyns are one of the key novel features, not the most appreciated, but they are vital.' The baron placed an unusual emphasis on the word vital. 'As we were leaving the cathedral I realised your specific interest. I noticed you kept turning to the babewyns as if you needed to say goodbye to each of them. Not to the statues of saints and bishops. Again, please, I do not mean to be rude. A master craftsman has eyes, not ordinary eyes, God blesses us with eyes for what others cannot see.'

Stephen drank the remains of his ale, not knowing what to say. As he hesitated De Juniac continued, 'Some people say your English word babewyn is derived from the Italian babbuino others, including myself, believe it is from the French babouin.' Both mean baboon. The word gargoyle originates from the French gargouille or gullet, hence in English your word gargle, which reflects the sounds of gargoyles draining water through their mouths. Gargoyles, humble plumbers as they are, are often referred to as grotesques. But I believe the grotesque that serves to convey a message without drainage duties has a certain superiority. But both are babewyns, are they not?'

Stephen listened with interest. 'It's true, I was looking at Exeter's grotesques—babewyns if you like—whilst awaiting you. Their eyes convey so much.'

De Juniac again fixed Stephen's gaze. 'My dear departed wife would look at me. Her eyes could take me to paradise. On other occasions, one look from her and I was a child caught doing wrong. May she rest in peace.' Stephen noticed that the Frenchman's sleeve had risen up revealing horrific scarring of his left forearm, as if it had been badly burnt. De Juniac must have noticed his look as he quickly pulled his sleeve down and hid his hands under the table.

'May she indeed; the pestilence has not left anyone

unscathed,' said Stephen, wondering about De Juniac's fore-arm and his quickly hiding it.

De Juniac hesitated. 'Carving the eyes must be exact—more than exact. Sometimes even I cannot tell why one result is so much more powerful than another. One of the skills of a master carver is to recognise which of his babewyns should be considered stillbirths—hard though this may be.'

Stephen was still picturing the scarred arm, thus missing the salience of De Juniac's remark—his talking about them as if they were offspring.

The master builder he sought must indeed have unusual talents to successfully transform his basic idea. 'I'm no designer but I have my reasons for wanting many babewyns. Does that present any problems for you?' Stephen said.

'As I have said, Father, perhaps we are a remarkable match. I love all aspects of the new design, the vaulted ceilings, the high walls, the buttresses, the windows that bring divine light, but most of all I like babewyns for they reflect the sorrows, and occasional joys, of mankind. They are children of the Mother Church. What is a home without its noisy children? But babe-wyns lead much harder lives than ourselves, someone must love them and...'

Stephen noticed De Juniac stopped mid-sentence—strange. 'Baron, some may consider my ideas are at the expense of beauty and virtue, but my reasons I believe may result in the inverse of this. Virtue may be enhanced.' Stephen raised his mug to call for more ale. 'As you know, light and shadow coexist. Light creates shadows, shadows provide contrasts that permit light to be all the more illuminating. My monks and babewyns are to be as light and shadow. Grotesques, babewyns have always been used to tell parishioners stories about good and evil, but it is not parishioners I am thinking of, for my brothers' virtues to shine my abbey needs to be a palace of babewyns. Thereby, the enhanced virtues of my brothers will better guide the people in the ways of the Lord.'

Stephen's thoughts were interrupted by De Juniac's lateral thinking. 'The Bishop of Laon once asked me, 'What good is virtue unless it is shared with one's brethren? Individual virtue is but conceit.'

Shared virtue? Stephen had never heard of or considered this philosophy. Other clergy might have been offended by it but he craved a united community of brethren for Torminster. 'I have explained my basic idea; now Baron, tell me more about yourself. Why might I need a Frenchman as my architect?'

'Father, you talk to someone who was raised with French cathedrals, which are the foremost in the world. All the world learns from us.' This grated on Stephen, but he conceded it was probably true. Was the Baron arrogant or just overly direct in his speech?

'Aside from working on Chartres Cathedral and the older Laon Cathedral, my major experience has been with Cathédral Notre Dame (Our Lady) de Strasbourg, in Alsace, not France I know, but it was where I last worked.' He drew himself up, 'Chartres is perhaps the world's greatest modern cathedral. Laon, though lesser known was one of the first of the new design. It is exquisite; it has six towers but no spires. The towers are elaborate with a light airy style that may be advantageous for Torminster.' They were interrupted by the door blowing open. The landlord secured it. De Juniac continued, 'I served an extended apprenticeship at Chartres and Laon, where I spent time in all the building trades: laying new foundations for extensions, performing general construction, roofing, stone carving, working on stained glass windows and more. By doing so, now as an architect I understand all the challenges presented and the scope for novel approaches.' Stephen was listening intently.

'Strasbourg has many grotesques, some of which I helped restore, some I replaced; I even added some new ones. I also developed a liking for cats there. Cats are said to be the guardians of the gates to the Otherworld. A link between humans and the universe; magical, mysterious, sensual. Some believe cats steal the souls of the dead.' De Juniac's eyes looked distant.

Stephen's face must have looked worried. De Juniac explained further, 'These of course are pagan beliefs, but if your babewyns are to have authenticity their evil looks should reflect such beliefs. In many churches—Exeter cathedral too as you have seen—the Green Man is featured. It is of course a pagan symbol representing nature. Torminster's symbols maybe need to be more unique.' De Juniac continued with a mischievous smile, 'It is said in real life cats can sense weather changes, as they prefer to find shelter well ahead of any rain. Maybe my cats in Dartmoor might take shelter while my gargoyles work?'

Stephen felt puzzled. 'Dartmoor will be a slave driver to gargoyles, rest assured,' he said steering the conversation to a concern he had raised with the other architects he had interviewed. 'One fear I have is the building project may take too long and undermine the spiritual project it serves. Salisbury Cathedral, not too far from here, is perhaps Britain's finest, but it took only thirty-eight years to build despite its grandeur.

How long might the reconstruction of a much more modest abbey take?'

'I visited Salisbury on my way down to Devon. The challenge of designing and building that spire—incredible. Tall spires reach high to grasp the extended hand of God, that He might prevent our fall to hell below. Constructing Salisbury Cathedral in such a time exceeds anything we French have managed. To answer your question, from what I know about your abbey perhaps it might be ready in about five years. I do not mean finished, but by five years it could be fully operational. Masterpieces may take lifetimes before they can be considered complete. Torminster may be a modest project but, I will take it.'

De Juniac raised his mug while holding Stephen's gaze, 'If you will have me of course. I do not mean to be condescending, your project holds special appeal to me. When I woke this morning I desperately needed work, now I want this project even more. Your plans are ideal for the crystalisation of my dream of leaving an indelible mark on history, as well as for my service of God. You have the brilliant idea for the redesign of the monastery. Some master builders are known for their spires—that of Salisbury Cathedral.' He pressed his finger-tips together as if emulating the spire. 'Others are known for their towers, their windows or whatever. For me I would be happy to be known for my grotesques. Better to have something modest but memorable engraved on my tombstone than nothing at all: 'Here lies the creator of the world's most famous grotesques.' Please remember that, Father, should you outlive me—which I am sure you will.'

Stephen gave him a quizzical look, noting the Frenchman

wrapped his coat more tightly around himself as if he felt a draught. Ignoring De Juniac's last remark, he asked, 'Why grotesques?'

De Juniac lowered his mug, 'Perhaps I too should have been a monk. I feel compassion for the unfortunate, the burdened, the oppressed, the discarded, the forgotten, those who people are happy to overlook. My carving of grotesques tells their stories, elevating them to higher positions where they are no longer ignored; they receive the honour of serving God alongside the saints.'

Stephen paused as the maid passed him to stoke the fire, taking the opportunity to digest the Frenchman's words. Following her moving on to other chores, he said, 'I will not beat around the bush, as we say in English. I have other applicants who appear well-suited to the task.' (Later Stephen chastised himself for this untruth.) 'Why should I consider yourself over them?'

'Your other candidates, they have already worked on cathedrals?'

'Some cathedrals, some abbeys.'

'They can make grotesques look demonic?'

'They can.'

'But can they make them sound so?'

'I don't follow you.'

'My question is straightforward. Can their grotesques sing?'

'Sing?'

'Yes, sing.'

'Are you suggesting yours can?'

'Bien sur, of course. Not the gargoyles, for their plumbing interferes with their vocal chords. But for the grotesques, yes,

49

I can make them sing. For you I can make them sing ugly, like Satan himself if you wish.'

'What can they sing? Surely not hymns and psalms?' asked Stephen.

'No, that they cannot do, not even in French. Satan does not allow it.' The Baron's eyes twinkled. 'What do I mean by 'singing'? Does an organ sing? If so, my grotesques can sing. Will they sing on command? No, they will not. Can they sing in major or minor keys? No, not reliably, though they prefer minor. Sometimes, when they so choose, they sing notes sounding like an organ? Often discordant, I accept. Can their songs move people? Oh, yes, indeed. And in those who don't understand them my grotesques have instilled far greater dread from their songs than from their looks.'

With little further ado, Stephen decided this unique Frenchman was sent to him by God—who was he to refuse?

God's light, shining from above, cast shadows from all those it struck.

4

Horace's seat

Douglas Wright, the new medical director, came in early to catch up on tasks. It seemed a good idea, but looking around his bare office he was struck by its aroma of disuse. He went to open the window for some fresh air—stuck. He put his hand on the radiator—cold. It's nippy, where's the tap on it? Seized up. He wiped the dust from his seat before sitting down at a scratched, chipped Formica-topped desk on which stood a phone that looked like a collector's item. Curious, he picked up the phone—dead, so he would not phone ahead to notify Ward 9 about his imminent debut appearance. He never expected to be treated as royalty, he told himself.

He ascended the spiral stairs to Ward 9, which once had been the night stairs to the lay brothers' dormitory. He smiled as boyhood memories of castles visited were triggered by the smell of damp and the stairs' uneven, smooth, shiny surfaces from centuries of use. The modern boarded up walls struck him as incongruous with the stone steps. By a window the cleaners appeared to have overlooked an impressive spider's web. He went to stroke it away but at the last second let it be.

'He's made his home here,' said a friendly voice behind him. He turned, seeing a shabbily dressed woman smiling at him in a welcoming manner. Her right hand shook, suggesting long term antipsychotic medication side-effects. He made a mental note to review this if she turned out to be under his care.

'A fine specimen deserves a good home,' he said, returning her smile. Oh, to be a spider.

'On you go Doctor, your time is more precious than mine,' said the woman, as the stairs left little room for passing.

Wright continued up the spiral stairs. Reaching the landing, he was confronted with the familiar ammoniacal aroma of long stay wards. Before entering Ward 9 he looked along the long empty corridor. It runs for what must be most of the length of the former nave of the church, he thought, but it's deprived of natural light by the wards on either side. 'Purgatory' was the word that entered his head—a half way station between heaven and hell.

'Peaceful,' said the woman who had followed him up the stairs.

'Yes, it is,' said Wright, stretching his imagination to agree.

Opening the door of Ward 9 he detected human activity. The ward overlooked the northwest corner of the former abbey's cloisters and looking out of a window he saw the green square garth, encircled by the cloisters, in which a few patients were milling around, shivering, rubbing their hands, oblivious of the drizzle. It reminded him of Melville's 'damp drizzly November in my soul.'

Further on he located the nurse's station, beyond which was the day room, with doors opening into small dormitories. Vacant faces greeted him, of patients unfamiliar with interruptions of their dreary existence by people who did not belong there. That would change.

The ward's charge nurse stepped forward smiling, extending

his hand. He appeared in his forties, fit-looking and was dressed in an outlandish leather waistcoat. His eyes were welcoming but Wright thinking of his hand and the previous day's introduction said, 'I hope you are not going to break it,' before realising his inappropriateness.

'You must've already met the Castle,' Fergus laughed. 'Can I bandage your hand for you? Or maybe you need something a bit stronger, though it is a bit early in the day for that. Welcome Doctor, I'm Fergus Anderson, I hear you've ventured down into darkest Devon to drag us into the twentieth century. About time too.'

'Sorry, I was rather rude. You are right about Mr Castle. I am as you have guessed the new psychiatrist, Douglas Wright. I am very pleased to meet you Fergus. Is it okay if I call you Fergus?'

'By all means. Many people call me a lot worse.'

Wright continued trying to make up for his earlier odd response to Fergus's amicable approach. 'I'm very glad to be here. I should have plenty to keep me occupied if the patients are half as interesting as their guardians on the roof,' he gestured through the window to the grotesques on the roof tops.

'Yes, they are an impressive bunch. The Proud Lion above Castle's office is in charge, so if they give you any stick, visit you in your dreams or the like, he's the one to go to—the Lion, not Castle. I'd like to consider them my ancestors but none of them wears a kilt.'

'From which part of Scotland do you hail?'

'Kinloch Rannoch in the centre, though I confess I don't recall ever living there. Shortly after I was born my parents decided to escape the freezing gales and wet of Scotland for the slightly less freezing gales and wet of Dartmoor. Hence my

Devon accent with a wee touch of Scottish thrown in.'

A pleasant chat ensued, including which nearby villages were worth visiting, where on this side of Dartmoor were the best walks and the village pubs not to be missed. There was no shortage of good will from Fergus. After a few more getting to know you exchanges they arranged a formal ward round for the following day, when all the patients' cases would be discussed, both so Wright could assess the lie of the land and to address any pressing patient needs.

'I'll leave you in peace now,' Wright said, 'but if it's okay with you I'll talk to a few of the patients before leaving.' He wanted to find his feet and to gauge the patient population.

'By all means,' Fergus nodded.

Wright walked through the day room fitted out with plastic covered chairs from earlier decades. Many had holes in them from which the stuffing tried to escape. Three patients were sitting staring blankly into the space in front of them. One wandered holding a cup of tea, struggling to prevent his shaking hand from spilling its contents. No one was talking to anyone else and none of them appeared interested in him, which was understandable. He would take his time and await their approach. He sat down on one of the several vacant chairs, choosing one that looked less grubby than some of the alternatives. No sooner had he done so than the three nearby patients, disinterested in him and the world at large only moments ago, turned and glared at him. Several others approached, though where from seemed a mystery, also with hostile expressions on their faces and dark staring eyes. It suddenly seemed awfully stuffy. As ever more patients appeared, he became alarmed. Never in his career had he been afraid of patients, but he felt most ill at ease.

As the patients edged closer enclosing him in a semicircle, the hairs on the back of his neck stood erect. Objectivity, being guided by evidence, was always preferable to new-age notions of gut feelings, but he recalled one research paper suggesting an exception to the rule. Gut feelings of imminent danger were found to be valid pointers to risks of staff assaults. Such dangers were not part of a doctor's day to day life, for the vast majority of patients are gentle folk. However, there is always an exception, and right now perhaps an alarming number of them.

Surrounded by staring eyes, he imagined people prodding the ground in front of him with their forelegs, like agitated bulls? Rising to his feet, he gestured he would like to pass. To his relief the patients promptly parted for his exit. Walking away he looked over his shoulder to find their angry scowls and disconcerting interest in him had dissipated. He left, along with his new-found companion—humiliation.

The following day he brought this curious incident to the attention of Fergus. 'Do you know, for a moment it crossed my mind they might assault me. And I haven't the foggiest idea why.'

'You weren't too far wrong. Forgive me Dr Wright, I should have warned you about the one way to turn our gentle flock into a mob of Glaswegians evicted early from a pub on a Saturday night. You have only just arrived and already I owe you a pint or three. You do drink beer, I hope? There's a good pub just beyond the main gate, The Tor Church Alms. Once was the old abbey's alms house. Round here it's known as 'The Torturer's Arms.' '

'I do indeed like a pint, provided it is real ale. I cannot abide the gassy stuff. Young's Best was my tipple in London.'

'Here I recommend Wadworth's Six X. About yesterday's experience, I should have warned you, but it never crossed my mind as they are such a peaceful bunch. My nursing colleagues envy me on this ward as we have fewer violent incidents than any comparable ward.'

'I'm relieved to hear that, I may keep coming.'

'Most nurses consider working in Ward 9 a holiday, but you must never sit on Horace's seat. To do so is to take your life into your own hands. As I say they are a peaceful bunch, but through no fault of your own, you weren't to know, you did the equivalent of sitting in her chair when visiting the Queen. Not quite a capital offence, but not far off.'

'Who is this Horace?'

'Old Horace is a delight. We could start our round with a presentation of him if you want?'

'Please, I'd like to get up to date with him before my next faux pas.'

'Horace Oldham—Old Horace to his friends—is a seventy-three-year-old former school teacher. He taught history at Dinsborough High, for over thirty years. He was loved by the pupils and staff and he in turn loved them. Lived for them. His wife died of cancer over twenty years ago. His only daughter, a right little madam, has had little to do with him and has never visited him here in all the years I've known him. While his family situation wouldn't have helped, he'd never been severely depressed until the Education Department's cutbacks resulted in the closure of Dinsborough. He was sixty-two at the time. Devon had an aging population and it was obvious some of the smaller schools were going to cop it and Dinsborough did. Redundancies were offered; pressure was applied on the older teachers. Horace offered to work on for free, but that of course would have caused all sorts of problems with the unions. Being the oldest of the Dinsborough teachers he was done for and no other school was going to employ an experienced teacher in his sixties when they could hire much cheaper youngsters, who'd in theory have many more years of service ahead of them. The irony is youngsters get bored around here so move on after a few years. Horace would have stayed till his dying day as he was so devoted to his work, and he was in good health.'

'Sad. An all too common story these days. But to end up in a long stay ward having not suffered depression before, or had he?'

'He'd had minor episodes of depression, easily treated as the school made up for his family situation. It was following his redundancy he first became depressed and psychotic with it; persecutory delusions and auditory hallucinations. He was tried on various antipsychotics and antidepressants, had a number of courses of ECT, but they did damn all for him. Eventually his psychosis eased and his depression lifted a bit, but each time he was discharged he'd relapse. Hardly surprising, as he had lost his whole day to day focus and purpose in life. So that's how he ended up in here. He feels at home here, told me so himself; he's a delight, never complains, though at times it's clear from his face he's suffering.'

Dr Wright asked the usual technical questions about Horace's treatments. His current medication regime appeared in order producing a partial but tolerable result. What interested him most was his unfortunate experience of the day before. 'Tell me the story of Horace's seat, so I remember never to sit on it again.'

'Yes, you'd better understand that one,' said Fergus, smiling. 'Horace is not our ordinary patient. Despite our rules and routines, he won't get up for breakfast with the rest of them. We once tried forcing him, but it wasn't worth the effort, it just caused him distress. Now he rises around nine o'clock. We don't have a second breakfast sitting but we give him a cup of tea and a roll. He will have another cup of tea at elevenses, then he sleeps in his chair, the one you sat on, till lunch. After lunch he goes back to his chair—which his many friends religiously reserve for his use only—he sleeps some more till he has his evening meal.'

'Not much of an existence for the poor old chap?'

'No, but it's not as it sounds. We used to wonder whether his medications were causing day-time sedation, but he said they weren't, and a few times we tried withholding his morning doses, but it made no difference. Come evening, when daylight departs and darkness descends, Horace awakens.'

Fergus paused looking wary and embarrassed. 'Horace, would you believe, is the reason this ward is so quiet and peaceful. Three years ago he developed pneumonia and was transferred to Freedom Fields Hospital in Plymouth for a month. More patient incidents occurred in that month than in the previous two years. When he returned to us it all settled down.'

'How strange.'

'Too right it was.'

'What is his secret?'

'His secret is not entirely clear to me. But each evening he gives the patients history lessons. They don't study as such, but they listen with great interest—fascination might be a better word. We are not sure when it started, but they'd look sheepish after tea, then they'd take off to the TV room, all of them, and close the door. Initially we were a bit concerned as we'd hear them switch the TV off. We are meant to keep an eye on them, but with Horace there's never been any trouble. I once asked if he'd let me sit in on a lesson. He said he'd prefer it if I didn't and his friends gave me the look, though not like you copped yesterday. He's even written a book about the hospital's history.

'After the lessons, if lesson is the right word, they watch a bit of TV, then they take themselves off to bed. Horace stays up later, having slept all day, but come ten o'clock we ask him to go to his bed. He won't go to sleep till well past mid-night.' Fergus looked down, wincing. 'More than a few times we have found him missing. We used to be alarmed and conduct searches but we never found him away. After hours of searching we'd find him back in his bed asleep. He'd never say where he went or why, other than to say he'd been for a walk. Of course, we told him it was not allowed, but that made no difference, so we let it be. Strange though it may sound this ward remains the quietest in the hospital.'

'Perhaps the National Health Service should employ more Horaces.'

'The Nurses' Union wouldn't stand for that; I'd be out of work if we had too many Horaces.' Fergus paused, 'I'd be grateful Doctor if you'd see for yourself how things go here for a while, before trying to change things. It's taken some trial and error to reach this stable situation and young Mabel, our senior nursing officer, took quite some persuading. Mabel, Queen of Sheba, oh wise one, visited us several times during his evening lessons. Put her ear up against the door a few times, but she agreed all she heard was Horace's quiet voice. She of course was more concerned about his going walkabout, but she looked at our incident book.'

A patient approached waving a teapot. 'Thanks, Phillip, and would you get the doctor one? Milk and sugar, Doctor?'

'No sugar, thanks,' Wright smiled graciously at the patient who was doing the honours.

'Mabel agreed the ward's incident figures were the best in the hospital, except for Horace's going missing, but he's never come to any harm. She's a good type, been here forever and a day. You won't have any trouble with her, except she doesn't stand up to Castle. She has accepted our situation, but Castle is a different kettle of fish. If he can make trouble he will. He knows nothing about Horace and that is the way we'd like it to stay if you don't mind, Doctor.'

'I don't mind at all. I confess Mr Castle did not strike me as the most understanding of individuals.'

'You can say that again, he's a right bloody idiot, though I never said that.'

Wright respected these confidences and thereafter always respected the sanctity of Horace's seat.

5

Torminster Abbey

*O**ur story turns to Torminster Abbey's brotherhood and its restoration. Now, where was I? Ah, here's the page.*

Hubert, Stephen's former fellow brother at St Madern's, arrived first; the others followed a few months later. He had written to Abbot Stephen imploring him to accept him into his new monastery as his situation at St Madern's had grown untenable. Though Hubert had never elaborated on the nature of his problems with Prior Paul, he had confessed his own shameful origins to Stephen. His father had committed crimes for which he would have been hung but for his useful contacts and his wealth, enabling him to buy his way out of trouble. Hubert had rejected his family's sinful values, turning his back on them to pursue the path of virtue. The rigid Carthusian order of St Madern's had initially provided him with the much-needed direction and structure to his life, but it ended in disappointment and a sense of failure, as it had for Stephen.

Stephen was only too happy to welcome Hubert into Torminster's fold. His old friend's dedication and efficiency would be useful.

Stephen led Hubert into the cloisters where they sat on a stone bench in the cool shade out of the summer sun. Through the archway they looked at the overgrown grass in the central garth. Hubert sat at attention with his hands clasped in his lap. His cheeks were even more sunken than usual. His skeletal appearance would improve with good food, friends and a new sense of purpose, thought Stephen. A large stag beetle lay on its back by Stephen's foot, with its legs waving ineffectually in the air. Stephen bent his somewhat corpulent trunk, attempting to roll the beetle over with the strand of grass, but that failed so he picked it up and set it back down upright. 'Would that all life's problems were so easily solved,' he said, pouring Hubert a mug of water, wearing his smile of contentment. 'Did you have any trouble leaving St Madern's?'

'Only the inevitable. Prior Paul reminded me that my abandoning him equated with abandoning God, and my leaving for a Benedictine monastery was proof I was a lost soul, destined for hell. But I'm here now.' Hubert looked even stiffer than usual, devoid of facial expression. Even his tonsure appeared unusually severe, his bald patch was skirted by a thin circle of closely cropped hair.

Stephen looked pensive. 'I believe God has directed me to pursue a different approach to virtue at Torminster, one that will elevate its brothers to greater heights. Perhaps he has sent you to help me.'

Hubert looked down humbly.

'I will tell you more in due course. Thus far building decisions and plans have consumed all my time. I cannot have a quorum of brothers while the abbey is in such physical disarray.' Stephen gazed around to illustrate his point. There were stone blocks lying all around, tools, pulleys and scaffolding lying yet to be erected, a crane with a treadwheel and everywhere signs of building. Though it was less than a year since the plague decimated monastery had been abandoned, many weeds sprouted from cracks in the original stonework. 'De Juniac is doing a superb job but in these early stages I need to consult with him regularly so the physical and the spiritual may develop as one.

'Building has delayed my addressing many of the ecclesiastical issues, especially the Rule of Benedict which needs to be made available to all future brothers and implemented according to the day to day activities that must be pursued within these walls. When it is more shipshape. I would be grateful if you would assume responsibility for developing the Rule for our daily implementation of it.' Stephen knew of Hubert's love of books and study, and how he would relish the task. 'Soon I hope to be recruiting brothers. I must have the Rule in place before I do so.'

Hubert thrived performing his duties, and later described this period as the most fulfilling of his life, despite the building chaos all around. Would that it had remained that way. He treated Stephen like royalty, strictly in a non-materialistic Benedictine spiritual manner. He made pertinent suggestions then set about their implementation as if they were his abbot's brilliant ideas. He had no desire for acclaim—service, humility and respect for authority being Benedictine tenets. Hubert worked late into the nights on these tasks—Rules from a divine Saint that he and his abbot would enforce.

Over the weeks, Stephen discretely noted the change in expression of Hubert's face. Gone was his frown and though Hubert succeeded in containing any unbecoming smiles, the creases in the corners of his eyes at times betrayed him. Life demanded Hubert's attention.

Hubert was much better organised than his abbot and was fastidious in his approach to ecclesiastical work. Their cooperative work arrangements went so well that a few months later Stephen asked Hubert to accept the role as his prior (second in charge, unlike the Carthusian prior who is first in charge, there being no Carthusian abbot).

De Juniac saw his abbot through the mist and waded across the boggy ground, his boots threatening to desert him at each step. He had willingly dispensed with his fine clothes worn at Exeter, substituting more practical ones which would not look so incongruous with stones, mud and the wet. His leather tunic had served him well for many years, scuffed without ever tearing. Joining Stephen at the main portal of the west façade, they sheltered from the drizzle under the arch peering out through the mist. Besides them the saints looked out upon the world. 'Another good day for gargoyles,' said De Juniac, smiling.

Stephen shook his head and grinned.

'Very well then, to business my Father Abbot. The foundations and the lower walls are all in good order; that will make the extensions easier. The repairs of the monastic buildings are coming on so well they will be ready for use before winter. As winter approaches we won't be able to continue the rebuilding of the church, but when the winter gales are not blowing, we may set about demolishing the abbey's roof so come spring we can raise its walls.'

'What have you decided about the tower?'

'The present tower is much too heavy to hold an extension. Its wide base is helpful but to reach high it must taper, so the upper two thirds of it will have to come down. As the wind here is so strong we must use the Laon style towers, which will let the wind blow through them unimpeded, reducing the structural strain. At the higher levels you'll see right through the towers.' De Juniac fiddled with his leather glove. 'Also, our choir of grotesques will be exposed to the air flow without the sheltering effect of walls behind them—much better for their songs. The central tower will have three levels with over twenty arches, each one providing a home for at least one large grotesque. The singing ones will stand forward from the archways as if they are taking to the stage. Twenty large grotesques, served by their minions. There will be many mouths for our Mother Church to feed.'

Stephen noted De Juniac wore a sheepish smile. 'Come on, out with it.'

'Father, I have a worry. I need your help. I have received a letter from Heinrich my former head mason in Strasbourg. He and most of the rest of my Alsatian team have been like family to me over many years. I am now well fed and content but my loyal friends and their families are not. They are close to starving for lack of work.'

'The pestilence has dealt severe blows to both our countries,' said Stephen. While the plague had caused the collapse of the Alsatian economy, as it had across much of Britain, De Juniac's Alsatian masons' lack of work was unrelated to this. So many masons died of the plague there was a shortage of their skills for the ongoing cathedral work. Bricks and mortar are vulnerable to the centuries but not to human diseases. Work was not available to De Juniac's masons.

'I have another concern, Father. Thomas and his masons are good workers, I am happy with them. Some of them have skills for carving basic gargoyles, but as I feared none has skills sufficient for my singing grotesques. If I myself were to do all the carving, much as I would like to, I could carve twenty-four hours a day and still not be up to speed. We need more masons with particular skills and the only ones I know who do are starving.'

'So, the solution to both problems is the same? Do they want to join us? Would they be allowed to leave Alsace?'

'Yes, the solutions are the same. Yes, enough of them want to leave Alsace to join us. No, they would not be allowed to do so, but nor was I. There are ways. I'd like to bring six of them with their families out to Devon to work with us, but neither they nor I have the funds for their passage. I am so sorry to have to put it to you this way, Father.'

'No problem. Our project is going well, unforeseen costs are inevitable. If as you say, the local masons haven't the necessary skills, I see no alternative. Can they be brought over safely?'

'There are risks, but Heinrich suggests if they stay in Alsace some will die; Otto has already lost one child to malnutrition. Heinrich and I have contacts all the way to the sea. The risks of their leaving will be minor compared with those of staying.'

Stephen paused, nodding his head, 'Then please make the necessary arrangements. I will pay their costs. Tell them all I expect in exchange is good will and good work.'

As Stephen returned to his temporary quarters in the priests' dormitory, De Juniac waded around to the north side of the church. He looked up through the mist to the tower contemplating its redesign. Through one of the alcoves in the belfry he saw someone or something moving. He squinted, staring, and shivered; the breeze was cold. It looked like a monk, but what he saw was unclear.

Curious as to who or what might have caused the movement he saw, he entered the church via the northern transept and climbed the spiral stairs of the tower. At each level he looked for signs of people or objects that might account for what he saw. There was an odour of decay incongruous with the old stone and timbers. In the spacious belfry the giant bells sat still, covered with spiders' webs, and were much too heavy to have been moved by the wind. The precision of the webs' constructions attracted his admiration. A feral cat, one of several, hissed at him before running off. 'So, the tower is part of your domain?' The movement he had seen from below was not that of a cat. Strange. He dismissed the image as an illusion, returning his attention to how he would dismantle the tower.

The six masons and their families from Alsace arrived in early September, towards the end of the construction season for that year. Stephen saw a bedraggled train of pathetic looking adults and children trudging up the hill. How emaciated they looked. The largest and most senior of them, Heinrich, was the only one who looked as if he could swing a mallet. Stephen tried greeting them in English but they simply nodded and smiled. He tried again in French with only slightly more success. They spoke Alsatian, a Germanic dialect, Alsace at the time being part of the Holy Roman Empire, adjoining but not part of France. Language barriers would create a distance from the Devon masons.

In the days following, their women folk in their long tunics with wimples covering their heads appeared relieved and uncomplaining, appreciative of their new boggy paradise. No matter how wet it was they laughed at their discomforts as if they were nothing. It amused Stephen to watch the smiling mothers looking on as their children ate their now plentiful food like ravenous puppies.

The women and older children kept busy clearing the abbey's neglected fields, overgrown with stinging nettles and other weeds. Come the following spring they would plant vegetable crops and Stephen would bring sheep, goats and a few cows over from the remains of his farm. The fields were mostly on south facing slopes with good drainage and exposure to the feeble filtered rays of the sun. The abbey and its fields became a picture of rural industry, the men toiling with stone, the women with the earth.

Some weeks after the Alsatians' arrival Stephen was in the cloisters when he was approached by one of the women who, with her minimal English, said, 'Father, please!' gesturing for him to follow her quickly. Her gestures and her eyes suggested something serious, perhaps an accident? Stephen followed her to the parlour, where, in the dim light to his amazement he saw Brother Frederick, an elderly priest who had ridden for more than a day from St Madern's. He lay on a large length of timber out of the wet, appearing almost lifeless with shallow breathing and was unresponsive to Stephen's questions, so much so Stephen feared he might not survive. Frederick was aged sixty-four, shrunken and frail even at the best of times, but he had been a model of virtue, respected by all at St Madern's. With the efficiency and the benevolence of the Alsatian women he soon regained his health.

As his strength returned Frederick explained he had followed Hubert's example, leaving St Madern's, but had underestimated the handicap of his years on such a long ride. He could not stay at St Madern's any longer, but again like Hubert, he would not elaborate. All three understood the Rule of Respect, seniors must never be challenged, and were glad of their now more conducive opportunities to practice it.

Frederick soon was back on his feet. At meetings with Stephen and Hubert he was so quiet and self-contained it was difficult at times to know whether he was awake. He was small of stature, thin and his tonsure was white, but thick. Both during monastic silences and when others were talking, he would close his eyes to tune into tranquility. Frederick was no fool; he possessed the power to retain awareness of all that was going on, even when he appeared to be asleep. However, his frailty rendered him unsuitable for most of Torminster's manual tasks.

Frederick's frailty contrasted with his well-preserved eyesight, perhaps the result of having his eyes closed much of the time. He was designated the role of scribe as the three brothers deemed the Torminster project worthy of recording for history from its earliest conceptual stages onwards. The brothers had accepted Stephen's plan that all brothers would be directed to purify themselves by transferring their sins through prayer into the babewyns. Eyebrows were raised when he informed them, but their St Madern's experiences facilitated their acceptance of a different approach. They agreed the abbey's history should be exact; Hubert was instrumental in this decision, knowing his abbot might be more casual, though he would never have described him as such. If they were to pursue a different approach in the service of God their deeds, their reasons for doing so and their results should be recorded for others to learn from—for better or worse. None of them would have realised how exact Frederick's records would turn out to be, partly as they agreed no one in their community other than Frederick—not even Stephen—would ever read them. For the outside world Frederick must be free to record everything— warts and all. And we here today are amongst his beneficiaries.

The first record of unrest dates from late that October 1350. Torminster had enjoyed a productive summer of construction surpassing De Juniac's timetable, thanks to the local Devon workers. But it gradually dawned on the locals that despite their good work some of them must be laid off for the winter, as the gales and ice would make construction too dangerous, and the ice would render fresh mortar prone to cracking. All the Alsatians would be kept on, mostly pursuing stone carving in the shelter of the cloisters through winter, but most of the local stone workers, the ones most lacking in skills, would at best have only occasional menial work, dismantling walls, clearing debris and such. They who had been so productive while taking orders from a Frenchman.

Thomas Pynn, the senior Devon mason and a good-natured man, met with his crew in the garth, explaining, 'The Alsatians have nowhere to go; they don't have homes as we do. Not even the money to return to Alsace for the winter. Do you expect them to sit around all winter doing nothing? And where? In the snow up on the tops of the moor? If they're to be housed and fed should they not work? The unfortunate reality is there will be times during the bad weather when we won't have enough work. That's not new to any of us.' He looked up to grey clouds galloping above the tower.

'But why should foreigners, enemies of England, be treated better than us who live here?' said Warren, with feigned confidence, looking insecurely to his friends for their approval.

'I agree it is unfortunate.'

'Unfortunate! It's more than that.'

'There's also the fact that someone has to carve the singing grotesques,' Thomas said putting his hands on his hips and puffing out his chest, 'Even I haven't a clue how to do so.' Relaxing, he added, 'I asked De Juniac if I could be taught how. He said I could, but my apprenticeship would take several years or more. All the Alsatians grew up as children watching their fathers develop these skills and started their own apprenticeships as soon as they could swing a mallet.' Thomas shrugged, shaking his head. 'The singing grotesques are carved out of granite; any of you ever tried carving granite? It's hard as hell, it takes much more skill, even for simple carvings. As for carving them in a way that makes sound—think about it. Over winter the Alsatians won't be doing jobs you or I could do.'

'They are better than us, are they?' said Stuart.

'They are not better people, but they have skills we don't. Tell you what, where tasks crop up we can do I'll insist we get them,' said Thomas.

'We know what you're really saying,' muttered Warren.

'This is getting nowhere. Get back to work.'

Thomas was true to his word, driving a hard bargain with De Juniac and the abbot. The tors of Dartmoor provided a bountiful supply of granite. The Alsatians would choose the stones, the local stoneworkers would hew them out and cart them the several miles across the boggy moor back to the abbey. But this proved back breaking work and resulted in injuries, including a large stone rolling onto one of the local worker's ankles crushing it, leaving him permanently lame and limiting his future work prospects.

Working over winter in the shelter of the cloisters the Alsatian masons concentrated on carving grotesques and the more difficult of the gargoyles, while some of the more skilled Devon masons carved less complex ornamental features. The clatter of mallets competed with the sounds of the wind and rain. The cloisters were open to the weather but they were afforded some protection by the square surroundings. They chose the west side of the cloisters as their haven as it was the more sheltered from the elements. They warmed their hands from time to time around a brazier, bringing the two factions together. The locals naturally spoke to their compatriots in English without being understood by the foreigners, but provocative looks were intelligible to all.

As the winter progressed, though De Juniac and Heinrich were careful to show their appreciation, the local stone workers increasingly felt judged as second rate. And the unskilled stone workers' families went hungry.

Amity provides such fertile ground for enmity.

6

The Castle

Douglas Wright approached the doctors' common room with a contrived sense of optimism. This time he would find signs of life, he told himself, as he straightened his tie. But yet again it was empty. The high-ceilinged room felt cold, musty and oppressive; not a living soul was to be found. He did find proof of life on a tea trolley laden with a large metal pot, which he touched to satisfy himself this was a contemporary provision, not the remains of something from a time past. Yes, it was hot. Discretely, he lowered his nose over a large jug of milk—no offensive aroma. Standing alone with the trolley in the cavernous room he felt like an actor in a play who had just gone on stage, but on the wrong night—there were no other actors and no audience.

He was due to meet Dr Peter Frank over an extended tea break. He helped himself to a receptacle from the stack of flimsy disposable cups. Instead of tea he chose a sachet of a cheap brand of coffee over which he poured luxurious hot water, following which he dropped a few coins into the tin in which the doctors paid for such delicacies. Aha, he espied a solitary used tea bag standing as confirmatory evidence some form of life had visited recently; but it appeared cold and dry so it might have been from the previous week. And there were no coins in the tin save his own.

Waiting for Dr Frank, he felt a nagging sense of loneliness and sympathy for the hospital's patients. At the end of the day he would go home to a loving family and a warm environment. Not so for Torminster's unfortunates—Les Misérables. He sipped his coffee wondering whether he should add a second sachet to it and, if so, should he add more coins to the tin?

Was he wise to have left his London hospital? It was huge compared with Torminster and much older. 'Bedlam' it was referred to in earlier times, its origins dating back to the Crusades in which King Richard I led the Christian attacks on the Turks with the aim of capturing the Holy Land—Christians slaughtering Moslems with the Pope's blessing. Torminster Asylum, serving Plymouth (originally called Sutton), was a late comer, so he had read. The Exminster Asylum serving Exeter, the capital of Devon, opened in 1845 but more than a decade later Plymouth to the west still had no corresponding service, despite its greater population. Eventually, a decision was made to use the abandoned Torminster Abbey. This Gothic wonderland.

He gazed out of the window of what once had been the lay brothers' dormitory. Across the north cloister he saw the tower below which was the row of Hell Hounds, some of which were so decrepit they were unrecognizable, but for the fact they were part of a group. Some appeared to have been restored and were even draining water from the old church roof.

With a sense of relief, he heard footsteps. He turned, 'Peter, good to see you. What will you have, tea or coffee?'

'Tea thanks, Douglas.'

Peter Frank was the most senior in years of Torminster's

psychiatrists and had served as director for a term of only two years. He was aged sixty-eight, had a slim healthy build, did not smoke but was gaunt looking with sunken cheeks making him look older than his years. Peter was different but was respected by both his colleagues and his patients. He spoke slowly with deliberation, unlike those who chat ten to the dozen without saying anything. He would run late for appointments, but only because he was so generous in his allocation of time for preceding patients. He was often the last doctor to leave at the end of the day.

Dropping more coins in the tin, handing him his tea, Wright said, 'Thank you Peter for taking the time out of your busy schedule to meet with me. I am keen to learn as much as possible about our unit from those like yourself who know it well. I am not one for charging in, knocking down walls, then deciding the walls were useful and should be rebuilt. I am keen to learn from you all how I might best help Torminster raise its clinical expertise to even loftier heights. I would value your observations of the place and how it works.'

'I am glad you have joined us, Douglas, you are most welcome,' Frank said with formality. 'You will find the consultants easy to deal with.' He sipped his tea but it was too hot. 'The registrars' training program is running well. The nurses are pleasant; they try to be helpful. But you will have your work cut out with our manager, Mr Castle. You would know a recruit from London was sought because no one could be found locally to replace Dr Symonds. That was because of Castle.'

'No, I was not aware of this,' Wright replied, a little miffed as he thought he had been selected on his exceptional merit.

'Frances Symonds was a lovely lady, but too sensitive for the challenge of Castle. He broke her; she has still not returned to work after being off now almost a year. That's common knowledge by the way. None of us other local psychiatrists were inclined to go another round with him. We all refused to volunteer to be acting director in her absence, so your appointment was rushed forward. Rest assured though, you will have our support.'

'Great,' said Wright feeling the reverse. 'What is the essential problem with Castle?'

'Simply, he is an idle bloody-minded crook.'

'Oh, is that all?'

'No, but I wouldn't want to overwhelm you. He controls everything; make a simple request of him, he will deliver the reverse. After fifteen years here he is an expert at opposition and has left his indelible mark.' Frank grimaced as he sipped his tea.

'How has he got away with this for so long?'

'He has contacts in high places. Also, Mabel Willing, is not one to oppose him. She does what he says, lovely lady though she is.' Frank stuck his fingers inside his collar as if it was constricting his throat, despite it appearing at least a few sizes too large and his tie being loosely tied. 'You will have to form your own ideas about how to work with him, but be careful. I never got anywhere with him; I gave up trying.'

'Thanks,' said Wright with another of his sinking feelings.

Though he'd barely touched his cup of tea, Dr Frank said, 'If you will excuse me, I must be getting along,' as though he was determined not to be late for the first time in years.

Back in his office, the rain pelting down against his window, on his fifth attempt Wright successfully contacted Castle's secretary. He said over the phone, 'Oh, good morning Frieda, I was wondering whether you could book an appointment for me to see Mr Castle, whenever he has a spare moment.'

'An appointment?' was her response, as though the word was alien.

'Yes, when would suit him?'

'Suit him? I wouldn't know.'

'Might you be able to look in his diary and at least pencil in a provisional time?'

'He doesn't have a diary.'

'Well how do you keep track of his commitments?'

'I don't.'

'Sorry, aren't you his secretary?'

'That's me.'

'Oh. Perhaps I should just pop my head in when I'm passing.'

'Do what you like, I don't mind.'

Wright put the phone down holding it between his thumb and fore-finger as if it he had picked it up from somewhere unsanitary.

Castle's office was situated up some steps leading into his secretary's office in what had once been the abbey's sacristy. The Proud Lion grotesque lurked above, but its decayed appearance suggested its tolerance of the office's current occupant might relate less to pride and more to senility. In the following week Wright called by four times. On the first two occasions neither Frieda nor Castle was there. On his third attempt Frieda was there but not Castle. 'I'm expecting him in soon,' she volunteered, with a strangely contemptuous look that left our distinguished psychiatrist wondering whether it related to himself or to her boss.

'Would you ask him to give me a call in Ward 2 so I can arrange a time to see him?' Wright asked with due politeness.

'I'll do that.'

Might Castle have escaped by the back stairs? Wright knew that Castle had had back stairs constructed beneath the Smiling Fornicating Peasant gargoyle so only she, her Devilish Goat Lover and Frieda, when she was in, would observe his comings and goings. The Smiling Peasant still had eyes to see as she sat in a sheltered location and had been restored.

On Wright's fourth attempt to visit Castle again neither Frieda nor Castle were in. He was tempted to ask the Smiling Peasant about their whereabouts. As he left, he noticed Matilda wheeling a large cleaning trolley along the long corridor. He had seen her a number of times since his arrival but tended to consider himself too busy to talk to her other than to offer polite greetings. She was only a cleaner, but he now would be grateful for help from anyone. He hurried to catch up with her. 'Good morning Matilda,' he offered with excessive enthusiasm in his time of need.

'Oh, hello my love? Are you settling in?'

'I am. Yes, nicely.'

'How do you like our friends?'

'What? Mr Castle?'

'Castle! Have you gone bonkers already? No, my love, I'm talking about our babewyns.'

'Baby whats?'

'Babewyns—grotesques and gargoyles—our stone friends. Didn't they teach you anything at medical school?'

'Oh them,' Wright said with a reassuring semblance of sanity. 'They are rather special. If only they could run this place.'

'Don't you worry, they do—with a little help from Brian, Horace and me. Have you met Brian yet?'

'No, but I've met Horace. Brian wouldn't happen to be the deputy manager, would he?'

'Well in a manner of speaking he could be, depending on what you're needing. He, more than anyone, keeps the hospital shipshape.'

'No, I'd better stick with the real boss for now. Have you any idea where I might find Mr Castle? I have tried to do so a number of times without any success.'

'Course I do my lover—if ever you need to know anything just ask me. I know everything that goes on hereabouts.'

'I wish I had known that earlier.'

'Well now you do, you have no excuses.'

'Is he in today?' Wright asked. It was 2.20 p.m. so he should be, but he might have appointments elsewhere.

'If he is, you'll find him in his office.'

'I have just been there and neither he nor Frieda was there.'

'I don't mean that office, you daft ha'p'orth, I mean his farm office.'

'I have not been to the farm yet. I didn't know he has an office there.'

'If Castle is in at this time of day, the farm is where he will be.'

'Then farm here I come. Thank you so much Matilda.'

' 'Ere Tilly to you. Don't you forget, if you need anything you come to Tilly.'

Relieved his frustrations might be over, Wright proceeded up the hill to the farm shed, lifting his jacket collar up to protect against the wind and taking care not to get his shoes muddy.

Entering, he noted a dozen or so busy patients working and a musty rancid apple smell. He approached one worker, introducing himself as the new doctor.

'Pleased to meet you, Doctor,' was the cordial reply in a strong Devon accent from an expressionless face.

Wishing to return like with like Wright remarked, 'This is an impressive set up; what do you do here?'

'We make cider, Doctor, with these here apples,' said the brew master pointing to a large mound of them looking none too inviting. 'We also grow and harvest these vegetables here. Might you like to try a glass of cider, Doctor?'

Wright was about to say no thanks, but he refrained as he did not want to appear aloof. 'I would be glad to, but just a drop as I have work to do.' The worker picked up a grubby pint tankard filling it half-way. Wright raised the glass noting the golden cloudiness and a slightly offensive aroma. Undaunted he took a healthy sip; good, not too sweet, it could pass as commercial grade cider, which was what it was. It may not have been exported, but most pubs within a ten mile radius stocked it. 'It is admirably full bodied. What strength is it?' he asked, being both interested and wanting to appear so.

'We usually make 'un around six to seven per cent, Doctor.'

'That's what I thought,' said the now congenial doctor who enjoyed his tipple. After offering a little more appreciation he asked, 'Do you know where I might find Mr Castle?'

'Try the office,' said the worker pointing to a closed door.

At last! I have him on the hook. Wright knocked on the door then wondered whether this was being a bit formal for what was a farm shed. No response so he opened the door. Inside was Frieda with another lady he did not recognise. 'Ah hello,

Frieda, is Mr Castle here?'

'Er, he might be under the bench,' Frieda replied, before bursting into the giggles with her friend. 'Just joking, Doctor. Here Jean, you must meet the new doctor. Dr Wright, this is Jean.'

While saying 'How do you do?' Wright thought, you Frosty Frieda are drunk and can cut the jokes. But not wishing to appear too superior to take a joke he responded, 'No, he is not under the bench. Might you have any other ideas where he might be?'

'Poor thing went home with one of his migraines, he did, about an hour ago.'

'Blast, I was hoping to see him.'

'You're not very sympathetic, you a doctor an' all. Migraines can be very debilitating you know. Never mind, I am sure you have plenty of patients you could be talking to instead,' said Frieda with a coy look.

Was she dismissing him? The impertinence. Before he said something he might regret he replied, 'Yes, you are right, I had better be getting along.' He took his leave with a forced smile. All the way back to his ward he seethed at his ever-growing frustration. His first day here he had been dismissed by a bloody-minded manager, now by the manager's secretary.

7

Family

This evening, my friends, it's time to introduce our grotesque family—our babewyns, I should say—grotesques may be the lords but we should not forget the workers, the gargoyles, our dutiful plumbers.

Winter gnawed at his fingertips as De Juniac gazed up at the main tower, square and heavy right to its top. Frowning, he shuddered with the unrelenting cold, slipping his icy hands beneath the folds of his tunic. It would be good to take it down as soon as possible. Its interior had been gutted but he would have to wait for spring before dismantling the tower's upper reaches.

Three crows guarded the tower, always three. Suddenly, as one they took off squawking in alarm. Then it was there, definitely, another movement in the same alcove as previously, not crows, something or someone much larger. It was a human figure, a monk in a black habit, he thought, but they know to avoid the tower as all the floors have been removed, it's impossible for anyone be standing where the hooded figure now stands—without miraculous powers of climbing.

The apparition returned his gaze with defiance, raising an arm beckoning to him. De Juniac wiped sleet from his eyes as the wind gusts eased allowing him a clearer look. He now saw the monk's face—a face of only bone, as was its extended hand, both devoid of flesh. 'Follow me; I offer you rest eternal.' Did he hear that?

'What's the matter?' asked Heinrich causing De Juniac to startle.

He turned to Heinrich. 'Do you see it?' pointing up at the tower.

'See what? What am I looking for?'

'There, the figure up there in the recess,' said De Juniac, pointing.

'No, my friend, I do not see it.' Heinrich saw a look of bewilderment on De Juniac's face. 'Remember Strasbourg? Could it be the same?'

Looking back up at the tower De Juniac no longer saw the apparition. 'The sooner that tower comes down the better.'

The passing of winter brought an early spring and like Eve the trees covered their nakedness with greenery. De Juniac's workers resumed building ahead of schedule; the discord between the two groups appeared to have settled. While the Alsatians installed the babewyns in the sites he chose for them, the Devon masons worked on the church, which was now his priority.

Stephen awaited his brothers. The hem of his habit was sodden from trailing in muddy puddles, but he did not notice such discomforts. He looked up at the recently installed line of Hell Hound gargoyles stretching the length of the southern roof of the nave overlooking the cloisters. Water dripped like saliva from their mouths.

He saw the brothers walking over towards him. Hubert

as ever appeared immaculate, while Frederick's habit seemed several sizes too large for him, trailing even more in the wet than his own. They were working well together, the older brother being content to let the younger take the lead.

'Good morning, Father Stephen,' Hubert said, while Frederick nodded. Hubert followed Stephen's gaze. 'These stone demons appear to have received the blessings of our Lord. How else could they appear so life-like?'

Stephen agreed, 'They must.' De Juniac would be happy to hear this. Stephen was yet to disclose the secret of the grotesques' songs to Hubert or Frederick. Was he wise to have kept the secret so long? With a pang of guilt, he thought, might his omission to tell De Juniac represent more deception than secrecy. Whilst his friend sought to protect the babewyns from their burdens, Stephen planned to add to them—they were to bear the sins of his brothers. They were only stone; he was the abbot and he was paying the bills.

There had been no songs as yet. Thus far the dry winds had been light and only a few grotesques had been installed, mostly those that would not sing, and gargoyles whose plumbing took the place of vocal cords were the priority. He must tell his brothers today before any grotesques burst into song. De Juniac had warned him he was uncertain about the precise sounds they would make, but they were likely to be deep and disturbing, reflecting the misfortune the congregation would seek to avoid.

Stephen ambled along with Hubert and Frederick. He looked up at one of De Juniac's creations, a lion with a shaggy mane, mouth wide and snarling, brandishing a raised paw. He quoted from the Rule of Benedict, chapter 72:

Just as there is an evil zeal of bitterness

Which separates from God and leads to hell,
So there is a good zeal
Which separates from vices and leads to God
And to life everlasting.

'The babewyns will manifest the zeal of bitterness contrasting with our good zeal,' said Stephen. Frederick's life had been dominated by good zeal. Hubert's drive was profound and with appropriate direction his virtues would flourish. As abbot, Stephen accepted responsibility for bringing out the best in his brothers.

'Good morning Baron,' he called to his approaching architect, who nodded and wiped his nose. Stephen, rubbing his cold hands together, smiling at Hubert and Frederick, said, 'De Juniac has agreed to take us on a tour to introduce us to some of his offspring.'

On cue the baron said, 'Good morning Father, Brothers, I have brought young Luke with me. Luke's the son of mason Ralph Scobbahull. He's been learning his trade under his father, who must be a very good teacher as young Luke is already an expert.' The red headed lad blushed with the awkwardness of adolescence.

'Tell them what you think about the stone carving of the babewyns,' said the Frenchman. Luke just shuffled, so De Juniac continued, 'The installation of the gargoyles requires connecting them up to drainage channels and Luke volunteered to help Heinrich with this task. Some gargoyles need to be mounted in difficult positions, even out on the flying buttresses that support our nave. The lad's agility and enthusiasm are a great help. But it's the singing grotesques that fascinate him most and he can't wait to hear them perform.' Luke smiled.

They approached the west end looking at its recently installed grotesques above the ornate arched main entrance. The scowling Demonic Abbot, wearing its mitre, berated those below for their sins. 'The face appears alive,' said Stephen, 'but not in a way I would wish for myself. Is there a story behind him?'

'There are stories behind all our babewyns,' De Juniac replied, pausing and looking pensive. 'I knew such an abbot many years ago. He said he cared for all, but his congregation feared him; he cajoled, he scolded, he said it was his responsibility to do so. He told them God loved them and he loved them, but they felt no warmth from him; their children burst into tears if he approached them. This he said was proof of their sinfulness; their parents should bring them to church more often. Later their parents beat their little ones for embarrassing them in front of the abbot. Thus, the little ones were to grow up to love the church.'

Stephen made a silent pledge; the Demonic Abbot would be his principal repository of any ill feelings towards others. He turned his gaze to four nearby Laughing Monkeys installed above the original figures of the saints. The monkeys appeared to be scampering around laughing and pointing to the world beyond.

De Juniac, noting Stephen's perplexed expression, said, 'Our monkey friends are the observers of life. They find the ways of their human cousins puzzling and amusing.' Hubert looked at them with disapproval. Frederick smiled as he saw the Monkey Scribe, a monkey with a slate and stylus who appeared to be recording what he saw.

Entering the church, glad to escape the drizzle, they gazed along the nave where building materials were scattered all around and upwards at the now higher vaulted ceiling—a work in progress.

De Juniac explained. 'The taller walls and lighter roof allow more windows, which now admit more light. There is as yet no glass in the windows but in time even the windows will tell stories.' Although the external roof was in place the ceiling was far from complete, yet light already penetrated the darkness drawing their gazes towards heaven. Light's rays shone down at an angle illuminating the droplets of mist, creating beauty from damp.

Hubert paused, looking upwards with his hands clasped in the fashion of prayer. He had never been in a church of this French design and wore an unusual look of interest.

They exited the nave by the door next to the southern transept, the transept being a structural representation of a cross, the north and south transepts depicting the arms of the cross. Entering the corner of the north and east cloisters, they strolled around the cloisters passing a small library to their left, beyond which was the chapterhouse in which they would hold their meetings. The brothers paused before entering, to inspect two new small grotesques on either side above the entrance. Each wore a wild harried appearance. One grimaced pressing its fists to the sides of its head; the other displayed a tortured scream. Both of their faces were distorted by expressions of agony; their brows furrowed, they stared at the brothers as if blaming them for their wretchedness. 'The Tormented Twins suffer for the sins of mankind,' said De Juniac, who was himself surprised by the power of their torment, as may a mother be pleasantly surprised by the beauty of her daughter.

Proceeding onwards to the southern cloister they paused at

intervals to admire other smaller grotesques on the walls and to look outwards at the growing array of different gargoyles ready for duty. From the south they gazed north at the magnificent southern aspect of the abbey's nave with its army of Hell Hounds, above the sloping northern cloister roof. De Juniac said, 'God's work is their duty, but some say Hell Hounds are the bearers of Death.' Stephen was impressed by their air of uniformity combined with the individuality of their expressions, some with their heads turned to one or other side, but all with mouths open as if baying, all working towards a common goal. Might his brothers also work as one?

De Juniac raised his hand signaling farewell, 'I have tasks to attend to so I'll leave you in Luke's capable hands, for he has given the babewyns their tasks.' Again, Luke beamed with pride. De Juniac took leave of the brothers, who Luke led out via the west door back into the cold and wet. Looking back above the lay brothers' dormitory they gazed at De Juniac's elaborate Human Lineage of many gargoyles and grotesques, ranging from bizarre fish and frogs at the south end, with animals becoming more sophisticated and eventually human in appearance. Stephen smiled at the profusion of grotesques. He had asked for them and De Juniac was delivering them.

Luke explained, 'Mr De Juniac has portrayed the increasing complexity of life, with mankind at the centre with an ape by his right side; further to the right are the Primitive Lower Creatures. Beyond man to the left is the Moral Decay lineage. I'm not sure what he means but as you move along the creatures become stranger, with evil demons at the far end.' The brothers saw sadistic expressions of the grotesques at the far end, with one biting the head off a baby.

Hubert uttered a snort of disgust to which Stephen responded, 'We must forever be on our guard. We three know all too well the depths to which even good people may sink. God created us in his image; he then gave us the burden of choice. The result is many fall from grace, so we brothers have to work all the harder at maintaining our reflection of the Lord.' Both Hubert and Frederick nodded in agreement.

Luke saw Heinrich beckoning to him, so he took his leave. Stephen decided it was time to be open with his brothers. 'I have told you the purpose of these stone creatures: their taking on the burden of our evil. Their ugliness will facilitate this, but they are more than ugly in appearance.' He paused. Hubert looked at his abbot until he chose to continue, while Frederick looked downwards with his eyes closed. 'The larger of them sing.'

Hubert failed to suppress a flicker of surprise; his eyes asked whether his abbot was being humorous. He awaited his abbot's elaboration.

Stephen walked on, giving them time to absorb his words. He continued, 'I hired De Juniac not only because he was an outstanding architect and master builder but also because he, and his stone carvers, have unique skills in the creation of grotesques whose expressions communicate with observers prepared to see—and to hear.' His voice faltered. He paused looking upwards and around as if he was afraid. They walked further on with none of them being in a hurry to end this intriguing exchange. Stephen, noting Hubert's formal self-restraint and Frederick's dreamy expression, was biding his time, summoning his courage to continue and waiting for their receptiveness to peak.

Stephen continued in a firmer tone, 'Some of the larger grotesques have been designed to sing with the wind. Their songs will test us.' Hubert raised his eyebrows; Frederick opened his eyes. 'De Juniac would not tell me all and I respected his decision. Their songs will not include words, merely tones comparable with those of an organ. He did say dry weather and strong winds will be essential to their songs. Remember as children the sounds created by blowing across the top of an empty bottle? Hubert looked uncertain. The organ and the grotesques' songs both work on the same principle. Their recitals will be occasional, not responsive to our demands, only to those of our Lord.'

Stephen felt a wave of relief as Hubert's facial expression appeared one of approval and Frederick looked serene. The brothers had received his secret better than he expected. His own more customary look of radiant benevolence returned. He added, 'The songs will at times interrupt our tranquility; I intend them to do so. That will make it easier for us to transfer our sins to them.'

Stephen watched the efficiency of De Juniac's chiseling. Rapid strokes, none wasted, carved perfect contours bringing the stone to life. Emboldened by his recent successful revelations to Hubert and Frederick, Stephen, yawned after another night of disturbed sleep. By now he recognised the theme of his dreams—deceit. He decided today he would come clean with his French brother in arms. Today he would confess his deception about his proposed use of the babewyns to his friend, their creator. If De Juniac's paternal feelings towards his babewyns ran as deep as he suggested, how would he take it? How might parents respond to those confessing ill-treatment of their children? This time he would not be averted from his task. Yet again, averted he was.

Before Stephen could commence his confession De Juniac looked up at him and said, 'Father Abbot, I have something important to show to you, which I would like to do with you alone.' De Juniac was beaming, he appeared as happy as he was that first day when Stephen agreed to hire him. De Juniac saw Stephen wanted to say something, but interrupted him. 'Yes, yes, Father Abbot later, first, I insist you accompany me to the west façade, then I will be all yours for you to instruct or berate as you wish. Come, it won't take long.' He took Stephen by the shoulders leading him out of the cloisters via the west doorway, then he turned him to face the western façade. 'Heinrich, the others and myself wanted to express our gratitude for your giving us all new lives here.'

Heinrich, the other Alsatians and Luke stood nearby, in front of a long drape covering a figure Stephen had noted earlier, by the outer side of the right doorway arch. De Juniac nodded to Heinrich and the others, whereupon they lowered the drape. 'Father Abbot.'

Stephen saw a life-like stone carving of himself standing dressed in an abbot's formal garments, topped with a mitre. At his feet lay a sleeping hound and sitting on its haunches by his right side reaching up to his waist sat a tall thin cat with its head nestled against his hip with a look of contentment, such that he could almost hear it purring. On Stephen's left shoulder sat a young monkey with its right arm wrapped around the back of the abbot's head, grasping the corner of his mouth while with its left hand it pointed to the world in front of them—with a facial expression of interest and understanding, free of contempt.

Stephen gazed at his statue. Somehow the light on its face gave it life, its facial expression was of the tranquility and benevolence he so desired, but which of late seemed so elusive. Its generous attributes did not belong to him, they reflected the sentiments of his Alsatian friends. Stephen embraced De Juniac. 'You have been too generous. If only my reward was warranted.' His left arm twitched agreement.

De Juniac smiled, 'Now, Father, is not false modesty a sin?'

Stephen embraced the other Alsatians and gave Luke a friendly pat on his head. After a few more polite expressions of gratitude to the Alsatians, Stephen and De Juniac walked on. 'Father, you had something you wanted to say to me, now I am all yours.'

'It can wait my friend. Thank you again.' Stephen nodded, forced a fragile smile with eyes lowered and left De Juniac to continue his work while he himself pretended to inspect the other works of the Alsatian stone carvers, conveying more thanks to them.

Frederick meanwhile approached De Juniac asking him what else inspired his creations, having noted that many of the babewyns were various forms of cats and dogs. De Juniac was reticent in his response, 'My children are for you to make of them what you will.' Little did he know how close to Stephen's reality he strayed.

'Quite,' responded Frederick, 'but there must be something of yourself in your 'children' .'

'I have always liked cats,' said De Juniac. 'Me and the ancient Egyptians. Not so Pope Gregory IX. As you may know he considered the black cat an incarnation of Satan. Therefore, he ordered black cats must die. Was the black cat really evil or might the cat simply have been different? Dogs relate to us humans as if we are God. They worship us to our face yet cheat us as soon as we turn our backs, as many of us do to our Lord. But cats…they do not worship or cheat us. They make no promises, so they break no promises, that's why I admire them.'

Frederick reflected on De Juniac's reference to lack of worship. De Juniac continued, 'The cat has suffered, being blamed for the pestilence, he's been persecuted for his sins, but are they his sins or might they be the sins of others? In Strasbourg I saw the hatred of humans towards cats; throwing them into rivers, which the cats do not appreciate; or worse, throwing them into fires. Then he who has done 'God's work,' purging us of Satan's helper, he laughs at the cat's suffering. Is this what our Lord encourages?'

'Why did Pope Gregory blame the cats? I have not heard of their link with Satan before.'

De Juniac continued, 'Both cats and dogs have been thought by pagans to be guardians of the Otherworld. I can understand dogs make good guardians. They follow their masters' instructions; when commanded to hurt someone they may do so with relish. But tell a cat to hurt someone. What does he do? Nothing, he listens only to his own commands. So much for the cat as a guardian of the Otherworld. I saw the cats of Strasbourg as suffering, bearing the burden of human sins. May they enjoy more peace at Torminster.'

Suffering from bearing the burden of human sins. Frederick lowered his head with misgivings.

A few days later, as dusk cast the last feeble shadows of the day, Stephen sat with De Juniac in the west cloister discussing future plans. He shivered, tucking his hands up his sleeves. 'My estate's funds, should get us through the first two stages of the renovations but only the Lord knows what will happen thereafter. But fret not, he will take care of things.'

'Thanks to your generosity, Father, that concern appears well into the future. When the time comes, though it is best not to accrue debts, if we have to, we can always take loans from the Jews.'

'There my friend, you are wrong, not about the wisdom of avoiding debts, but about the Jews. We got rid of that lot long ago, and none too soon.' Stephen failed to notice a tensing in the Frenchman. He continued, 'They caused so many problems King Edward III got rid of them about fifty years ago.'

'He got rid of them? Your king did not kill them?'

'No, no, no. Some were killed much earlier, around 1190. Despite Devon, particularly Exeter and the tin mines of Cornwall, carrying more than their fair share of Jews, we did not kill them. But there was the tragedy in York. The Jews there took refuge in the castle as some returned Crusaders demanded it was time they converted to Christianity. Things became unruly, then their rabbi ordered them to kill themselves rather than convert. Only a Jew would give such a command. It is for God to decide when life should be taken. The father of each family proceeded to kill his wife, children and himself, before their leaders set fire to the keep, killing the rest of them. A few survived but were killed by the locals, who were outraged by their behaviour.'

'You said fifty years ago, not 1190, earlier father?' Stephen noted the Frenchman appeared agitated.

'Yes, I did. It was a hundred years after the York fiasco that King Edward decided enough was enough. Before he did so, King Henry III had taxed them for their money lending. King Edward continued this, but then the Jews had the nerve to call in their debts from us Christians ahead of schedule, while declining to charge fellow Jews any interest at all. They never belonged in England, having been brought over by King Mark of Normandy, starting a problem that never existed here before. So, as I said, Edward decided enough was enough. Solved it by shipping them abroad; any remaining would be executed.'

'What, all of them?'

'Yes. No Jews, no problems.'

'But even Jews should be allowed basic rights.'

'Should they? Why? That has not been the way we treat the heathen in England. They never belonged in England. Some have even suggested the Jews were Satan's helpers, but I myself do not believe this.'

'Don't Jews have children who need parents and security?'

'That is a difficult one. For the children it was sad, but it was their parents who insisted on defying our Christian faith—and their children in turn were contaminated. So, we won't be seeking any loans for our plans from any Jews.'

Little did Stephen know it, but just when things were going so well, he had ignited a slow growing cancer in his closest friend that was never to heal.

Observe good faith and justice toward all nations. Cultivate peace and harmony with all.

George Washington

8

Unlikely heroes

A sequence of three tones rang out, the first two short and slurred, the third longer, louder and more emphatic.

'Bach's Toccata and Fugue in D minor, if I hear right,' called Wright to a man high above on a ladder, attending to some guttering. Brian Shields, balding with long grey hair in a pony-tail and baggy jeans, Torminster's head of maintenance and general factotum of many years, looked down at the new doctor. Wright could not have got off to a better start with Brian, witnessing this sonic miracle and correctly identifying the music.

'Gloating Priest over the southern chancel; can't see him from here. Hasn't sung in years,' said Brian. 'Singing it in F sharp minor, not D minor,' he added.

Wright, musical though he was, did not have the ear to challenge this assertion. 'Will any of the others sing today?' he asked, but Brian was away with the fairies. Wright was not to know that Brian had been working on the Gloating Priest for several months, nor that this was the first time anyone in recent memory had heard a song during daylight hours. Not even Horace knew why they only performed at night—till now.

Wright proceeded along a fluorescent-lit corridor to Ward 2, where he was due to meet his senior registrar Dr Young and the new junior registrar Dr Simpson. Rosemary Young had completed her Membership exams, was competent, reliable and awaiting a suitable consultant position to become available. She tended to speak softly, as if she was trying to put her children to sleep, but on this occasion she snapped to attention as her new boss entered the ward office. 'Good morning, Dr Wright.'

'Good morning Rosemary, good morning Roger. Any particular problems today?'

'Not here sir,' said Rosemary, 'but Dr Finch has asked if you wouldn't mind giving a second opinion on a young female who has been admitted to the forensic unit on an involuntary detention order. It's a bit complex. I have treated her myself intermittently over the years, though not recently. She has been prone to self-cutting, but on this occasion she cut her boyfriend—his throat to be precise. She has been charged with murder, bail was refused, but she then slashed her arms in prison so voilà, here she is.'

'I'd be delighted. Sounds interesting. We'll get this lot out of the way first, then you might pop over with me and give me some introductions.'

After their round with the ward nursing sister and the nineteen patients who presented only the usual issues, Wright walked with Dr Young the 300 yards to the secure forensic section at Torminster— 200 yards if you risked walking across the lawn, which on wetter days did a good imitation of the quicksands on the other side of the moor in Conan Doyle's Hound of the Baskervilles. It was in a small ugly 1960s purpose-built unit, catering for up to ten involuntary patients, usually all males, many of whom came from the nearby Dartmoor prison when they became psychotic.

The doctors entered the forensic ward via two locked doors and a charge nurse escorted them to Dr Finch's office. Finch, a lanky weather beaten individual of sixty-one years, skillfully transferred his cigarette from his right hand to his left and extended his nicotine stained fingers. 'How do you do Dr Wright? Good morning Rosemary. I'd be grateful for a second opinion on this girl. She has no business being here. If every criminal learnt that cutting themselves entitled them to a get out of jail free card there'd be no one left in prisons and we psychiatrists would all become correctional officers—and be paid as such.' He gave a wry smile.

'Yes, it's a perennial issue we faced at Bethlem Royal, but we had more backup and disposal options in London than here. Anyway, I'll be glad to see what I make of her. Is it all right if I use Rosemary as part of the process as she has previously treated the lady, what's-her-name?'

'Celeste Lewis. Involving Rosemary would be fine. Before you start you might like to have a picture show, see the skills of the leading lady, the femme fatale.' Finch rummaged through a heap of papers on his desk before coming up with a large brown envelope. Dr Wright opened it and pulled out half a dozen photos of presumably the ex-boyfriend, whose ugly face was not improved by a gaping bloody diagonal gash on the left side of his neck, travelling from just under his ear down across his lower middle throat.

'Charming, eh?' said Finch, lighting another cigarette. 'How are those fine boys of yours, Rosemary?' Finch was a habitual grumbler when it came to his patients, but relatively human beyond his work. One astute observer said he grumbled so much about his patients it was a wonder he ever became a psychiatrist, adding that perhaps it was having the pleasure of locking patients up, but no sooner did he do so than he would strive to secure their release.

Drs Wright and Young spent the next hour in a small stuffy interview room with Celeste, a young lady with a slim boyish figure, and dark but disheveled hair. Rosemary took notes while her boss asked most of the questions, addressing them to a sullen Celeste. Her crime involved her lout of a boyfriend of two years, her longest relationship to date, which went reasonably for the first six months but it was all downhill thereafter. After many lesser altercations, he first seriously assaulted her eighteen months into their relationship. Saturday night beatings became a regular feature, along with takeaways, mostly Indian. As with many individuals prone to major self-cutting Celeste had suffered many years of childhood sexual abuse, first by her father and later by her mother's numerous boyfriends. She left home for the streets of London at the age of fourteen.

The night of the crime was three days after her boyfriend raped her. He came home from the pub drunk again and demanded she get out of bed to cook him some eggs and bacon as the Indian takeaway was closed. She complied, fearing another assault, or so she claimed, which did not sound unreasonable. Her partner was calling her everything under the sun—compliments excepted—taking pleasure in taunting her while she was preparing his food. She was cutting a loaf for his toast when he approached her from behind and started getting fresh with her. She told him to stop, but he laughed at her, telling her that her saying 'Stop' was her way of saying 'Give me a rough one.' He then grabbed her and clamped her to his groin, while she still held the bread knife. Celeste claimed her next memory was of her boyfriend being on the floor surrounded by blood emanating from his throat, but the blood was no longer flowing, the river had run dry. She also claimed that the bacon and eggs were burnt to cinders. Both observations suggested minutes rather than seconds had passed before she realised what she had done.

After their assessment Dr Wright said to Dr Young, 'The essential questions are: firstly, did she know what she was doing was wrong? As in cutting his throat. She probably did, but her not having recall for that moment and for some time afterwards raises the possibility of dissociation, though lying to help her case is, of course, another possibility.'

'I have previously heard her describe dissociative episodes when she has cut herself, feeling no pain; and of course, her childhood sexual abuse is a risk factor for them,' said Rosemary.

'Yes. The second question,' Wright continued, 'Was she suffering from an irresistible impulse depriving her of self-control? The skeptic in me is happier to agree to this one. Furthermore, Dr Watson, our young lady appeared left-handed when filling in the questionnaire we gave her. A deliberate forehand slash from a left-hander would cut the right side of the throat, but if she was held tight up against her assailant and struggling to break free while holding a bread knife, a backhanded downward slash across the left side of the neck is quite plausible. Also, if you were planning on cutting someone's throat would you not prefer a straight edged carving knife over a serrated bread knife. Either might do the job, but straight edges glide more smoothly, producing neater and more satisfying results.'

Dr Young agreed with his assessment and the two headed off to Finch's office to discuss it with him, but they did not provide him with the answer he wanted.

Finch protested, 'And what am I going to do with her over the years it may take for the Court to deem whether she is fit for trial, then for the duration of the proceedings, not to mention beyond? And from your experiences Rosemary, it sounds as though she will cause mayhem in here and put my staff at risk of injury.' Finch was never known to have supported his staff, but there is always a first time. 'Maybe you'd like to change places with them. See how you like dealing with murderous slashers?' Drs Young and Wright paused until Finch's diatribe spent itself.

Rosemary volunteered, 'If it would help, I'd be happy to co-manage Celeste under your supervision, Dr Finch. I have had a reasonable relationship with her to date and with her being detained here I might be able to pursue more effective psychotherapy with her, without the interruptions of her dropping out of contact as she has tended to do as an outpatient.'

Finch paused to calm himself, inhaling on his cigarette. 'That is a kind offer Rosemary. Yes, I would appreciate your co-management offer, if it is okay with you Douglas?'

'Oh, yes by all means.'

In the forensic ward the following Saturday both of Celeste's arms were leaving trails of blood wherever she walked. She had been agitated for days. She had kicked chairs and thrown aluminium ash trays and waste paper bins. A male patient alerted a nurse who arrived exclaiming, 'Not again. Look at the mess you are making.'

'I tripped and fell across all this glass on the floor. I could sue you and the hospital, you know.'

The duty registrar was called in, requiring a wait of over half an hour for his arrival. In the meantime, the nurses applied dressings to stem the bleeding. Although the longitudinal cuts were long, they were not deep; bleeding was venous without any arterial spurting. The nursing attention was delivered without drama or sympathy, the staff unimpressed by this common occurrence and appropriate responses took care not to reinforce self-destructive behaviours by paying them too much attention. The doctor stitched her up with a similar lack of concern.

Matilda was called, as usual, to clean up the floors and walls. The nurses always preferred her no-nonsense approach to those of the other cleaners who tended to fuss about the possibility of catching diseases such as hepatitis B, or worse still that new AIDS doctors were beginning to talk about. Some of the cleaners were at times sympathetic to self-cutters, even suggesting patients cut themselves because the nurses were so uncaring.

Matilda was mopping when a young female patient with bandaged arms approached her and gave her a daggers-look and hissed at her. Matilda had no doubts who she was but carried on unconcerned. This young lady with matted fur-like long hair prowled around Matilda inspecting her from all angles.

'Aren't you afraid of being alone with a murderer?' Celeste asked with a smirk.

'Can't say I am, my love.'

After a pause Celeste said, 'I bet I've spoilt your day, bleeding all over the place.'

'No, my love, you haven't, I like cleaning, simple soul that I am. Blood's no problem. Now if this was red paint, I'd call that a problem—that would get up my goat. But blood comes off easy, so don't you go feeling sorry for me.'

'I'm not feeling sorry for you and don't you call me 'my love' you fucking cow.'

Ah, the sweet voice of youth, Matilda thought. 'I call everybody my love, it's the way I am.'

'What are you? A lesbian? Fat bitch. I bet you can't you handle men?'

'Oh, I've had a few. Some good, some bad. I hear your last one was a bad 'un.'

'Have these idiots been gossiping about me to you, a bloody cleaner?'

'No, but I did see your pretty face on the news. A bit extreme wasn't it? I've always thought it is easier to leave the bastards rather than cut them up. But then again maybe you couldn't leave. My lot of losers have always been too scared of me to try to stop me leaving.'

'Scared of you? They must have been right pansies.'

'If you say so, my love.'

'I told you, don't you call me your fucking love.'

'Would you prefer me to call you fuckface or fuckwit? Which'll it be? Move over now, I've got to mop behind that chair. Careful, you're almost smiling and might look prettier for it.'

'Don't you patronise me, bitch.'

'As you like, fuckface.'

As her abuse was not working on Matilda Celeste tried a different approach. 'I cut my fella's throat. You should have seen the fountain of blood; makes this look silly it did.'

'Yes, I bet it did. That sort of quantity is not so good for carpets, that's why we don't have them here. I remember way back when I was not much older than you the thought murdering my ex- crossed my mind. I decided he wasn't worth the trouble, and that's how I get to go home tonight, whereas you are stuck in this dump.'

'Dump? I've been in worse. My home, years back, was worse.'

'Assuming you're not daft in the head—and you don't look it—I'm proper sorry to hear that.' Matilda stood up straight stretching her back. 'I've finished now, I'd best be getting along. I've enjoyed our chat. Now don't forget what I said. No paint or you'll cop it big time.'

As Matilda turned her back and left a rare smile crossed Celeste's feline face.

9

Stone

Stephen felt uneasy about his discussion with De Juniac of the Jews but was puzzled as to why? Standing in the nave, he gazed at the chancel where the altar would stand. Something about the Frenchman troubled him. The image of his scarred forearm peeping out beneath his left sleeve in the ale-house in Exeter when they first met returned to him. Why had he been so quick to hide it? He felt sick in his stomach about his own deceit involved in hiding his proposed use of the babewyns, who visited him in his dreams, tormenting him almost nightly. Yet again he resolved that today he would own up.

When Stephen met De Juniac in the nave that morning he saw an unusual frown on the Frenchman's face. De Juniac took the initiative. 'Good morning Father.' He fidgeted picking up an offcut of wood for no apparent reason, only to put it down. 'Please come with me, I have a confession to make.' De Juniac led Stephen to the north chapel, where they sat down safe from prying ears. 'I am not who you believe me to be,' he said looking down at his calloused hands. The Devon masons have been talking and they are right, I am not a baron; barons do not do my sort of work. Their hands are soft unless they have wielded a sword, not rough and dirt-stained like mine.' Looking Stephen in the eyes, he said, 'My name is Swarber,

Sebastian Swarber, though my mother's name was De Juniac, and she at least was French. My father was Alsatian. I wonder if you will be able to forgive my deceit.'

Stephen was taken aback but felt a sense of relief, preferring to be on the receiving end of sin than to be its source. 'Deceit may be forgiven if it is fully confessed,' he said.

'And now must be the time, though I hoped to delay it longer. May we sit?' The two sat side by side on a large stone block. 'I fled from Strasbourg as sooner or later I'd have been killed; accidents are easy to arrange in my trade. I'd already once been nearly lynched and would have been but for the loyalty and quick wits of Heinrich and my other masons.' De Juniac paused, clenching his fists.

'We were working in the north aisle of Strasbourg Cathedral when the mob came for me. About eight of them. They were only after me, the master builder.

'Are you the boss?' I was asked with contempt.

I recall replying, 'If you mean am I in charge of my friends here? the answer is yes.'

'They work for you?'

'For me and for God.' It was then I noticed the blood stains on the fellow's jerkin and the sneer on his face.

'And you pay them well?'

'I pay them as much as I can afford and I consider that to be a fair wage,' I replied.

'And which of you earns the most?' the thug asked my crew. 'Might it be the boss? Oh, what a surprise, the boss does all right for himself. Wouldn't want a serf's wage, would he?'

My masons saw the direction this interrogation was going. Heinrich stepped forward and said, 'Friend, might I ask you to shake hands with my employer?'

'Now why would I want to do that?' he replied.

'If you were to do so, you'd find his hand was much rougher and much stronger than yours. Roughness and strength from manual work, not from counting coffers. And he pays us more than any other master builder; not because of his wealth, but because of his generosity. You have the wrong target, my friend. Kill him and you may as well kill all of us.'

The thug shifted from one foot to the other, his right-hand straying towards his dagger, unsure what to do next. Then my mason Otto took a risk and said, 'Kill him and you will have to kill all of us.' They all stepped forward as one. Part of me wanted to stop their becoming involved, but I realised it was my only chance and but for my men that day I would have met a similar fate to my father and brother. I am ashamed to say sometimes since I have left Strasbourg, I have wished they left me to that fate.'

Stephen asked, 'Why did they want to kill you? Because you were an employer and more wealthy?'

'No, no; robbing and a beating would have sufficed. Heinrich's diplomacy, Otto's threat and the show of solidarity from my other men saved my neck that day. It was much more serious than money and for that reason I knew they would one day kill me. My father and brother had already been killed several months earlier. My father was the brother of Peter Swarber, I was his nephew. You've not heard of him?' De Juniac asked, noting Stephen's vacant expression. 'He was the mob's number one enemy. I was guided by him, but I was insignificant enough to be killed without many people noticing or caring—other than Uncle Peter. Killing me would have

107

been a way of persecuting him and he was the one they hated most.' De Juniac paused, adding, 'He couldn't be killed, that would have been too obvious, too public, so they hurt him via his family. They'd already dealt with my brother and father. As another master builder I was a suitable next target.'

'I confess I have not heard of Peter Swarber,' said Stephen.

'But you have heard about the pogrom?'

'I heard Strasbourg experienced some problems with its Jews, with tragic consequences.'

The words 'problems with its Jews' seemed to grate on De Juniac, who drew a deep breath and swallowed in silence to maintain his composure. After a pause he said, 'Strasbourg, unlike England, didn't solve its problem by sending innocent families abroad.' He coldly stared into Stephen's eyes. 'Instead, it sent them by the hundreds to their deaths—in infernos. Yes, burnt masses of them to death. My uncle Peter Swarber was the leader of the master tradesmen and it was they, the master tradesmen, along with some of the church who opposed the masses, insisting the council had a duty to protect the Jews.

'The masses wanted to blame the Jews for all their hardships, some of which arose from the pestilence and some from the greed of the wealthy. The Jews were accused of poisoning the wells with corpses of those who died of the pestilence. One Jew was tortured into implicating the cantor of Strasbourg in the poisoning of wells. Pope Clement of Avignon instructed the clergy to tell the people such accusations were the lies of Satan, but their words fell on deaf ears and eventually the Church switched to the winning side. And the wealthy survivors of the pestilence could escape their repayments to the Jewish money lenders, if they let the masses have their way.'

'The guilds, including our own, whose existence was meant to support us, turned on us and became some of the most vocal liars. The former noblemen and the Bishop of Strasbourg—yes, God's messenger—replaced the council who tried to protect the Jews. Then there was no stopping the evil, the Jews were killed en masse, the flames consumed them.' De Juniac pulled back his left sleeve exposing his horribly scarred forearm. He paused. He was no longer angry with Stephen, who was listening to his account with obvious sympathy.

'The master tradesmen including my uncle and myself did have some vested interests in protecting the Jews. They were a vital part of Alsace's economy and we were amongst its beneficiaries, but the suggestion that we accepted bribes from the Jews was a lie. That was a convenient strategy used by the masses to overthrow us, the wealthy protectors of the Jews—fail though we did. Some of us may have been arrogant about our entitlements, but such problems did not justify violence and should have been dealt with by truth, not lies. In time many of our artisans also turned against us.

'It was hopeless. I was stripped of my land and money. Then many artisans, other than my masons and a few others, would no longer work for me. Most did not want to, but the few who did knew they in turn would be persecuted if they did, so better to join the masses. Some of the more decent defectors warned me after the incident in which I was nearly lynched that the radicals were still determined to kill me.

Stephen looked bewildered and was lost for words.

'I fled to France, with my mother's name and hoped to start afresh, but it was not to be. My reputation followed me to France, so to England I came. My title of Baron was a lie.

I knew the English, like the French, are impressed by titles, unhappily for me, not French ones.'

De Juniac looked Stephen in the eyes. I am sorry Abbot Stephen, I have disappointed you. I have engaged in the sin of deceit, all the time justifying it with the notion I must maintain my secret and that of my Alsatian friends for our safety, when I should have trusted in our Lord.'

Stephen desperately wanted to share his own deceit but again balked at the challenge. Later, that evening as the sun sank beneath the hills to the west the monkeys smiled, reflecting on man's folly.

How foolish be the wise!

Charles Reade (1861)

10

Intelligence

Rubbing the back of his neck, Wright asked himself, 'Is Castle playing silly buggers?' He looked around his now fully functional office that Brian had fixed up, gaining momentary relief from Brian's competence. It was eight months since the funds for his research grant had been sent, yet he had not received a penny. The grant money had to pass across Castle's desk and in the year Wright had been at Torminster he'd had only a handful of meetings with Castle beyond their original introduction. He must confront him, infuriatingly evasive though he was.

Frowning, his thoughts turned to the ethics of the patients' cider production. It was not that the hospital might not have a license to manufacture cider that worried him, nor the selling of it to local pubs—those were Castle's responsibilities—Wright was more concerned the patients were working under Castle's direction, which could be seen as exploitation. As their chief caregiver he must be their advocate, he could not turn a blind eye to patient exploitation. Also, while rates of alcohol related disorders appeared no higher than expected in Torminster's acute wards, they should have been lower in the long stay wards where such patients supposedly did not have access to alcohol. Yet, he had several times encountered intoxicated long stay patients staggering around the hospital. As yet he had not done anything about it and the longer this went on the greater the chances of his being judged as being complicit.

He decided to take Matilda up on her offer of help. Their paths crossed one morning in the former cloisters when no one was around. 'Of course we do,' she said, 'we're always seeing patients away from their wards mooning about barely upright and sometimes lost. We take them back to their wards where they get more tongue-lashings from their nurses. We're often called to clean up pools of alcohol smelling vomit. Like a turn, Doc? Sometimes we find broken furniture and the odd broken window pane which we report to Brian. His dockets pass over Castle's desk, so he knows all about it.'

Matilda sensed the doctor was more concerned than he was letting on. 'It's not just the cider, is it Doc? What is really getting you about Castle the Arsehol?'

Wright looked around for potential spies. 'Tilly, you should have been a psychiatrist, you understand people too well. Yes, there is something else, but it is sensitive and lies outside your domain.'

'Oh, it does, does it? Maybe you being the understanding psychiatrist don't understand there is very little that goes on round these parts this here director of sanitary services doesn't know about. So out with it, what's up?'

'For what it's worth, I've been waiting on a research grant of close to one hundred thousand pounds, but Mr Castle keeps telling me it hasn't arrived, yet it was posted months ago.'

Matilda replied, 'God you're a slow learner. You'll never make it to professor unless you lift your game. Didn't I tell you way back if there was anything you needed to know or any little problems you were to come to Tilly?'

'You did indeed, and I am. Perhaps I should have done so earlier.'

'No perhaps about it. The trouble with you psychiatrists— an' I don't want you to take offense now—is you have no bloody understanding of people. Now I'm not suggesting you don't understand madness, you being mad experts and all, but you don't understand people, not how they tick.' She paused to let her words sink in before proceeding. 'Your problem sounds very simple to me. The word is Castle has money problems, big ones. He has a big swanky house, presumably with a big swanky mortgage; and he and his missus like expensive holidays in the sun, when the rest of us are shivering through winter. A friend of mine happens to be a bookie; says Castle is one of his best customers, bets regular like, large amounts and loses.'

'You don't say.'

'You deaf or something? I just did.'

'I'll bear that in mind when I'm dealing with him.'

'And where will that get you? He's not a total idiot, close I'll admit, but he won't go telling you what he's up to—what he's not meant to be doing. You leave this to Tilly.'

'I appreciate your offer Tilly, but even you might find this one tricky.'

'Here you go again. Us cleaners have a saying, 'If husbands want to play up, they better not have married a cleaner.' We get everywhere—into every room—as part of our cleaning duties. Into every drawer, though I never said that. Who has the keys to every room in Torminster? Only Tilly does. Even Brian doesn't have them all. Also, my friends on the outside include more than bookies. Give me a few weeks and I'll tell you what I can about your grant money. I'd best be getting along now. You

113

doctors may have the time to stand around gossiping all day but some of us have work to do.'

That reminded Wright he was running late. He grinned, shaking his head as they went their own ways, but still asked himself whether Tilly might be overstating her abilities.

Wright went to Ward 2 where through the glass partition he saw Rosemary Young writing in some patient files in the nurses' station. He entered the office, said good morning to the nurses, then went with Dr Young to see a few patients who were causing concern. They then adjourned to Rosemary's office where he asked her how she was getting on with Celeste.

'We're making progress. Her father appears to have been a sadist and as is often the way she still tended to love him as a kid. On the odd occasion he did not beat her into sexual compliance he made her feel special and told her she'd make someone a wonderful wife one day. Feeling special she then loved her Dad except for the yucky things he did with her, or until the next beating. Her mother must have known all about it, but the arrangement presumably suited her. Fewer beatings herself, and less of the other. As a result, Celeste does not trust anyone and that is a challenge. But there is something different about her compared with the usual borderline personalities. While she has problems with trust, her spats and her self-cutting, at times she radiates an unusual degree of confidence and independence, which I don't claim to understand.'

Switching tack Wright said, 'Hmm. How is Finch?'

'He's settled down, seems quite happy with me working with Celeste. He is agreeable enough to do all the paperwork for the courts and the tribunals; he at least spares me those chores. Actually, he appears to prefer paperwork to contact with patients. Should have been an accountant. And how about you sir, have you heard any news about the grant?'

'No, not a thing.'

Wright passed Matilda most days and said hello, but he knew she'd advise him of any progress when she was ready. The sun was shining, casting dark shadows where his car was parked outside the main entrance that day. 'Good mornin', Doc,' said Matilda, walking over to him. You know your car has a stone chip near the lower edge of the passenger side door. I noticed it the other day. You want to get that fixed you know. The cow shit flying off the road when it's wet will eat away at it.'

'Blast, another few hundred quid. The problem with owning a sports car is the repairers double their charges. 'Such is life' as Ned Kelly used to say.'

'Ned who? He's not from around here is he?'

'No, no,' he laughed, having for once come up with a name Matilda did not know. 'No, Kelly was a famous Australian criminal of the last century. A bit like our Robin Hood, but not as generous.'

His grin subsiding, he asked, 'Tilly, have you made any new local discoveries, spoken to the Cray Twins about daylight robbery or such?' Wright surprised himself at his new found humour.

'I'll have you know you are talking to a now respectable lady, you are, one as is happy to leave the London crims to the likes of yourself. I still can't understand how eight million people are daft enough to live there. Anyway, enough of this chatter. As it happens, I have made some progress.' Tilly looked up at the skyline, then asked, 'You've never been up on the roof and met our friends up close, have you?'

'No, I have yet to have the pleasure.'

'Well if you've got the time, I've got the keys. It's private, the only ears are stone ones—maybe that's where they get the saying 'stone deaf' from.'

It was still early morning. The nursing day shift had arrived but it was much too early for Castle or Frieda to make their appearances. Matilda used a large old key to unlock the door, waiting till Wright passed through before locking it behind them. She then unlocked a second door leading them to a spiral stairway taking them up to gallery on the southern side edge of the church overlooking the cloisters, where they sat down on a couple of crates surrounded by cigarette butts. The ornately carved shoulder high balustrade hid them from those below, but Wright could see through it to the world beyond.

Looking up, he said, 'She's a striking looking lady if ever I saw one,' referring to a grotesque on the tower. 'I wouldn't want to get on the wrong side of her.' A decrepit female form with angry hollow eyes and a snarling expression stared down at him.

'Oh, that old hag, the Banshee; miserable bitch, a bit like my mother was, all doom and gloom. Banshees are known for screaming about coming family deaths, screeching like they can't wait for them to occur. You take care what you say around her, or she'll add you to her list. But, believe it or not, it's the pixie beside her you really need to look out for, devious little bastard, not as cute as he looks Any excuse and before you know it, he'll lead you into the shit up to your neck and enjoy doing so. So, Horace says. Good job his wings have fallen off and Brian hasn't yet replaced them.'

'That little fellow?'

'Goebbels was a little fellow too and look what he did. I once dated a Jew, nice bloke he was, but his parents didn't approve of me.'

'Surely not?'

'Well, enough of my prattling; as you might have guessed all is not right. Your grant came through months ago. The date on it was November 20th last. It took a bit of finding. It wasn't in his in-tray and not in his regular cabinet. It was in his locked cabinet, which only he has the key to, but if you know the numbers of the keys, which are conveniently stamped on the locks, you can get the right ones and as it happened, I already had one of them in my draw of odds and sods.'

'So, the grant was for how much?'

'Ninety-three thousand quid. You could have a fine party with that.'

Wright of course knew how much the grant was for, but he now knew Matilda had seen the real thing.

'Only I'm sad to say you won't be getting all of it, even if we do make him hand it over,' she paused, 'as the blighter has gone and spent some of it. I suspect about half at least. That was what took me such time. It was one thing finding the grant, but another thing finding out what he's done with it.'

Wright scratched his jaw. 'He can't have. It would be illegal.'

'He can have and he has.'

'How? How do you know Tilly?'

'Those Doc are questions you aren't allowed to ask, so of course you never did. Certain people around town have received payments they were owed long ago but weren't expecting. Large ones.'

'The bastard!'

11

James the Curious

Abbot Stephen saw a rider approaching from the trail east of the abbey. As the stranger drew near Stephen recognised him as Mark Redvers who bought most of his father's estate. He put down his shovel, left his brothers to continue their work in the muddy fields and wiped his hands on his dirty habit as he walked over to Redvers who dismounted from his frisky stallion.

'Tie him up under the tree here, Mark,' said Stephen.

'Be still,' Redvers whispered to his beast. Turning he said, 'I hope I am not catching you at an inconvenient time, Abbot Stephen? If only my workers followed the example you set to your brothers,' Redvers said. Stephen knew Redvers ran a tight ship, that was one reason he sold his land to him for such a modest sum.

Stephen stroked the horse's neck. It seemed to recognise him as no threat. 'Welcome Mark, it is good to see you, I'll gladly take a break with you.' They shook hands and walked over to the abbot's cottage. They sat on the two wooden chairs in the spartan room. Stephen enquired how Mark's farm was progressing and Mark asked about the abbey.

After a pause, Redvers put his hands together as if in prayer. 'You have never met my son, James, the only one of my brood still living with his mother and I?'

'No, I have not had the pleasure.'

'My older children have their own homes and growing families. James is not ready to start a family and I suspect may never be so. I wonder whether you might consider his becoming a novice at your abbey?'

Stephen's eyes looked up with a smile. 'You have come at a good time as I have been recruiting recently, now that we have accommodation ready and a church in which we can begin holding services.' He wondered why Redvers had not brought his son with him so he could assess his suitability first hand. 'How old is James and is he ready for such a commitment?'

Redvers cleared his throat, 'James is eighteen, yes he is ready, at least I believe so as he has expressed interest in the monastic life.' Mark shifted on his bench, seemingly ill at ease.

'Come Mark, feel free to tell me about him. We know each other well enough not to prevaricate. The idea of your son joining my brothers is an appealing one. So, tell me about him, what is the lad like?'

Redvers looked down at the floor summoning the courage to raise his eyes and continue, 'James is a remarkably intelligent young man, caring, studious, diligent—characteristics well suited to life as a monk. But he is different, very different, and I fear his mother and I, try though we have, have not succeeded as parents. Not as we would have wished.' Redvers looked upwards as if seeking help or forgiveness from above. 'Vanity is a sin of which we have both been guilty. God presented us with a challenge and, well, we fear we have disappointed our Lord. It is time to make amends and surrender James to his service.'

'Vanity, you say? I don't follow you.'

Redvers hesitated. There was a long delay before he continued, as if he was breaking the news of a death. 'James was born with a facial deformity. He had…he still has a gap between his upper lip and his left nostril. It is most unsightly. His appearance at birth was a shock to us. His mother believed it was the mark of Satan.' Redvers looked imploringly at Stephen, who nodded. 'I tried persuading her he was not Satan but a challenge from God—some type of punishment for our sins. My wife must be forgiven, she did try, poor soul. She would feed him as a babe only to find her milk leaked from his mouth and nostrils and he tended to choke, for the deformity extended into his mouth. She handed him over to a wet nurse, who herself was not blameless. She too was devoid of compassion for his infliction. I busied myself with farming and spending time with my more presentable children, as much as possible—to forget James.' Looking Stephen in the eyes, he continued, 'We hid him from our neighbours. He grew up thin and unhealthy looking, although in his later years he has become surprisingly strong for all that. He was a lonely child and but for the love of his sister Anna, four years older, I fear his problems would have been even worse.' Redvers looked away, again struggling to maintain his composure.

Stephen volunteered, 'God sends us challenges. It is difficult to understand why he does not target the more sinful, but he has his reasons. The role of a parent is not an easy one, even with healthy children. All a parent can hope to do, is to do their best.'

'Their best!' Redvers looked up, wincing. 'That is what we did not do. James was like a stranger to us through most of his childhood. But for our daughter Anna he would have remained a stranger. She taught him to read, she took him for long walks on the moor and she cultivated his love of nature. When older with her help he studied the Bible. He learnt to read Latin far better than Anna, his teacher. He now reads the Bible to us each evening—it is a delight to us. He reads as if it was written in English, yet when his mother or I look at it we cannot understand a word. We can only read English.

'Anna's love of James also helped awaken us to our errors. My wife realised several years ago when he was becoming proficient with the Bible that he really must have been a child of God and our relationships with him began to improve, but we can never make up for our deficiencies during his early childhood. Since then we have shared with him our love of the Bible and that has brought us together. It has been a source of great solace. Yet he has rarely been inside a church.' Stephen's facial expression turned to one of amazement. 'Apart from his appearance scaring people, his speech and singing are awkward.'

'In the service of God these are not insurmountable obstacles.'

Redvers responded to Stephen's encouragement. 'James has unusual talents. He understands animals and plants like nobody else I know. Animals do not judge him as we have; they accept his ugliness and his lack of social graces. They judge him by other criteria, if at all. James has looked after our horses, sheep and cattle with great skill—self-taught. He is well-read, but it is also as if he can read the minds of these dumb beasts, whatever their minds may be. Even with wild animals he is uncanny.' With a look of pride Redvers said, 'I once watched him walk over to a pair of foxes. When thirty yards from them he lay down as if he was going to go to sleep. The foxes responded with curiosity, and a little caution, granted.

Slowly they approached him. I feared they would bite him, but they sniffed him while he pretended to be asleep. After a few more sniffs they sauntered off, but subsequently the same pair became interested in his visits and when they had pups, they brought them over to our house to show them off. James' scent appeared enough to reassure them his mother and I were not threats to them. They became like pets to us—though we did lose several chickens to them.'

'His animal skills would be an asset to us,' Stephen said.

'He also has healing skills with humans. I cannot remember when any of my family last needed another healer.'

'A vet and a physician in one, now that would be useful. You're sure he wants to join us?'

'He does. All the more so as his sister has recently married and left home. He needs to mix with people nearer his own age. His aging parents with their deficiencies are not enough for a young man.'

'Would an aging abbot be any better? Tell him he will be welcome.' Stephen did not volunteer he felt as if God was talking to him, telling him he was providing Torminster with a special brother.

'One other thing, Abbot Stephen,' Redvers said with formality, 'I want to make a donation to the abbey.'

'That is not necessary; your son more than suffices.'

'Father, I beg to differ. For too long we neglected many of James's needs and we need to atone for this. If you will allow us to make a donation it will ease our burdens of guilt. And it did not go unnoticed from my business eye you could have asked double for the land you sold me and even then, I would have considered such a price. I have watched the abbey's restoration from afar. The speed of the work has been remarkable. I have heard you have opened an alms house for the poor and the infirm. Such work, if you will excuse my presumption, might suit James, so it is fair I make a donation. I am aware my level of affluence is not enjoyed by many; I want to share it with those most in need.'

'Most generous of you Mark.' Stephen felt unusually serene. Was his Lord indicating his approval?

'I also note the church has many missing windows. May I contribute to their installation?' Noting Stephen's opening his mouth to express objection Redvers interrupted him with a mock look of disapproval, 'You would not come between me and the Lord, Father Abbot?'

Stephen smiled, 'There will be vast expanses of stained glass, which will be very expensive. You are being most generous, I will gladly accept a donation towards the abbey's windows. I will introduce you to my master builder, he can tell you what costs may be involved and you can discuss with him which window you wish to fund. When would James join us?'

'If it suits you Father Stephen, he could join you next week.'

'Fine, tell him to come over on Monday and my prior Brother Hubert will help him settle in and arrange for his instruction.' With a welcoming smile Stephen added, 'Mark, we have now opened the church to the public, although our congregation is limited as Torminster's villagers are accustomed to attending other churches in the nearby towns and villages. We have no wish to disturb well-established congregations, but perhaps Mrs Redvers and yourself might like to come to a service some time? You'd be very welcome.'

'We'd be delighted.'

'I will tell my prior Hubert to expect James on Monday, but now let's visit my master builder De Juniac and he can show you and discuss with you his plans for the windows.' Stephen took Redvers over to De Juniac who ended up spending much of the remainder of the day with him.

Later De Juniac told Stephen, 'It has all been agreed.'

'Which window did he volunteer to fund?'

'Which one? Which one was it? The rose window of the west end, those of the celestory, those along the knave.' De Juniac struggled to contain his smile, then gave up, 'All of them.'

'That's a fortune!'

'Certainly, a considerable sum. This means more than just windows. All of Monsieur de Redvers' donation will go to the windows, but I'd already set aside a modest amount for the start of the windows. That amount can now be freed up to finish the walls and the roof which are the essentials, that way you will have a church more fit for a congregation. Certainly, the interior will remain a little bare but even Chartres is a little bare. It helps focus the gaze on the light out of darkness.'

On Monday, as James rode through Torminster on his ass he looked up to the abbey's towers. The main tower, still incomplete, stood so tall that he thought it might topple. It was not until he was half way up the ridge before the grotesques high in the main tower became visible, standing forwards from their archways, as if stepping outside for the day's activities. There were so many, even though many archways remained empty as yet. One grotesque was a bizarre tall cat with a sinister and aloof expression, mounted on a high pedestal. James smiled—a strange looking smile, involving only the normal side of his mouth and a twinkling of his eyes. As he came closer to the abbey, he discerned the cat's stiff look of superiority. He sensed it warning him.

He rode around the church. It stood so tall with windows, lacking glass, reaching up to the heavens. Their pointed arches, instead of the usual round ones, made him imagine his finger-tips meeting at the commencement of prayer. How could the windows stand so high? The contrast between the lower level weather worn limestone and the much lighter new stone above created a strangely beautiful effect. He smiled at their builder's daring and defying of conventions.

He came across some carpenters at work. 'I have been told to ask for the prior,' he said to a man sawing a plank of timber.

'Say that again,' said the carpenter who looked up, staring with unease. James repeated his statement more clearly.

'Try the cloisters through there.'

James tied his donkey to the gate. In the cloisters he found no one as all the brothers were out working in the fields.

Stephen was the first to spot him, as he awaited James's arrival with interest. Stephen had never seen a person with a hare lip, and checked his uncharitable feelings of disgust, replacing them with sympathy and understanding. Smiling a welcome, he said, 'You must be James, I am Abbot Stephen, you are most welcome. We are doing our morning field duties. Perhaps you'd like to join in, but first I will introduce you to the brothers. Stephen had warned them that their new brother would have an unsightly facial appearance, nevertheless, some of them looked away as if they might withdraw. The gap in his left upper lip travelled into his left nostril producing the air of an ugly sneer. James stared down at his hands. He had encountered similar reactions many times before and it never became any easier for him, but on this occasion it mattered more as he craved acceptance in this new home.

Hubert, never the warmest of individuals, though often the most correct, walked over to James and Stephen and even more stiffly than usual said, 'Welcome Brother James,' to which James responded by biting his lower lip and looking around as if Hubert was not there.

'James, this is Prior Hubert,' said Stephen. 'He will be responsible for your education in the Rule of St Benedict and will help you settle in here. Prior Hubert is in the process of setting up an alms house beyond the abbey's gate where we will help the sick and the poor. I'd be grateful if you would help Brother Hubert, who will give you directions.'

By the day's end the prior had named the newcomer 'James the Curious.' It was never clear whether the name arose from James' curiosity causing him to ask so many questions or whether it was more a statement about Hubert's reaction to the odd young man.

In the following weeks Hubert found conversing with James did not come easily as he appeared to have hearing problems resulting in his tending to stare at his prior's lips, making Hubert in turn inclined to return the stare, only to be repelled by what he saw. It was easier to tolerate when James looked down or away, which he often did. Also, James's speech displayed a predominance of vowels over consonants, having particular difficulties with ms and ns, so he said 'aass' instead of 'mass' and 'hads' instead of 'hands.' But the speed with which he learnt the Rule of Benedict amazed Hubert. He did not parrot the text as most novices did, he grasped its deeper purpose and this would enable his being ordained sooner than any of the other priests.

But James also questioned the Rule of Benedict, causing Hubert to struggle with how to divorce James's understanding from his unappreciated questions. Over time this became more problematic. Hubert thrived on accepting the Rule and other ecclesiastical doctrines as sacrosanct—they commanded, he obeyed—but James raised the possibility that the path to righteousness might not be so straightforward.

One day the two met and walked around to the chapterhouse. Rain poured down in torrents and the Hell Hounds vomited in unison a sheet of water blowing sideways. James struggled to prevent the chapterhouse door from slamming shut with the wind. Shaking some of the wet from their habits, the two men sat down at the table. James said, 'I have no difficulty in accepting I am but a 'worthless workman' according to the Rule. I have tried considering myself 'inferior to all'. But are the two not incompatible with being respectful to my brothers.'

'In what way?' asked Hubert.

'Do the rules not apply equally to all brothers?'

'They do.'

'Well therein is my difficulty. If we all are worthless how do any of us deserve respect? Also, if I am inferior to Brother Peter how can Brother Peter be inferior to myself as one of the 'all'? With the greatest respect to yourself and to Abbot Stephen, if you too are bound by the tenet of inferiority to all, does this not contradict the respect for authority I owe to you?'

Hubert, stony faced, hands tightly clasped felt doubly irritated by the nature of James's questions and by the slurred manner in which they were delivered. He gave himself time to contain his feelings of which he had limited awareness, other than he knew he felt uncomfortable and might be vulnerable to saying something he might later regret.

Having composed himself and deliberated James's questions Hubert said with a pained expression, 'Those are challenging questions. The issues do at first appear contradictory.' He again paused. 'We must not forget you refer to the Rule of St Benedict and as such, they must be correct. The Rule says I share your inferiority. Perhaps as a result I find I do not have the answers at hand to your questions; this is part of my inferiority. Let us reflect on this in the weeks ahead and await the answers from our Lord. He will provide us with guidance—when he is ready.' Little did Hubert foresee the time when he himself would doubt the Rule of Inferiority.

A more serious rift between James the Curious and the prior arose following a chapterhouse meeting. The brothers were crowded into the cramped room, with a damp oppressive odour. Hubert standing at the lectern, lit by candles was discussing 'The Confessions,' the most widely read text of St Augustine of Hippo from 398 AD. St Augustine came to the Church late in life, after a life spent '…floundering in the broiling sea of my fornication…' Hubert found it reassuring that someone with such an evil past had risen to become not only a saint but one of God's key representatives.

Brother James at a suitable moment asked the meeting, 'Father Abbot, I do not understand how St Augustine spoke of 'a Just War' in his work 'The City of God.' How is any war compatible with 'Thou shalt not kill' or with 'Love thy neighbour?' '

Hubert froze, his face turning dark, and a long silence

followed—not a divine one. Hubert glanced at Stephen who nodded. Hubert looked into James's eyes and in a controlled but icy voice he asked, 'Do you presume to challenge St Augustine? Do you know better than he? Might you set up your own church?'

James turned to Hubert. 'No, to all three of your questions, Father.' He waited, as Hubert was struggling to maintain his composure, then continued, 'I understand 'Love thy neighbour' as a commandment going beyond those living in adjacent farms. I have learnt through deliberations that 'neighbour' extends to all of mankind. Without a better understanding of St Augustine's wisdom, I might be at risk of duplicity—one moment loving my neighbours and the next declaring a 'Just War' on them.'

Abbot Stephen saw James was being deliberately provocative; he had Hubert in a corner. There was already tension between them and Hubert was struggling to contain his response so Stephen stepped into the fray. 'St Augustine's wisdom is unparalleled, other than by the words of Christ, Son of God. Hubert is correct in expecting greater respect to be paid to the Saint and so I suggest James you consult the original text and reflect further on the issues. Your confusion is understandable; a more diligent reading of the text is the solution. I suggest you search, thereby you will find answers. That will be all for today.'

Hubert's jaws were tightly clenched. James had insulted himself and St Augustine only for his abbot to fail to deliver the outright condemnation clearly warranted.

Later Hubert raised with Stephen James's difficulties in accepting directions from above. 'Abbot Stephen, brother James's disrespect of St Augustine and the Rule of St Benedict is growing to intolerable proportions. Must it not be addressed?'

'It must, but we need to exercise understanding and compassion for James, as before entering our monastery the unfortunate lad had to learn everything in life on his own. He has done so through observing life and asking himself questions about the world—seeking there answers. He has done remarkably well given he grew up shunned by his parents and all others, except his sister. We must take care not to add ourselves to that list.' Stephen had forgotten Hubert's own disadvantaged early life that he dealt with by self-discipline, not by questions.

Hubert continued, 'Are we to treat James differently from the other novices? Are there to be two sets of Rules for the novices?'

'Yes, for the moment.'

Hubert was speechless. His abbot was defying St Benedict.

Beware the ugly and the curious—they share the sin of difference.

12

Victory

'Doc, he's arrived,' Matilda said over the phone, 'I'll keep an eye on him till you get here.'

Wright laughed with glee. 'Thanks Tilly, I am on my way. No disappearing tricks this time. We've got him.'

Heart pounding, the doctor knocked on Castle's door but did not wait for a reply before entering. 'Good morning Mr Castle,' he said, knowing it was going to be anything but for the manager who was hiding behind a cloud of cigarette smoke. Wright was not going to lose him now he had him on the hook.

' 'Allo Doctor,' Castle glared, 'I'm busy so get on with whatever you're here for.'

'I have come to advise you to resign your position.'

'You what? What did you say?'

'You heard me correctly. The alternative is I will notify the police.' Wright paused so his threat would sink in. 'I do not take kindly to my grant money being misappropriated.'

'Oh, that's it, is it? You are put out, as I, the manager, put the money temporarily to good use for the benefit of your patients. The swanky doctor of course doesn't give a toss about his patients; it's all about cultivating his reputation that matters. But not round here it don't. Bugger off back to London if it's fame you're after.'

'It sounds like you want me to call the police without further delay.'

Castle pushed his chair back from his desk. 'No need to waste their time. Everything is as it should be, the hospital should be in a position to release the first installment to you within a few weeks.' He stared around the room as if notifying the walls to order a flurry of bank notes.

'It is not the first installment I am concerned about, it's the rest that's my concern. I have heard from reliable sources you have used tens of thousands for paying off some of your personal debts.'

'Poppycock! Who on earth told you that? Do you believe every two-bob bit of gossip?'

'I did not expect you to see sense. I was merely making a gentlemanly offer, easier for you and it would settle this distasteful situation more quickly than by involving the police.'

'You wouldn't dare!' Castle roared. 'You go blabbing and you'll find yourself on the receiving end right smart. The hospital board and I go back a long way.' He crossed his arms leaning back on his chair. 'They know I'm reliable, and some of them have relied on me in more ways than you would know. They don't have the option to get rid of me—if you know what I mean?' he said with a sneer.

'The Board can do whatever they like. It is the police who I expect to take the definitive action.'

After a lengthy staring contest, Castle was the first to break the silence, 'You've never met my brother, have you?' Castle's fists were clenching, his nostrils flaring, spittle flying. Then with a smirk, 'He's a scallywag that one; known as 'The Enforcer' around here. You definitely wouldn't want to go messing with him, he's three times my size and has always looked after his little brother, he has. And he enjoys every minute of it.' Castle held his hands behind his head smiling, letting his words sink in.

Wright rose to the occasion, 'That is as may be, but I am duty bound to notify the Board. I am familiar with scandals and committees' preferences to avoid them. However, if you are not prepared to resign, I will be notifying the police shortly after speaking to the Board's Chair.'

Castle was rattled, despite Wright's voice starting to croak. He looked sideways at the doctor and said with venom, 'How are your wife and kiddies settling in? Such a peaceful lifestyle down here. Wouldn't want to disturb them, would we?' He suddenly leant forward on his desk as if to pounce. 'Not everyone around here deals in clotted cream teas. Some make their living out of being a bit more physical, know what I mean? And my brother knows all of them, not that he needs them as he's more than capable of handling things himself.'

Wright was determined to stand his ground. 'Very well, you have chosen your path. Be advised I will be notifying the police this morning about your theft and about every word we have just exchanged, sorry though I may be for implicating your brother. However, it has to be done. I will advise the police if anything untoward were to happen to myself or my family…'

Wright struggled to maintain his composure, his facial expression and tone of voice stood on the brink of an undignified descent into vulgarity. There is nothing like threatening someone's family for activating rage and valour, but perhaps the Proud Lion on the roof above helped him, having witnessed Castle's antics over the years. 'If anything unusual—anything

133

at all!—happens to any of us the police are to assume you and your brother are the culprits. Good day to you Mr Castle!' Our usually controlled medical director, walked out of Castle's office, slamming the door behind him. As he emerged, he saw Matilda sitting in Frieda's chair. Surprised though he was, he stormed past her still fuming.

Matilda let him leave. After thirty seconds or so, she knocked on Castle's door, walked in and with a forced smile said, 'I was cleaning Frieda's office and stopped for a rest break. Your walls are ever so thin, I heard every word. Have you met the Doctor's family? His wife is ever so nice, a real lady she is, and as for his two kiddies, they have lovely complexions, such healthy little ones they are. And they'd better stay that way. If not, I might have to call on my police friends, or maybe I should use some of my friends in your brother's hotel up the road? I'd best be getting along now.' She quietly left, closing the door.

Adrenaline does funny things to people. Dr Wright could tell you all about it, but even he was surprised at his reaction. He felt light headed and was shaking. He knew he was unfit to return to his ward office in this state and needed to calm himself down before he made the necessary phone calls. He walked outside to a bench that sat in a discrete but sunny position. Matilda guessed where he had gone, but was surprised to find him sunning himself.

'Oh, there you are, Doc. You are looking proper out of sorts. A touch of heat stroke? Or are we having one of those tiresome days? A good strong cup of tea is what you need. Come along with Tilly.' He rose, following Matilda like a child who has had a big fright. She led him into the cleaners' tea room, closing the door and hanging out a sign saying, 'Do not disturb—unless you want a dirty mop wrapped around your head.' She sat him down on the bench at the table near the sink, and gave him time, putting the kettle on and lighting a cigarette.

'Tilly, can you spare me one of those?'

'But you don't smoke, do you?'

'Not in the last twenty years I haven't, but I used to enjoy it.'

'Are you sure?' Matilda asked, doubting the wisdom.

'Come on, give me one.' She handed him one which he took, but his hand shook so much that without asking she took it back, put it in her mouth and lit it from her own before handing it back to him.

He took a couple of deep inhalations and within seconds turned green and looked as though he was going to be sick.

'Here give it back, you daft prat. You should know better. Take deep breaths and in a few minutes it'll pass.' She put four tea-bags into the tea-pot and poured in boiling water. She set a tea stained mug down in front of him and said, 'I'm not going to risk our best china on you in your state.'

'Did I go too far, Tilly?'

'How would I know? You think I goes snooping into other people's affairs and conversations?' She poured some milk into the two mugs and shook the tea pot to strengthen the brew, before pouring it. 'No, you were a proper gentleman. If it was me, I'd have smacked the blighter, even though I promised myself many years ago there'd be no more of that. But, then again, maybe I'd have had an attack of a cute ambrosia. No, you did fine Doc.'

'I will be phoning the Board, I meant it. Regardless of what they say I will then phone the police, as soon as this tea has settled me down. But it is best I know what I am up against.

Do you happen to know anything about his brother—The Enforcer?' He felt silly asking.

'Oh, Christ. Funny you should ask. A couple of my friends are lodging with him.'

'You do know him then. What is he like?'

'I know him alright, The Enforcer,' she paused. 'A real giant he is. Must stand five foot four—in heels that is. Good for slapping a few kids around when they are late on paying his drug deals. My friends—the ones lodging with him—say he made a fourteen-year-old cry so much his father went to the police and reported him. The father was never seen alive again, poor fella.' She looked up catching Wright's nervous look. 'Just joking, before you have another one of your funny turns. They did The Enforcer for assault, but it was his long list of drug missesdemeanours that resulted in his lodging with my friends in Dartmoor Prison, up Princetown way.'

'Near here, isn't it?'

'Yes, up near the top of the moor. Walking distance if you are in the mood—a long walk, and you being you'd probably get lost. It's one of Her Majesty's palaces it is. Not as dusty as Buckingham Palace they say, as they all take their turns in cleaning at Dartmoor, unlike Buckingham Palace. Word is Philip refuses to take his turn cleaning up the corgis' messes.'

She looked the doctor in the eye, 'Yes, The Enforcer's name is well known to my friends and the prison guards, all proper gentlemen. They laid on a special for him. Poor sod tripped and caught one eye on the edge of the table and the other on the edge of the bench. Ended up all black and blue and he'd not had a drop to drink. Afterwards he somehow became afraid he was going to get 'back door parole'—might 'die in prison,' to you. Quiet as a mouse he's been since, so my friends tell me. And before you going thinking nasty thoughts about Tilly, I am referring to my friends the prison guards—well mostly.'

'That's a relief. Thanks, Tilly dear.'

'Now watch it Doc. Don't you come on all amorous with me. I've got a dodgy heart—'tattycardia,' my GP called it. Go on with ya. Go call the police before your knees go weak again. And if they say they are too busy, tell them Tilly sent you and can help fix 'em up with all the paperwork they'll be needing.'

Wright phoned the chair of the Hospital Board, who was left speechless on the other end of the phone, but the doctor made it clear this was a polite notification preliminary to his duty to report a serious crime to the police. The chair was a habitual wimp who, like the other Board members, had never summoned the fortitude to stand up to their manager.

The police suggested it might be better if Wright came to their station rather than they turn up at the hospital. He went in and found them receptive and did not have to play the Tilly card. They knew the Castle family and appeared not to consider them drinking mates. Following a phone call from the police to the Board, Castle was stood down as manager that same day, pending the outcome of police enquiries. The missing grant, as the police detectives suspected, was the tip of the iceberg and they were glad of the opportunity to improve their conviction statistics. The trial process took several months, as these things do. Then Castle did a spell lodging with his brother and friends at Her Majesty's-on-the-Moor.

13

Choristers

There was a faint rumbling. A problem? Stephen's frown changed into a smile as he realised De Juniac's grotesques were breaking into song for the first time. De Juniac had said that the songs always occurred in the dark of night for reasons not even he understood, adding that he gave birth to them, but thereafter he had little control over them, much like a mother of wayward children.

In bed, Stephen listened hoping they would continue and continue they did, fluctuating in time with the ebbing and flowing of the wind, with longer and clearer tones lasting over a minute. Unlike anything he'd heard before, mysterious, disturbing.

As the night went on the wind gained strength and the sounds became louder and even more unsettling. While De Juniac had warned him they would sound so, Stephen was not to know the unusual tone of the songs that night was alarming even De Juniac himself. Ugly they were expected to be, but so sinister?

A few weeks later the grotesques performed a veritable opera. Young Luke listened from his bed in the non-ordained dormitory with rapt attention, noting the wind was resulting in distinct sounds. A sound he heard one minute appearing to come from the sacristy, the next moment came from the refectory, a different direction. A loud 'Wwwwhhhummm,' lasting about a minute, fluctuating in intensity, caused him a sick sensation in his stomach. It was such a dominant fear-inspiring sound, like a prolonged roar and the depth of the resonance suggested a large grotesque. Might it be the Lion Prince on the north wing of the cloisters? As the roar subsided a plaintive sound, much more fragile in its tone, like weeping, arose before trailing off into a few minutes of near silence.

Another resonating roar came from the south side of the main tower. That must be one of the lions, if not the Lion Prince then the Pious Lion, but a few minutes later the same sound came from over thirty yards further to the south. Were the lions on the prowl? They couldn't be—fixed stones don't move—it must be another grotesque. Yet which? Oh well, God's the conductor, he thought, so no need to worry.

As the night progressed the noises became more elaborate and even Graham the farmer, the senior of Luke's room-mates, took it upon himself to reassure his brothers all was in order, agreeing with Luke it appeared as if the makers of the sounds were moving around, as might buyers at a market. Impossible, but so it sounded.

Meanwhile, in the priests' dormitory the noises grated on Hubert, interrupting his meditation. Nothing should interrupt his meditations, he told himself, but the grotesques were deaf to his commands. The sounds put him on edge, despite their being only the products of wind and stone. He tried telling himself they would make it easier for him to transfer his anger to the stone demons and his years of meditation should serve him well for this. Anger begs to be transferred to others once it is awakened and all he needed to do—in the pursuit of virtue—was to let his wrath flow to these repositories of sins. As the night progressed, he became angry as never before, and not just with the grotesques—anger took him by the throat. Sleep did not visit him at all that night.

Following rising for prime at 6 a.m. the brothers met, with Frederick reading to them from the spiritual writings of the Holy Fathers. The candle illuminating his text kept flickering. Stephen struggled to suppress yawns and noticed Hubert wore an uncharacteristic scowl.

After Frederick's reading Stephen spoke about their night's visitors. Smiling reassuringly at his brothers he said, 'So we had a major visitation from our stone friends last night. Let us not forget they are inanimate stone and as such they have no essence other than that which we ourselves inject into them. It is my hope they will alleviate us of our burdens of sin through their evoking emotional responses from ourselves, God's fallible servants. Troubling though they may sound, it is not a sin to condemn a demon.' Stephen, smiled with a look of not being entirely convinced by his own utterance.

Following the meeting Stephen, curious about which grotesques had sung during the night, walked around his abbey looking above and around for answers, also noting work still needing the baron's attention. It was drizzling with not a breath of wind. Instead, there was the pitter patter of tiny raindrops, settling on his habit like dew on a spider's web.

It was incredible they had achieved so much in just a few years. The rebuilding remained well ahead of schedule and captured both the spirit of the old Torminster and that of a new more vibrant one. Even their services for the local community were now well attended.

Walking along the east side of the abbey still wondering about the previous night's choristers, Stephen read an inscription on the exterior of the chapterhouse he had not noticed before:

Incepto ne desistam

'May I not shrink from my purpose.' Quite so, he thought. Further on, also at eye level but this time tucked away in a shaded area confined by the north side of the chapter-house and the end of the southern transept, he saw another inscription:

In absentia luci, tenebrae vincunt

'In the absence of light, darkness prevails'. Why would such an important message be hidden away in this dark spot? De Juniac being humorous? Applying a literal interpretation to a deeper message?

Looking up to the light filtering down he saw a large gargoyle of a twin horned goat apparently having intercourse in the manner of animals from behind, with a peasant woman whose face was turned towards himself with a smile of delight. Stephen shivered as if Satan was draining his body of its warmth and hurried away.

In the corner of the northern transept he looked long at a figure, the 'Blind Monk,' which he'd seen many times before, but previously he had only given it cursory glances. It was a large monk standing almost as tall as the saints on the west façade but it stood banished to this dark cold corner. Its appearance was ominous due to its hood lowered over its face symbolising blindness. Below it he saw:

Quo lux lucet, et omnes qui non vident caeci sumus

'Where no light shines and all who see are blind.' Strange, he thought.

Walking around to the west end, he stood admiring its façade with its sculptures of saints by the main entrance—so life like, so human, fallible, not at all superior. At their feet the saints were attended by numerous tiny demons, which must have been scribes, judging from their writing materials. Perhaps the devil kept notes about the saints? Some of the imps at the feet of the saints were using abacuses. Were they assessing costs? Unlikely. Might they be deliberating the world's problems in mathematical terms? De Juniac had spoken of mathematics and spirituality, including God being infinite.

He saw the sculpture of himself but looked away, returning to the sculptures of more worthy individuals. As he continued his inspection, Stephen saw De Juniac walking towards him. Guilt suddenly grabbed him by the heart. It is time I told him about our use of his babewyns, he told himself once more. 'Good morning De Juniac, I have been admiring your creations. I have been pondering their stories from which we might learn and benefit, disturbing though some are.'

'Yes, Father.' De Juniac paused looking down at the ground, before continuing. 'Life is strange. Once life was good. Then my wife and our newborn were called to return to our Lord, then my father and brother were taken, leaving me with no immediate family. These last few years have been longer than all my life before, but my loved ones are now at peace. I am left with the role of master carver of God's loyal servants, whose calls may awaken the beholder.' He walked on with Stephen beside him.

Stephen said, 'Can stone demons be said to be loyal or to

serve our Lord? They may serve us mortals, keeping rain from our heads, even looking over us and stimulating reflection on good versus evil, but stone demons serving God? Surely not.'

De Juniac again looked down at the ground as if he was taking a much needed breath; then he looked at Stephen with a terse look in his eyes. 'I understand Father. You think my master carvers and I mess about with stones; we make funny faces out of them.'

'No, I did not mean that.'

'I beg to differ, Father, I believe that is exactly what you meant.'

Stephen's arm twitched. He berated himself for the evident offense he'd caused his friend, but decided now was not an opportune time to confess.

De Juniac's irritated expression moderated, 'It is not just priests who communicate with God. You Father have never been to Chartres. Perhaps more than anywhere, in Chartres it is apparent its architects, master masons, stonecutters, glass workers and all the other cathedral tradesmen have used stone, wood and glass to reflect the divine. You Father and your priests, you use words and reason to do God's business. Very important is your work. You explain the ways of God to those less knowledgeable; you tell of his kingdom of heaven and if they do not listen the threat of hell below; you guide them towards salvation. Dionysius the Syrian believed we know nothing about God, not just because on the divine scale of things we have a brain like an ant, but also God is more than everything, he is beyond all reason. Yet Dionysius taught we can witness some of God's manifestations around us and thereby be in union with him.

Stephen listened with sincerity, open to learning more from his unusual friend who continued.

'Church builders, including simple labourers, give the people a taste of heaven on earth, through the stones and glass shining light out of darkness, through the perfect proportions of the walls, the arches, the carvings and more. All this from stone, wood and glass. In the faces and behaviours of our grotesques and gargoyles we give the people a taste of hell below. We carvers, we call these tormented beings, our 'children.' We are responsible for who they are, who they become, is that not the role of a parent? We do not invent their expressions, we borrow them. Each expression of torment has its origins in human suffering, often combined with corruption of their values, as they have failed to hear the messages of priests.'

Guilt gnawed ever more fiercely at Stephen's heart.

De Juniac looked Stephen in the eyes. 'To carve a saint we experience some of that saintly feeling. To create these images of torment, to carve a demon we must sink to the depths, we have to be them, we have to suffer with them. And what demons they have become. Look up, what do you see? Hell, damnation, tortured minds. You visit them and rejoice they are not you and you have no experience of being them, but we carvers temporarily became them. Why? So, we may serve God though them.

Stephen's gaze lingered looking towards heaven lest his tears might fall to the ground below.

'The Mother Church has two faces,' De Juniac continued, 'One is an organisation, a large family, governed by you priests. Her other face is her physical structure in which she provides the weary with shelter and her loving embrace. But our Mother, she is not happy, this was evident in their songs last night; they were not what I expected; they are unlike anything I have heard before.' He looked Stephen in the eye, with a look that spelt darkness.

Stephen, lost in thoughts of how to appease his friend, missed the significance of De Juniac's concern about the songs. 'Forgive me Baron, I spoke out of order without thinking. Of course, your work is important, it employs skills few on earth possess and your results are more than I ever hoped for.' Stephen then looked afresh at De Juniac's creations, feeling for the first time the true depth of their suffering—and sensing their evil. God was teaching him humility through De Juniac.

'Forgive me if I have been harsh to you Father, but perhaps now you are beginning to understand? But only beginning. Do you not agree the sounds of torment are even more disturbing than their appearance? Do not ask me how it is achieved, it is much more than a trade secret, it is a subject I cannot discuss with anyone other than the best of my master carvers. Through their work alone I know they too have suffered. Forgive my temper, of late God's work has been a heavy burden, I have grown weary, but the work must go on.'

Stephen's friend for some reason was suffering and he, Stephen who prided himself on his powers of listening, had been oblivious of it. He looked De Juniac in the eyes. He saw torment, harshness. To his surprise he also saw disbelief. Did De Juniac suspect the brothers' real use of his babewyns? De Juniac knew. Stephen's heart sank as it dawned on him monks are human and humans talk. The Alsatians did not speak English but did they understand more than the brothers realised?

Shuddering in the chill wind, ashamed of his deceit, Stephen endeavoured to reassure himself that his brothers' ridding themselves of their sins could only bring good.

The Devil said, 'Give me your hate.
Fear not, I will return it in kind.'

14

Torturers

'Douglas, isn't that your fifth pint and it's not even 10 o'clock?' said Mary Wright with a good humoured frown. The Tor Church Alms, known to locals as 'The Torturer's Arms,' once was the old abbey's alms house, and was packed, tonight with rowdy drinkers oblivious of yesteryear's diseased and poor, or the relevance of the names Hubert and James.

'Come on, darling it's not every night that warrants a celebration,' her husband replied.

'Can't argue with that,' said Matilda.

Mary conceded, 'I suppose I am the nominated driver,' failing to recognise even she was already a tad over the limit.

Matilda had organised a celebration at the Torturer's following Castle being stood down and suggested the doctor bring his wife. Whether this was more out of diplomacy or to have someone fit to drive him home was unclear. Mary, younger than her husband, was plainly but expensively dressed and very sweet.

Fergus was at the bar, but it was unclear whether he had come or simply never left.

Paul Frank made the effort as he had seen many changes over his years at Torminster, but had always believed Castle would outlast him and was delighted to have been wrong.

Brian came along as Matilda told him to and even he was glad to be rid of Castle. Matilda and Brian were a pair, not in the romantic sense, that was beyond Brian, but she was one of the only two humans he was close to, the other being Old Horace, because of their shared fascination with Torminster. Matilda took an interest in Brian's stone friends without interfering and on occasion he would even chat with her. Mostly she did the talking.

Young Mabel wouldn't have missed it for the world. To her St George may have been brave taking on the dragon, but he was not a patch on Dr Wright. It was a quarter to ten and she was already well oiled, having in her excitement said 'Yes,' each time Dr Wright asked, 'Who is ready for another?' In the early rounds he ordered large glasses of house white for her but by this stage, despite feeling a bit lubricated himself he changed her orders to small glasses. He handed her another drink, charming her saying, 'Here you go Mabel. Just you and I now Castle has gone.'

'Poor Mabel,' Mary said, 'If my husband gives you any stick you just come to me and I'll sort him out for you.'

'Mary! I couldn't imagine your husband ever giving anyone any stick.'

'Don't you believe it. Why do you think we were run out of London?' Perhaps I didn't quite mean to say that, she thought, and I've only had two gin and tonics. I hope he hasn't been feeding me doubles.

'Well I won't be running you out of Devon,' replied Mabel beaming. 'You can't imagine how grateful I am to your husband.'

'Steady on Mabel,' said Matilda, 'no tears before midnight.'

Grateful? thought Fergus, he hasn't taken you out the back

shed, has he? The image of this caused him to grin.

Matilda, never one to miss a thing said, 'And what's making our Master Fergus look like the cat that's got the cream?'

'Just happy for Mabel,' he replied knowing the others might believe him, but not Matilda. To cover himself he added, 'Does anyone know who is going to replace Castle or what we are going to do without a manager in the meantime?'

'I can tell you the little I know,' said Wright. 'The Board have secured a stand-in from Plymouth who starts next week, holding the fort pending a permanent replacement. I put to them we must look to the development of community mental health services in the coming years and the managerial challenge of the gradual reallocation of hospital funds to the community will be huge. The Board agreed and will advertise nationwide. They accepted they cannot preempt the police's prosecution of Castle, but even if he were to get off on a technicality, they won't have him back at Torminster. His having used patients as he did for cider-making without a license is something even he cannot dispute. As for the embezzlement…'

'Does that mean no more cider?' Fergus asked.

'Sadly, I think it does,' said Wright.

'Oh well, better have another round, and it's my turn,' said Fergus, refusing to hear the doctor's protests.

'What will happen to Mr Castle if he is convicted?' Mabel asked.

'He's hardly Gregor MacGregor,' interrupted Brian, who had woken up at the word 'embezzlement.'

'And who is Gregor McGregor when he is at home?' Matilda demanded.

'Don't tell us. Might he have been a Scotsman?' said Fergus.

'Yes, a Scot,' said Brian, 'an adventurer, served in the Navy in the 1800s. Could have taught Castle a thing or two about embezzlement. 1817 he said he'd been appointed leader of a new Central American nation, Poyais. Wrote a book about it. Got people to invest their life savings in the booming country. Two ships of settlers left Britain for Poyais in the early 1820s. Trouble was, it didn't exist. All they found was jungle. McGregor got away with it.'

'You don't say!' exclaimed Mary.

'Brian does say,' said Matilda, 'If he says it, take it from me, it's for real. Who's for another? My turn.' Matilda bought another round for all but herself—tonight she would not disgrace herself. The doctor, with her help, had the potential to improve the patients' care, especially now Castle was gone.

They carried on in riotous spirits till closing time and how they got home is best left unsaid. That was the end of Castle. But the end always brings a new beginning.

At their first meeting Wright was impressed with Peter Jackson, the new (permanent) manager. No Devon yokel, he found himself thinking, with a twinge of disloyalty to people he was growing to appreciate. Jackson wore an immaculate three-piece suit, dripped with after shave, spoke with a public-school accent and appeared in fine physical shape. 'I used to be a competitive squash player, but now I only play socially,' he explained. 'Any time you'd like a game…'

'What made you leave London for these quaint back roads? Torminster is hardly a London teaching hospital,' Wright asked.

'Quite. I had a no-win situation. My elderly parents live in Salcombe and I was driving down here almost fortnightly to help them out, being their only offspring. Eventually, it got too much and I saw Torminster's advert. I miss London though. Enough of me, I expect you want to know about your research funds, you've been waiting an eternity for them I'm told, dreadful business, it is hard to fathom the mentality of someone who'd behave like that. Anyway, don't you worry, I've sorted it all out, the funds can be released to you this week.'

Wright beamed, relieved his woes were over.

On the Thursday he arrived at work to find his parking spot occupied by a large new Mercedes. At the front of the Mercedes he saw a newly installed sign, standing proudly, 'Manager Mr Jackson.' What cheek! Should he take it up with him or might that sound petty? He decided it would sound petty, but all morning he could not stop the argument that raged inside his head. He had to settle for a spot under the trees where the leaves were bound to fall and stain his Porsche.

That afternoon he received official notification from Jackson that forty-three thousand two hundred and ninety pounds were now available to him. His heart sank. The grant was for ninety-three thousand. He dialed the manager's number, 'Peter, I am grateful for your notifying me about the funds, but where is the rest of the ninety-three thousand?'

'I'm afraid that is long gone. Unless Castle has an unusual attack of generosity, I can't see your getting it back.'

'But what am I to do? The research project will cost ninety-three thousand to conduct, not forty-three thousand.'

'You might apply for a top-up grant.'

'But that could take another year or more. And who is going to give a grant to a research establishment whose former manager has embezzled the original funds?'

'Yes, a difficult position. You may have to make do with what you have got.'

'But that's impossible. Can't the hospital find the rest? After all it was their ruddy manager who stole the money.'

'I understand your position entirely, but sadly the hospital has no spare funds. Oh, one other thing. I've notified the grant body this unfortunate incident has occurred. They were very understanding. They said they have great confidence in your project and are happy for their funds to finally be delivered to you, but if the project for any reason does not proceed without further delay, they'd expect the funds to be returned. All ninety-three thousand, so you'd better get on with it. Sorry I can't do more, old boy.'

Wright was flabbergasted. Did Jackson call me old boy? To abandon the research project by the sound of it might cost him personally nearly fifty thousand. Somehow, he must salvage the situation on less than half the funds he needed.

A few days later, as Dr Wright arrived, he saw Matilda on the steps flick a cigarette butt onto the path. I shall have to complain to the director of sanitary services, he thought before noting the expression on her face. He parked his car in a doctors' space and walked over to her. 'You're not the only one who offers free consultations,' he said. 'What's up?'

'That stuck up prick from London!'

'Which one? Me or the new one?'

'Not you, my lover, the new one.'

'Well don't keep me in suspense. What's he done to you?'

'He told me one of my cleaners has to go as his budget can't afford her. She's worked here five years and has two kiddies to raise on her own since her old man wiped himself out in an accident a few years back. How's she going to pay her bills? And Jackson told me I'm just a bloody cleaner—not in so many words, like—but everything else I've been doing to keep the place afloat has to stop, as he's taking over. He said the same to Brian—that he's just a maintenance man. Brian. He and I have been running this place all these years, with a bit of direction from the Fisher.' She pointed up to a huge grotesque on the roof. 'Then he told him if he wants to spend his spare time repairing the grotesques that's his affair, but he's to stop using any hospital materials when doing so, or pay for them himself. Tight bastard even told Brian to stop replacing any old fire alarms that don't work. At least Castle didn't interfere and left us to the day to day running of this place. No wonder you chose to escape from London. Are they all like that? S'pose not, as you're half human.'

Tilly looked at her watch which read a quarter to nine. 'It's all right for you doctors who have nothing to do, but some of us work around here.' A glint of a smile lit up her face.

'That's more like my Tilly.'

Matilda turned to look him in the eyes, 'Oh, one more thing, an' I don't mean to spoil your day Doc,' but before she could continue Wright interrupted her.

'Don't you go apologising. You are a human being too, it's only human to be upset when treated like that.'

'Doctor, I know you mean well, but keep your trap shut will you. What I'm apologising for is about what you don't know but is about to learn. I know about your grant problems; missing fifty thousand in cash. Before I tell you what's what, have you taken your pills?'

What was coming next? He felt all clammy.

'What you'd not be knowing, Doc, is Jackson has ordered a total administration block refit starting Monday. A little birdie told me it's costing at least thirty thousand, including new desks, carpets and a lot more. Me and Brian have to have all the furniture out of his office, the secretary's and the conference room by the end of today, so they can start Monday.'

15

Deceit

Hubert cleared his throat and clutched his crucifix with his boney fingers as he watched Heinrich and other masons use a crane to haul their latest grotesques up to the roof of the lay brothers' dormitory. The crane was a triangular wooden construction with a treadwheel powered by a worker walking inside it. It seemed remarkably efficient. The grotesques were wrapped in sacking to prevent damage during the manoeuvres and their positions faced the chapterhouse where Hubert was standing. Come nightfall their task remained unfinished.

The following day the masons were still at it, but by midday they finally started unwrapping the four figures. Instead of the usual hideous grotesques, Hubert saw they were maidens in various states of grief. One sat sideways on a pedestal with her bare feet on the step below, her elbows resting on her thighs and her hands covering the lower part of her face as if weeping. Her upper face was hidden by her hood. The folds of her long cloak were exquisite, complimenting her female form. The other three were variations on this theme of grieving maidens.

Hubert grunted. What accounted for De Juniac's change in topic? He stared at the beauty of the forms, at the flowing folds giving shape to their hips and thighs. How the material clung to their thighs bringing them to life—a combination of beauty, allure, innocence and grief. Stirrings in his loins awoke him from his reverie with words of rebuke from Thomas Aquinas, 'In the realm of evil thoughts none induces to sin as much as do thoughts that concern the pleasure of the flesh.' Had Satan taken the form of the alluring Maidens to tempt him? Would that these beauties appeared more demonic, making it easier for him to condemn them.

Stephen saw Hubert looking at the new forms and wandered over to him. As if aware of Hubert's thoughts of only seconds past, he said, 'The Maidens of Temptation. Beauty paired with innocence; I fear, Brother Hubert, De Juniac is testing us further.'

De Juniac, Satan or both? Hubert silently asked himself.

During his evening reflections Hubert considered might even he himself have been unwittingly serving Satan? Might his abbot's experiment with the babewyns be empowering demons?' When had he last been blessed with a good night's sleep? If only sleep would come to his rescue, transport him to the comfort of oblivion, but that night once more sleep did not visit him.

Hubert rose in the night quietly leaving the priests' dormitory, walking barefoot along the cold stone passage to the sacristy to seek solace in his passion for theological texts. He returned to the works of Thomas Aquinas. For much of the 13th century theologians were preoccupied with Satan, the fallen angel; and with demons, Satan's followers. Aquinas viewed angels and demons as intermediaries between man and God, inferior to God but superior in intellect to humans. Angels and demons possessed immediate understanding, whereas man needed to deliberate matters before understanding them.

Demons more intelligent than himself?

Hubert wrapped his blanket more tightly around his habit. Might the transfer of his brothers' and his own sins to the babewyns—the demons—have been at their command? Might they be more than stones? Might the brothers have been setting their sins free, releasing them beyond their control, for the demons to feed on? All in Abbot Stephen's pursuit of virtue.

As Hubert was changing, so too was De Juniac, for not altogether unrelated reasons. The smiling benevolent Frenchman was becoming increasingly withdrawn and worked harder than ever, as if to finish his project as soon as possible. The only time he felt at ease was when he was supervising Luke, but Luke the young scamp was becoming increasingly mischievous. He was often seen clambering around the skyline of the church when working and at other times, pursuing his fascination with his stone friends.

It was now April and while the church exterior appeared sound at the start of winter De Juniac wanted to check how his restoration had stood up to its winter challenge. It would have been tested by the frequent gales, deluges, ice and snow. He took Luke up with him onto the roof to inspect it, looking for any unexpected cracks due to ice and for any excessive build-up of leaves in the drainage system, but they found it all in excellent order.

De Juniac valued Luke's agility. He could reach awkward structures such as those situated on the ends of flying buttresses. De Juniac had first-hand experience of a number of stone workers who had fallen to their deaths—a few had been his own, so before giving the lad instructions, he asked, 'Luke, could you climb up the outside of the tower to that third level arch?'

'It would be difficult, but yes,' Luke replied.

'I am not asking you to do so, this is a hypothetical. Let's return to mathematics a moment. You understand the risks of structures failing can be expressed in mathematical terms. If a roof is likely to collapse within a year, it should not be considered a finished structure. If it is expected to stand for a thousand years it may be considered finished but it still requires review inspections to re-determine estimates of risks arising from unexpected aging and weather. Now what if I asked you to climb up to that arch every month? How many months or years before you fell? And how long does it take to become a master builder?'

They both nodded; words were unnecessary. A rascal at times Luke was, but one with a level head on his shoulders.

At other times, when Luke was not with him, De Juniac appeared morose. The resumption of construction of the interior, following the return of the Devon masons, did nothing to improve his mood. This was apparent the day Stephen and he were reviewing the building progress. As they wandered through the southern cloister De Juniac came to a halt and gazed up at the southern aspect of the abbey's roof. He asked Stephen, 'Tell me Father, have my friends performed to your satisfaction? Have their songs enhanced your virtue?'

'They have performed as you said. You told me their sounds would instill more fear than their looks and you have been right. You may have noted after their more vocal nights my brothers have risen with tired and troubled expressions. Fortunately, we have not had too many dry and windy nights, but there have been enough. Yet I am unsure if my experiment is succeeding.'

There was no point in Stephen hiding his deceit any more, now De Juniac knew of it.

De Juniac was not going to make it easy for Stephen. 'You are not allowing yourself time Father. The church's interior is far from finished, you can't expect to build up a proper congregation until it is. It will now be my priority.'

Before Stephen could unburden himself De Juniac continued, 'A few weeks ago, Father, I had a curious dream. In my dream it was not Christ who was nailed to the cross, it was a burning part-cat part-monk grotesque. In his dying breaths he said, 'Father, forgive them, for they know not what they do.' I woke with an unfamiliar sense of horror.'

Stephen looked at the ground. 'I should have told you at the outset.'

'Yes, you should and if you had done so there would never have been an experiment, for I'd have told you what you risked and walked away. I'd do so now, if it were not for my countrymen.'

'What can I say?'

'Words, words!' De Juniac calmed his raised voice, 'Always words and thoughts. Why do you men of the Church consider them more important than deeds?'

'Words and thoughts reflect intentions. Intentions reflect morality.'

'And deeds do not?' growled De Juniac.

'If I spill your mug of ale, does it not matter whether I intended to do so or did so by accident?'

'Oh, now I see,' De Juniac said, with a drawn-out smile. 'We are both right. In your act of hiring me you deceived me, and most importantly from the Church's perspective, you intended to do so.' De Juniac pointed to the babewyns above, 'Stone they may be but they have inherited the sins, the evil of the living—of you and your brothers.' He clenched and shook his still raised fist. Lowering it he said, 'Do you remember the first time we met at Exeter Cathedral?'

'How could I not, my friend?'

'I asked that on my tombstone be inscribed 'Here lies the creator of the world's most famous grotesques.' Now I may be remembered—if at all—as 'the creator of the world's most infamous grotesques.' Their spirits are no longer as I created them.' With a bewildered look, he murmured, 'And what does the Mother Church think?'

'Come now, they are just stone,' said Stephen, his arm twitching, his voice quivering.

> *Oh, what a tangled web we weave...*
> *when first we practice to deceive.*
>
> Sir Walter Scott

16

Team work

The renovations of the hospital's administration block were finally complete after months of inconvenience. It looked more like a four-star hotel foyer than a neglected hospital, a distinct improvement, but Jackson was accustomed to five stars.

He ascended the outside rear steps, a feature commissioned by Castle so he could come and go to his office, unnoticed. Jackson cursed the Smiling Fornicating Peasant gargoyle who, deaf to his curses, looked down on him from her centuries old perch now situated above the more contemporary concrete steps. A disgusting sight, Jackson thought, the remains of a smiling female peasant being held from behind by some unrecognisable devilish beast. Why should he tolerate her dripping God knows what on his suits? He might catch something.

Later in the day, returning from lunch, Jackson noticed the Smiling Peasant was no longer dripping despite more rain. Wonders never cease, Shields must have fixed it. As he approached the top step, he heard a sudden vomiting sound from above, followed an instant later by a deluge of sodden leaves and a torrent of damned up filthy water. The cascade landed on his head and shoulders, causing him to leap to one side too late. He slipped on the wet steps and fell down them, landing on his backside. It was a good job he was athletic;

though his rear hurt it appeared he had not suffered any broken bones, but he was saturated. He rose from the puddle in which he sat; his trousers clung to him intimately and he stank from the decomposed leaves. Or worse?

He climbed back up the steps swearing profusely, entering the back of the foyer where Matilda was vacuuming the fluff from the new carpet. 'Here, you get out! Don't you know we have just had this place done up? Don't you come in here all muddy. Buzz off!' She said this with such authority he retreated outside without hesitating. He returned to his car deliberating what to do. He'd drive home and change; he couldn't spend the day in wet filthy clothes, new carpets or otherwise.

Some hours later he returned to his office in a fresh suit. He was not game to risk the Smiling Peasant again, so entered via the west side of the cloisters. As he passed her desk, Frieda said, 'Slept in did we? Did you have a good night out?'

'Don't be so bloody impertinent, you...'

Frieda looked at him, taken aback. 'Frieda's my name, Mr Jackson. I'd be glad if you did not shout when I am only being polite, greeting you. You wouldn't want to bring on one of my migraines. You know they can last for days.'

'Shut your mouth and get me Shields.'

'Get him yourself. But I will be putting your words in a complaint memorandum about abusive language to the manager. Oh, you are the manager; it will have to be to the Board.'

He entered his office slamming the door behind him. He called the switchboard operator demanding, 'Get me Brian, Shields...no, I won't hold on. You tell him to get here quick smart,' whereupon he slammed down the phone.

Almost two hours later Brian, who worked by his own set of rules and did not appreciate anyone telling him what to do, knocked on his door.

'What time do you call this, Shields? I called for you hours ago,' said Jackson.

'It be half-past four and you did indeed your Lordship, but I'ze been busy attending to your earlier instructions.' Brian was not sure precisely which character he was playing, maybe it was from Thomas Hardy. He doffed his cap, bowing for added effect. Like many introverts, when it came to acting a part he became almost eloquent.

'That obscene, that disgusting gargoyle above the back entrance is to be removed and replaced with proper modern drain pipes by the end of the week. Whoever designed a stairway with a gargoyle above it must have been retarded.'

'You are correct, Squire. He was—as some managers tend to be. I did warn him, but you know what managers are.'

'Well we no longer have that idiot Castle, I am the manager now, and that stupid gargoyle must be removed.'

'Sorry Sir, we don't have any stupid gargoyles around here; but as you say managers can be a trifle dim.'

Jackson gave him a look of disbelief. 'Just remove that gargoyle,' he eventually managed.

'I would not advise 'ee to do that, Sir.'

'I am not asking for your advice. Just arrange it!'

'I can't do that Sir; he and she are family, like.' Brian was not just referring to the nuptial bliss of the Smiling Peasant and her consort—the babewyns really were family to him. That was why he spent his weekends restoring those with any realistic futures and even those that were little more than unrecognisable stumps still commanded his respect. Some fools thought they were just stone, Brian knew better.

'Family? Are you feeling all right? You need a few days in Ward 2, you do.'

'I didn't mean human family, they being stone. The original architect Baron De Juniac, genius he was, installed them as part of the babewyn family and it would not be wise to go interfering with family. Even the police don't like interfering with families.'

'I don't give a toss about your Moron the Maniac. Just do it.'

Brian rankled at the abuse of his hero and the heretical order. He struggled to maintain self-control. 'As I said sir, I'd not advise that. It might have far reaching consequences the likes of you would not understand.'

'Do it! Or find yourself another job and I'll get a proper tradesman to remove it.'

Brian tried to repeat his warning but words would not come. He left the office feeling like a serf evicted by his lord, taking his family to live in destitution.

He wandered along the cloisters and climbed the spiral stairs to the external south gallery where he found Tilly, sitting hoping for brief glimpses of the sun while her hair blew in the wind. He pulled up a crate that was not too wet.

'Christ, Brian you look dreadful. Don't tell me you feel sorry for the prick. They got him a bull's eye, all over his nice shiny suit. You should have seen him; now you've got me spillin' my tea,' Matilda said, coughing and choking as she drank, inhaled and laughed about the Smiling Peasant's bullseye.

Brian sat next to her without a word. Matilda said, 'Here you have this tea. Looks like you need it. And I'll light you a fag.'

'The idiot says I've got to remove them. He wants a drain pipe instead. If I don't, he'll get tradesmen to do it.'

'But they've stood there for over five hundred years.'

'Six hundred and twenty.'

'Six hundred and twenty then. He can't do that. The Fisher would never allow it.'

'I hope so, but he's been awful quiet lately.'

'Wake him up then.'

'Bit easier said than done.'

'Don't you worry Brian, I'll have a word with him. Fisher'll tell you how to fix Jackson.'

At the end of the day, on leaving via the back steps Matilda looked up at the old goat shagging the Smiling Peasant. Ancient and pock-marked though they were, she could have sworn they had twinkles in their eyes.

While Matilda and Brian were regular visitors to the church gallery by day, it also had occasional visitors by night. Old Horace had been going up there for years and constructed his own ramshackle shelter in the gallery of the north east corner of the southern transept. This location was sheltered from the wet westerly winds, ideal for the now all too rare nights when the less decrepit grotesques might attempt a performance.

Brian sometimes met him in the evenings after his history lessons, but never past midnight. They enjoyed each other's company, sharing their knowledge of the abbey, particularly of the babewyns. Horace had researched the names of all the major ones, including over one hundred gargoyles and at least sixty grotesques. Originally there were double that but the ravages of time had taken their toll.

It was well past midnight when Horace heard footsteps and rose to his feet and saw a dark-haired young lady. She saw a small thin white-haired old man with a kindly expression. They stood staring at each other in silence not knowing what to say. Breaking the silence Horace said, 'Here, come and sit in this corner or you'll get cold, I won't hurt you, I am just a stupid old man.' Horace, wrapped in one of the blankets he'd smuggled up there pointed to a cavity in the masonry where he kept them dry. 'There's another blanket in there. It's cold.'

'It's not going to rain is it?'

'No, I don't think so.'

After a pause Celeste accepted Horace's offer. 'You won't tell on me, will you?' she asked as she sat down, the blanket wrapped around her.

'Not if you don't tell on me. How do you like my friends?' asked Horace pointing up to the Pious Lion.

'They're cool, but I don't really know them.' But how I want to, she thought.

'Would you like me to introduce you to some of them? Oh, by the way, my name's Horace.'

'Celeste, and yes please, especially to the cats, I like cats. I prefer being out after dark too.'

And so started an unusual relationship between two lost souls—one, an old man who had once known happiness and the other, a young lady who had not. Their lives had been so different, but they came together through their both being lost and through their bonds with their stone friends. Male though he was, Horace's age and withered stature presented no threats to Celeste. Her youth and lack of knowledge reminded him of his former pupils.

Celeste thereafter often came to visit the gallery late at night, hoping her new stone friends would be more trustworthy than humans. It might be asked how a patient from the secure wing of the hospital could leave a locked ward at night and pass through more locked doors to the gallery stairs. Indeed, it might be asked, but in fairness it is better the question remain unanswered. It is sufficient to know she had her own keys and she did. It was easy compared with getting into Torminster from prison.

Sometimes Horace was already in the gallery, other times he was not. Horace told her many stories about the babewyns over the months, to which she listened enraptured. Having grown up in a world of ugliness and neglect she felt at home with the babewyns.

One night when she was alone, she did a circuit of the gallery extending around the entire external circumference of the church. The Black Dog situated high up in the tower facing north east was huge and carved out of unusual black stone. It appeared mysterious, with protruding malevolent eyes. Curiously, she never saw it by day from the ground below, presumably because of the angle, but it was all too visible in the dark of night. Horace described it as a guardian of the underworld, a portent of Death.

Walking along the north gallery to the west she braced herself from the chill wind. Gazing back up the peculiar main tower with its array of other large grotesques she saw what must be the Headless Monk and his servant with a head on a platter. Horace had told her about them. They were to become her favourites; they shared something in common with her. Further on, she saw the mischievous Monkeys below her on the west façade and wondered what the Monkey Scribe would record about her? Maybe his fingers were too arthritic. Then there were the Hell Hounds below to the south; would they protect or savage her if she were to approach them?

This night her exhilaration was close to overflowing and as she walked along the southern gallery her heart pounded. Tonight's the night, I'm ready, I've waited so long… There he is, there's him, up in the main tower, Death, the Skeletal Monk. Are we going to become friends, oh bringer of eternal rest? No, not yet.

The Fisher must be somewhere near. There he is overlooking the green, yipes, looking straight at me, De Juniac's other masterpiece, the Fisher of Souls. He's bloody huge, maybe not what he once was, but Jesus is he giving me the creeps. Look at those eyes. I hope he can't move. Come on, it's not the time to go all wimpy, now I've finally done it, met them both and who would look at Satan and Death and feel all cosy like?

The moon came out from behind the clouds creating the opportunity, illuminating the Fisher who seemed to look down at her with approval. Then the clouds returned and The Fisher said goodnight, to which she returned, 'Till next time.'

'Is that water?' Jackson touched a wet spot on his desk and looking up saw a damp patch on the ceiling. It had been pouring for days and there was a definite drip so he placed a waste paper bin on his desk under it to prevent the beautiful old mahogany from being spoilt.

Later, there was a knock at his door. 'Come in!'

'You called for me, Sir,' said Brian.

'Look at this,' he said pointing to the receptacle on his desk.

'It's a waste paper basket, I do believe,' said Brian.

'I know it's a waste paper basket you clot. It is what it is doing I am referring to.'

'It is collecting water, that's what it is doing. Good job too, otherwise your papers an' all would be getting wet.'

'Heaven help us! Why is the roof leaking and how soon can it be fixed?'

'The first question easy. Leaking 'cause you made me remove the nice lady gargoyle and her gentleman who was looking after your office as they had done since long before we was born. Doubt if the former chapterhouse, now your office, ever leaked before.'

'The nice lady? She was obscene, she was being fucked by a goat and she was enjoying it. She was not being kind.'

'And why should she not have enjoyed it. Nature's way, it is.'

'Nature's way?'

'The birds and the bees an' all that. Did no one ever explain it to 'ee? And she didn't do it all the time, as she and him had jobs to do like the rest of us.'

'That pair of stone demons were doing it when I came to work and they were still doing it when I left. They never stopped, because they were stone, so how the hell could they do other jobs? Did they drive to work or perhaps they flew? Heavens, now you've got me talking as if they were people. I cannot be having such a conversation; this hospital is driving me mad.'

'Well I never. You queer in the head like your predecessor? They were stone they were; how could stone drive, let alone fly? They didn't move around as they were gargoyles and gargoyles have to stay at their workstations in case it rains, for drainage was their job and very good at it they were. It's the grotesques that move around.'

'Come now, do tell me how do they move around?'

'How'd I know? Do you expect me to be a bleedin' encyclopaedia as well as sorting out all your darn cock-ups? Just 'cos I don't see them move, don't mean they don't. I know some of their friends change places, how they do so is their secret. I suppose you still believe the earth's flat and if you sail past the Scillys you'll drop over the edge. You better take care if you are ever down Penzance way. 'Tis getting awful close.'

'You talk absolute claptrap man, that's what you do. Talk of grotesques moving around, but you haven't the faintest idea how.' The manager stood scratching his neck.

'Maybe it's quantum mechanics,' said Brian, 'Quantum theory says one object can be in two places many miles away at the same time, not that it looks that way to us. The grotesques might be up outside here and at the same time enjoying some sun in Australia and you'd never know it.' He pointed outside as if there were kangaroos hopping around in the rain.

'Are your mechanic friends as mad as you?' Jackson was starting to have doubts about his own state of mind.

'It were not my mechanic friends,' Brian said with a scornful look, 'it was my friend Eric the physicist who taught me about quantum theory.' With a more conciliatory expression Brian continued, 'It's difficult at first, but when you open up your mind it gets quite easy, it does. Eric, when he was a youngster worked in America and even met Albert—Albert Einstein; Einstein was no fool—no bloody administrator, that is. Mind you he started out as a clerk, so don't you lose heart.'

'Enough of this drivel. Let's start again. Why has my ceiling started leaking since you installed the drain pipe? Drain pipes are things we all have on our houses. They keep us dry, they work, they are simple, they don't take brains to install.'

'Ah, but it is what happens before the water enters the drainpipe that is the issue.'

'I'd worked that out, Brian, I'm not totally stupid.'

'Now don't you go selling yourself short, Mr Jackson, Sir.'

'What has gone wrong with the water flow before it reaches the downpipe. Have you got the channeling wrong?'

'What me? I'ze been looking after Torminster since you were having your school dinners and there were no troubles with leaks till you went interfering. I did warn you.'

'It was a simple job of replacing one gargoyle, two if you prefer, with a drainpipe.'

'Simple?' Brian said in disbelief, 'You don't know what you are talking about. One out an' they are all out. I expect we are going to have leaks all round the hospital. They have gone on strike, they have. That's what the problem is.'

'Who's gone on strike?' shouted Jackson.

'I just told you, who.'

'No you didn't.'

Brian paused, allowing Jackson time to calm down enough to hear him. Softly, he said, 'I repeat it's the gargoyles who have gone on strike. They didn't take kindly to what you did to one of their sisters and her fella. I told you you'd be courting trouble but no, you wouldn't listen. You managers are all the same.'

'God help me! You are going to be telling me the gargoyles are marching around the roof tops with banners next.'

'I reckon you be a bit touched in the head, a bit mazed. I'ze already told you gargoyles are made of stone; stone can't walk and they'd never leave their workstations. I'd have thought you with your fine education might have known that.'

'But you said they have gone on strike.'

'That I did. The proof is before your eyes.'

They both looked up, noting the drips were now a steady flow.

'Shields, we cannot waste any more time having this stupid conversation. Get up there and fix it.'

'No, I can't do that, Sir, as you said the lady must go, gone she has. And her gentleman goat, seeing he was so attached to her.'

'Just get up there and fix the drains.'

'That won't stop the strike.'

'There is no strike you fool!'

'And no water flowing through the hole in your ceiling, Sir?' They both looked up at the increasing stream.

'Look I don't care how you fix it, just do it.'

'Do I have your word as a gentleman, Sir?'

'Yes, for God's sake—anything.'

'Very well, I'll ask the lady whether she wants her old job back. Let's hope she and her fella haven't taken another while we've been wasting time.'

'You mean putting that disgusting duo back. Have you kept them?'

'Of course I have, they be heritage pieces they be. I reckon the police would have nabbed you if they'd been dumped. You've got me to thank for that.'

'Okay, put them back. Now. Without further delay.'

'One problem, Sir, maybe two,' said Brian looking up at the stream of water. 'I think you be needing another bin, before that one overflows.' Brian stepped out and returned with Frieda's bin, with which he carefully replaced the original. 'Until it stops raining I can't fix it, not with those new health and safety regulations you introduced. You'd not go ordering me to break your own rules, would you now? Have me break my neck and you'd be in court an' all over the front pages. Anyway, the mortar wouldn't set properly in this wet, but not to worry, I can work in the shed. I'll get working, no delay now, on repairing the damage done to the gargoyle's base from taking the old lady and her fella down. As soon as it stops raining, I'll have the crane out again and get my lads up the ladder in a flash. Oh, did you know you have another leak over in that corner. You'd better get Frieda to organise a few more buckets, the weather forecast is for this storm to get worse. I'd better be gettin' along now.'

Brian left Jackson's office, closing the door behind him, struggling to hide a grin as he passed Frieda, who gave him a strange look. Tilly had been right about the Fisher.

17

Grotesque

Drizzle gently falling on the abbey's roof. What a delight, no risk of infernal songs tonight, thought Hubert, surely I will sleep.

Some nights the wind howled as it chased the angels around the abbey and the rains dashed their wings as if saturated, they might fall from the sky. Even those nights were preferable to ones with demonic songs. On the quieter nights Hubert would relax then ask himself with alarm whether he heard the first notes of a grotesque performance? The songs would start quietly with isolated short-lived low notes. Before long Satan's choir would be in full swing and the noise would increase, at times until he feared a wall or roof might collapse.

On other nights the grotesques put on different performances; much quieter, almost melodious, but he who sang from the north then sang from the east; where there was one, were now two or three. How was that so?

Tonight, the gentle pitter patter. And still Hubert did not sleep.

It was two nights later, after dark as usual, that Luke and others in the lay brothers' dormitory listened to the grotesques beginning their song. They started with the familiar 'Wwwwhhhhummmmm.' But something was different, they sounded ill at ease. Young Eldred was whimpering. Graham tried to reassure him.

After about an hour another sound with a higher pitch was heard, one they had not heard before, it had a more human plaintive sound. There it went again, 'Ooohhh.' It sounded to Graham to be coming from the north but others disagreed. The fragile 'Ooohhhs' sounded more feminine than the Wwwwhhhhummmmms'.

Near on midnight Luke, unable to contain his curiosity any longer, rose to leave the dormitory but before he reached the door Graham, his elder, asked, 'What are you doing?'

'Silence, Graham,' he cheekily replied.

'Where are you going?'

'Don't ask. Guess if you must.'

Graham like everybody else liked the young rascal so he said, 'Don't be too long, it's freezing outside.' It's also scary, he thought.

Half an hour later Luke had not returned and Graham wondered where he might be. It's an unusually cold night—well below freezing—rules do not permit wandering at night. What mischief is he up to?

The songs continued unabated, becoming more complex with distinct wailing tones. They also now came from several directions at once, none of which Graham could reliably pinpoint.

Alfred, the cook broke the silence. 'Graham, where might Luke be? He's been gone a long time.'

'Yes, he has.'

175

'What is a banshee?'

Graham, normally placid, was taken aback, perhaps because of the context in which it arose. 'What is a banshee? What are you talking about?'

'The 'Ooohs' keep moving around.'

'So?'

'Well, Matthew, the stone layer, told me no good would come from the old hag with the wild hair above the south transept. He called her a banshee, whatever that may be. The 'Ooohs' started there but they now are coming from all over the place. I don't like it.'

Graham was more familiar with Irish folklore than Alfred; this talk of banshees unsettled him further. Banshees were said to have foresight and to wail for good reasons. Luke had been gone long enough, there might be something wrong. If there was, he did not want to be in trouble for having ignored it. He rose, wrapped a blanket around his habit, descended the stairs from the dormitory and walked along the southern cloister. It was bitterly cold, even for winter. His eyes stung and his nose started watering. Why did Luke choose to stay out in this? If only there was more moonlight to guide his path. Graham feared tripping over tools or materials left by the stone carvers.

A noise further along the cloister. 'Luke?' he whispered. No response. Motionless, he listened, his heart pounding, hoping for more signs of life. What's that scraping noise? It is like something being dragged along the stone floor. He tried catching up with it but no sooner did he arrive at the apparent source of the sounds than they stopped; he found nothing.

Looking up across the garth, lit by the moon, he saw the Hell Hounds along the abbey's south wall. They appeared to be asleep, but something was different. I don't like it, he told himself. Perhaps it's the cold. As his eyes adjusted to the dark, he found the silhouettes of grotesques and gargoyles disturbingly alive. What's that high up in the tower beneath one of the new empty arches? Something like a skeleton with a limb raised, as if pointing. He moved to his right for a better view but received a sickening thud to his forehead. He had walked straight into a protrusion from a stone carving. As the pain eased, he looked back to the tower, but the image was no longer apparent.

He shook himself and proceeded with his lap of the cloisters with his arms stretched out in front of him as if he was blind. He would complete a full circuit for Luke, but no more. Luke might have ascended the stairs to the gallery, but no way was Graham going to follow him up there on such a night. Who knew what might be on the prowl? He snuck past the priests' dormitory. The sounds of the grotesques were moving around all around him, as if the choristers themselves were aware of him and moving. Completing his circuit, he decided it was time to tell the ordained brothers, though he hated to think of the trouble this would cause for Luke.

Graham knocked on the door of the ordained dormitory. No response, so he knocked again a little louder. He heard a shuffling. Brother James opened the door, suspecting someone might be sick and in need of him. In whispers Graham explained the situation. Luke had been missing for almost an hour. The two brothers proceeded to the lavatories next to the ordained dormitory but Luke was not there. They returned to the dormitory where James said, 'Stay here, I'll tell the prior.'

Hubert stepped outside with James, closing the door so as

not to disturb the others, if any of them were able to sleep that night.

'What is the meaning of this?' Hubert asked.

'I don't know, Brother Hubert. I have asked myself that question with no answer,' said Graham. James explained the situation.

'Don't worry, Brother Graham,' said Hubert, 'you were correct to disturb us. Where can Luke be? You say he is not in the lavatories. Where else might someone who is sick go?'

'If he was hungry he might have gone to the kitchen,' James said. In which case he is in big trouble, he thought. To protect Luke he added, 'Not being able to sleep on such a terrible night he may have felt troubled, in need of Our Lord's succour and gone to the church to pray.'

'Kitchen first,' said Hubert. On the way they passed the dining room, but there were no signs of Luke, nor was he in the kitchen where nothing appeared to have been disturbed. They proceeded along the western cloister, entering the nave via its western door. 'James take the north aisle, Graham the south, I will check the nave,' ordered Hubert.

Graham's heart was racing as he searched in the dark, at intervals calling 'Luke?' All three froze as a near deafening bass resonance sounded above the nave. What could this mean? As it receded, they continued on, reaching the choir without any responses to their calls. James then searched the north transept, Graham the south, with Hubert searching the presbytery and the high altar.

'Please be here,' Graham whispered.

There was no sign of Luke. 'He is not in the church and he has not gone for food, unless we have missed him and he has returned to his dormitory,' said James. Graham was shivering uncontrollably. Hubert said, 'I fear there is no more we can do till daylight. It is possible he has returned to his bed. We should retire to ours, but Graham if you do find him back in his bed come and tell me.'

'Yes, Father Prior.' Hubert and James returned to their dormitory clutching their habits close to them in the frigid air.

Graham headed along the north cloister to his dormitory but on reaching the stairs he decided he'd check once more. Perhaps he was in the kitchen. Reason dictated to the contrary as they had already searched it, but worry outplayed reason. Luke was not in the kitchen, nor in the refectory beyond. Graham decided to complete one further circuit of the cloisters. He passed the ordained dormitory and the chapterhouse, reaching the north eastern corner of the cloisters. In the corner of the garth he saw what appeared to be an unfamiliar long rock. He stepped down into the garth and approached the object. The hairs on the back of his neck stood on end as another sad wail came from high above.

He approached the rock shaking worse than ever and wanting to run. 'Is there anybody there?' he said, as if the inanimate object might reply, or perhaps there was someone hiding behind it. Touching it cautiously, he felt cold cloth around a body. He felt further: a limb, an arm, a face. It was cool. 'No, No.'

He ran to the ordained dormitory and barged in without knocking.

'What is the meaning of this?' asked Hubert, although he must already have grasped it portended calamity.

Graham stood shaking with a look of horror, his mouth fixed open, brows furrowed. He struggled to speak. James approached him placing his hands on Graham's shoulders staring him in the face. 'Easy Graham—what is it?'

'He's…he's…he's in the courtyard.'

'What is he doing?' asked James.

By way of answer Graham raised his blood-stained hands.

Only Evil yearns to kill a friend.

18

Money

It rained non-stop for a week. Jackson's office renovations were trashed, there was no getting around it. New carpets ruined, new paint peeling off the ceilings and walls, floorboard damage and some of the dated electrical wiring would now have to be replaced. Total costs of the original renovations and the subsequent repairs—sixty-seven thousand pounds, give or take.

Wright was livid when Matilda told him this, but they only knew half the story. Believing the repairs of the renovations would be covered by the hospital's insurance Jackson decided to slip in a few little extras here and there—ones even he could not have justified if they had to come out of the hospital's budget. Now the subsequent repairs would provide him with the five-star office suite he felt he deserved.

A rude setback arrived several weeks later when the insurer retracted their undertaking to pay anything at all for the repairs, as it had come to their attention that the water ingress causing the damage resulted from the removal of the original adequate drainage system and the substitution of inadequate measures.

Jackson called a meeting with Dr Wright under the guise of 'Service Standards of Excellence,' a pretext for discussing budget repair issues. Seated in Jackson's new office suite Wright noted Jackson's coffee was an altogether different drink from that of the doctors' common room. No cheap sachets, plastic cups and drop your money in the tin. No, much more drinkable, and out of bone china cups, with presumably Jackson paying as there was no tin. Wright decided he'd better not comment, as if he got started…

'Dr Wright, so good of you to come,' Jackson said with a somewhat supercilious air. 'Do you take sugar? Don't the hills look green? Devon has not got the culture we both enjoyed in London, but the opportunities for country walks are right here on our doorstep—if only it would stop raining. How are your wards going? Patient care must be so rewarding; I wish I had chosen your career path, so much more rewarding than this. But then of course I didn't put in those long years of study you did. Now let us get down to business, the tedious type that falls my way—the budget. Things are very tight currently.'

Wright pointedly looked around the luxurious office, noting the smells of new carpet and polished woodwork, before saying, 'I thought this meeting was about Standards of Excellence.'

'Indeed, it is. We have to consider how—or if—we can maintain them. You see Castle left the hospital accounts in very bad shape. I am sure you understand.' Not even Dr Wright could disagree with that one.

They both paused to sip their coffees. 'Funding for the inpatients is straightforward. X number of beds attracts Y pounds of funds per annum,' said Jackson, 'Though the acute beds of course attract greater funds, as they are more demanding of staff. I hear you visit Ward 9 yourself? How often? Might there be any scope for going more frequently and our redefining it and some of the other long-stay wards as acute? Give it some thought if you would. No hurry, as next year's budget does not have to be in for some months yet. Your outpatient figures are the ones we need to get on with. Yes, yes, I have them here.' Jackson pointed to a sheet with his pen. 'For the number of doctors we have, the numbers of out-patient attendances don't appear that many.'

'I assure you my medical staff is working to full capacity.'

'Of course, of course, they are so devoted to quality patient care. I am proud to have such dedicated staff working in my hospital. But might it be possible to have shorter appointment times and squeeze a few more in as a result?'

'At the price of quality care?'

'I'd never ask that. Never! But there are degrees of quality.' Jackson put his finger tips together as if in prayer and tilted his head. 'Of course, another option much easier for everyone would be to recheck the figures.'

'Recheck the figures?'

'Yes, recheck the figures.'

'To what purpose, and why would you want to?'

'I wouldn't, but you might.'

'Why?'

'Well, you might recheck them and find they are inaccurate.'

'They're not.'

'But what if they were, say, you might recognise when all out-patient contacts are considered the real figures might be, how about, 40% greater. That would not overstretch the imagination.'

'Are you asking me to fudge the figures?' Wright shifted forward in his chair as if he had an unpleasant itch.

'Goodness, no. I'd never ask that. But they could be made more accurate.'

'How?'

'As I have just described.'

'As you have described?'

'Look Doctor. May I ask? How much do you care about your patients?' Jackson saw Vesuvius was glowing red, but was not to be deterred. 'It's a simple equation. The current budget allocation based on outpatient attendances amongst other things, dictates fewer staff. Fewer staff equals fewer patients, or some other reduction in care.'

'You are asking me to behave unethically!' Vesuvius was now blowing clouds of smoke.

'Doctor, please don't take that line. I'd never dream of such a thing, but the bottom line is in your hands, is it not? I'm merely the pawn who has to balance the books, you are the king here, as it were. It is what you do and what you want to do for your patients and the community that determine the outcome.' Jackson gave the doctor a lingering look. 'When the figures go up-line, figures are all they are to me, but those figures determine pounds, shillings and pence.'

Jackson's phone rang. This interruption involved a new feature from London. A button under Jackson's desk, if pressed, resulted in Frieda calling him. 'Would you hold the line for a few seconds, I'll be with you,' he spoke into the mouth piece. Turning to Wright, he whispered covering the mouthpiece, 'Doctor, thank you so much. This is an important call from Westminster. Please give it some further consideration and get the final figures back to me?'

Dr Wright was dismissed.

19

Investigation

Constable Richardson responded to Abbot Stephen's noti-fication by visiting Torminster Abbey the day after Luke's death and was led to the location where Luke was found. It indicated a fall from the south west corner of the main tower and apparent proof of this was found in the cloister gully below by way of four broken roof tiles, from which Luke would have bounced to the ground.

While the constable was satisfied the direct cause of death was by a fall from a height, much to Stephen's and Hubert's dismay he insisted on a further step. 'Forgive me, Father Abbot, but I have legal responsibilities as you have spiritual ones. The next step I have to consider is how he came to fall.'

Hubert clasped his hands more tightly, grunting. 'He must have slipped.'

'Quite possibly. In support of your suggestion Prior Hubert, it was a very cold night. Although it was a dry night it is wet up on the gallery and only a few minutes ago I observed some of the moisture is still frozen. Ice is of course slippery.' The consta-ble paused. 'However, a slip on ice involves one or both legs giving way with the body collapsing downwards. Yet to have fallen from the gallery Luke's body would have had to pass over an upper chest height balustrade.' He paused again for them to digest what he was saying. Hubert shuffled, looking to each in turn as if something was missing, while Stephen wrung his hands and his arm twitched. The constable continued, 'Despite this I agree Fathers, an accidental fall is still the probable cause of death. However, I have to consider all alternatives.'

'And these are?' asked Hubert looking away from the constable.

'First principles of death investigations involve four possibilities. Natural causes such as diseases; these are eliminated by the finding he fell to his death. This leaves accidents,' he paused, 'suicide, and murder.' He gave them time for his words to sink in; sink in they did. If an accident was excluded, which alternative was worse? Suicide constituted self-murder, a major sin against God—unthinkable in a monastery. As for murder...

Stephen trembled with a sense of dread. Hubert shook with anger. 'You must do your duty constable,' Stephen said.

'I will need to interview each brother, one at a time.'

The constable conducted his interviews in the chapterhouse over the following week, at times interrupting the brothers' prayer schedules, much to Hubert's disgust. He also interviewed all the workers including Luke's father, who in his distress tended to make wild accusations: 'He should've been supervised up on the roof...shouldn't've 'ad to work at night when it's cold...'e was afraid to say 'No'... wouldn't get no abbot up there, nor no prior...'

Several days later Constable Richardson went to the Abbot's cottage and knocked at the door. 'Come in,' said Stephen.

Good morning Father. 'If now is convenient I'd like to advise you of my progress.'

'Please; please sit down,' said Stephen pointing to a chair.

'I have interviewed everybody of relevance. Their testimonies, with only one exception, point to the fall having been an accident.' The constable detected Stephen breathing a sigh of relief. 'The one exception is your master builder, whose testimony cannot be lightly dismissed, given his expert knowledge.'

'De Juniac?' Stephen choked. 'Excuse me.' The constable with interest observed Stephen's arm, which had started twitching. Stephen caught his breath. 'Er, what, what does this mean?' De Juniac had told Stephen he had lost two other masons over the years in similar tragedies, so he more than any of them would have thought through the issues involved.

'Quite, and with that in mind I have arranged for De Juniac to explain his views to me once more, in your presence. He is ready to do so and waiting outside, if you are agreeable.'

Shaking, Stephen said, 'Please.'

De Juniac was called in. Stephen was shocked at his appearance. His face was downcast, his broad shoulders were slumped and his clothes were filthy even by a builder's standards.

'Might De Juniac be allowed to sit Father?' asked the Constable

'Yes, of course,' said Stephen looking around, as his cottage only had two seats. De Juniac saw Stephen's overnight bucket had been emptied, so he turned it upside down and sat on it.

The constable spoke. 'Mr De Juniac, I'd like you to return to our conversation of two days ago, but this time in the presence of the abbot.' De Juniac looked at the floor.

'Do you still agree with me, on the night of Luke's death it was cold with widespread ice?'

De Juniac nodded. 'You do,' said the constable. 'If Luke had slipped on the ice could he have fallen over the balustrade?'

187

'No.'

'Why not?'

'It is too high.'

'Could he have slipped and fallen through it? There are some wide gaps in places.'

'No, he could not.'

'And why not.'

'Even a fool when he slips puts out his arms to break his fall. To get through the wider gaps in the balustrade Luke would have had to squeeze himself up tight and even then…'

'Even then… and it is unlikely the boy would have done so accidentally?'

'Yes.'

'Do you believe he fell from the gallery in the south west corner of the southern transept?'

'Yes.'

'Why do you believe that?'

De Juniac looked up to the roof, 'Nearby and above stands the Banshee grotesque that has been an interest of his. More importantly, there were the broken cloister roof tiles below that suggest he fell from there and the trajectory of his bounce would have left him where he was found.'

'A fall by accident?'

'No, not by accident.'

'Baron!' Stephen gasped, with a look of amazement.

'Father, please let me continue,' the constable said. 'He was a youngster and if what I have heard is right, he was known to be a rascal at times. Could someone else have been up there with him? Perhaps the two of them were larking around and he fell? Might that be a possibility?'

'No.'

'Why not?'

'A rascal he was at times, but he knew when not to be. If he was up there that night and the patterns in the ice combined with how he fell suggest he was, he would have been far too careful to allow any larking around. He would not have stood for it. None of the masons meant him any harm and none of them would mess around on ice that high above the ground. Also, there was only one set of footprints.'

The constable played the devil's advocate. 'But supposing there was another person with him and they were larking around—purely hypothetical—could he not have toppled over the balustrade?'

'No, he would have had to be lifted, or to have climbed up it himself.'

'Indeed, which brings us to the next possibility, might he have jumped?'

Stephen's mouth hung open as if he were about to sneeze, or had been stabbed in the back.

'Definitely not.'

'Why not?'

'Of all my workers he was the brightest, the happiest. He had a loving family, he loved his work, he was devoted to God and he talked about the future with enthusiasm.'

'Let us say it is established he did not fall accidentally. Do you believe any person might have wanted to harm him?'

'No, definitely not.'

'Let me sum up what you have said, Mr De Juniac, and correct me if I am wrong. You say he fell to his death from the gallery at the south west corner of the southern transept. You say he cannot have fallen accidentally? Yes or no?'

'He did not fall accidentally.'

'And you have no reason to believe anyone wished him harm.'

'No, nobody.'

'And you do not believe he committed suicide.'

'Most definitely not.'

'Thank you Mr De Juniac, and thank you Father.'

'But what is the cause of his death?' asked Stephen with a beseeching look.

'That, I must further deliberate. For now, I wanted your architect's testimony to be clear to the three of us. I will report back to you Father in due course.'

Stephen gazed at De Juniac in bewilderment as the constable left. De Juniac returned the bucket to its usual position, before taking his leave without further comment.

Abbot Stephen, troubled though he was, rose to the demands of the crisis, providing direction, but Hubert floundered. Both took their responsibilities for the novices seriously and now one of them was dead. Stephen was gentle by nature, Hubert was not, and they both treated themselves as they treated others. Guilt plagued Hubert no matter how much he prayed for forgiveness. One moment he felt God was expressing disappointment with him, the next moment Hubert would insist it was the abbot who was responsible; then he felt more guilt for his sins of disrespect and disloyalty. He also found himself blaming De Juniac, the demonic babewyns' creator, and then Ralph, Luke's father for not properly raising his son. Incessant turmoil.

Then Hubert blamed himself, whether his transfer of his

anger to the grotesques might somehow have contributed. Could spirits bring stones to life? After all they were more animated than ever that night. That was absurd. He prayed again for forgiveness.

The remaining mystery of what caused Luke to venture up the tower that tragic night and the unknown cause of his fall did not help. The constable's final report reached an inconclusive verdict, adding to everyone's unease. If his death had not been a murder—heaven forbid—and he had not fallen accidentally or deliberately, how else had it occurred?

Over time Hubert's anger and guilt grew further, while Stephen embraced his responsibilities to express remorse, repent and reiterated his order that his brothers transfer their sins to the stone beings.

Hubert became irritable with Wilfrid, his new assistant, who previously could do no wrong. Ambivalent and floundering, Hubert again accepted this direction, aiming much of his anger at the infernal Banshee, the harbinger of Death, who everybody targeted in one way or another. Hubert also targeted the nearby Averted Gaze, a little seen priest figure, hidden by the cloister roof, but visible from the south west cloisters. His location mirrored that of the Blind Monk of the northern transept but the monk depicted in the Averted Gaze alongside the Banshee would have witnessed what happened that fateful night, had he not been looking away. What must he have heard? He might have been able to spare Hubert the guilt he now felt.

In the meantime, De Juniac carried on carving grotesques to the exclusion of all else. Stephen interpreted this as his way of coping with the loss of Luke, his surrogate son, and left him to it. The noise of his chipping away late into the night infuriated Hubert, whose nocturnal reflections were further disrupted. De Juniac was often still carving when the brothers rose at 2.30 am for nocturns.

With De Juniac's withdrawal, Heinrich took over the day to day direction of the workers who remained during the winter recess. Ralph Scubbahill, Luke's father and one of the more skilled Devon masons, stayed away in his grief, but Thomas Pynn tried to maintain morale in the others.

In the weeks following Luke's death the grotesques' songs, when they came, tended to be quiet, gentle as if mourning, as if they too regretted Luke's death. Hubert and others had no difficulty identifying their main source, the Maidens of Temptation who had foretold of their grief. For Hubert, these demonic creatures tormented him with their tender tones, reminding him of both Luke's death and of his own lustful temptation. In bed he would do battle in his mind fighting his twofold enemies. Those nights there was no chance of any sleep at all for Hubert. He would lie awake tormented, cursing the Maiden—Satan in disguise tempting him—begging God to silence them.

After such nights, he was particularly tense in his interactions with his brethren, and had to restrain himself from behaving angrily with them, even with Wilfrid, a young ordained brother, who helped Hubert locate relevant documents. He was studious and readily accepted his prior's directions, but he was a strange young man, a master of lingering, watching, waiting for whatever might one day bring rewards.

Stephen noticed the changes in Hubert. He asked Hubert to meet him in the chapterhouse in the hope of encouraging him to unburden himself and confess his troubled state. Hubert told himself if he were abbot, he too would have taken similar action, but baring his troubled soul to Stephen did not come easily. Stephen, benevolent as ever, probed into Hubert's theological musings with some success.

Some days after Hubert's initial confession Stephen said, 'Hubert, my loyal prior, I have read Pope John XXII decreed in the Clementine Constitutions '…if the madman, or child, or the sleepwalker harms or kills a man, he incurs, by that fact, no irregularity…' Hubert took great interest in this. The two deliberated the associated ecclesiastical issues, agreeing this would also apply to self-killing, be it accidental or otherwise. Luke must have fallen while sleepwalking. Death by sleepwalking definitely did not involve murder; it was not compatible with suicide per se, as no intent would be formed. It was closer to a death by accident, but unlike regular accidents it permitted an individual to climb a balustrade. It was the only possible explanation.

This masterful conclusion brought some relief to all concerned, but was insufficient to fully extinguish Hubert's sense of guilt. Worse, over time it reinforced his sense of inferiority, his beholdenness to his abbot, who with little effort discovered what he, the prior, had overlooked in his studies. Then Wilfrid brought to his attention some theologians believed sleepwalkers were vulnerable to demonic influences. This undid all the good Stephen's research had done for his prior, filling him further with doubts.

Brother Frederick appeared to cope best with the crisis. One of the advantages of old age was he'd seen it all before, so little surprised him. He had lost count of the number of brothers' funerals he had attended, though few had died under such peculiar circumstances as Luke's. His role as a scribe may also have helped him. He had much to record in relation to these events and it gave him a sense of purpose. Furthermore, by hearing the troubled and divergent thoughts of his brothers, De Juniac and the workers Frederick developed a greater understanding of the issues than anyone else.

He was sympathetic to Brother Hubert's state. His suffering was all too apparent, even when Hubert tried to hide it. Frederick tried shielding his prior from some of his duties. Hubert appeared to respond to Frederick with some relief and was ever respectful in his interactions with his elderly brother.

While Frederick himself coped well with Luke's death he recognised the threat it posed to the community. One foggy day, when he would not be spotted from below, Frederick ventured up the stairwell of the southern transept. The spiral staircase was steep but he managed them and opened the door to the south gallery. The old man was so shrunk with age he could not look over the balustrade; even glancing through the gaps in it the fog was so thick he couldn't see those below in the cloisters.

He turned around looking up to the lower reaches of the tower. In turning he found himself close to the Banshee. He stared long into her eyes, undaunted by her staring hollow eyes and scathing facial expression. She was stone, not flesh. Her companion monk averted his gaze. There was also a little pixie, cute but somehow sinister. Were they responsible for Luke's fall? At very least they had witnessed it and now guarded its secret.

Frederick shuddered as he looked upwards to the higher reaches of the main tower. Was it the freezing fog he felt? There was more. He sensed Death—more than Luke's death. Above him were some empty archways, awaiting the larger grotesques that were yet to be housed in superior positions. He thought he saw a figure, but looked again and deemed he was mistaken. He found himself trembling and felt cold beyond anything he had ever experienced. He wrapped his habit more tightly around him. It was many years since he had felt such unease, having accepted the faults of the world and been at peace with himself. Death was here, he felt its presence.

And why not death rather than living torment?

William Shakespeare.

20

Tribunal

With an artist's skill Celeste painted her face: black tears flowing from her left eye and an openly weeping scar across her right eye. That will do, she thought. She put on her black jeans and a black top—black now her preferred colour. Looking in the mirror she decided yes, now she looked like her grotesque friends. Shocking that the monks in the olden days 'dumped shit' on them. So, Horace told her. 'You are not alone,' she said out loud.

Celeste was due to attend a Mental Health Tribunal review of her ongoing detention at Torminster. Matilda and Horace assured her the Tribunal was unlikely to discharge a patient charged with unlawful killing this early, but she had been much more settled on the ward since making friends with Matilda 'the Bitch,' Horace and his stone friends. Her improvement was likely to be reflected in reports to the Tribunal by Drs Finch and Young. In her only recent serious outburst, two months ago, she smashed a few cups, called the nurses '… fucking whores… [and]… perverts,' threatened them with a bread knife, and then inflicted a few more cuts on her forearms. Dr Young told her she was making good progress with their psychotherapy sessions, which was both good and bad. Good she was doing all right, bad that she liked where she was and didn't want to be moved on. Finch told her the coming tribunal might approve her transfer out of his unit to a less secure one in a different hospital and that worried her. Worry is a good motivator and Matilda had given her some helpful suggestions.

After waiting outside the Tribunal's room with a ward nurse she was called in. The Tribunal members were taken aback at her ghoulish appearance—one coughed and convulsing nearly choked, spilling tea from her bone china cup. The Tribunal members made efforts to be civil and professional, going through the usual formal introductions and explanations of the purpose of the meeting.

No sooner had she sat down as instructed than Celeste rose from her chair, gliding over to the window. 'Please carry on, I am listening,' she called over her shoulder as she looked out of the window. Such behaviour by Tribunal patients was very unusual and quite unsettling. 'It's very good of you to explain all this to me,' Celeste said. She walked to the long table at which the tribunal sat, and she put her hand on the back of the chair of the middle-aged lady sitting next to the Chairman. She bent down whispering in her ear, 'I do like your ear rings. Are the stones real or are they costume?' Her warm chewing gum breath enveloped the lady who went white, staring at the table, fixed as if turned to stone.

'Miss Lewis,' the Chairman interrupted, coming to the member's rescue, 'would you mind sitting in the chair over there, then we can carry on; we have a tight schedule today, if you wouldn't mind.'

'I don't mind; but you poor things, being made to work so hard. I don't have to work at all in here and they provide all my food and stuff for free—for nothing like. Good hospital it is, I reckon.'

'Now according to the records you were admitted here in January…er, er,…' said the Chairman as he searched for his pen. He always brought this pen with him; it was a valuable old fountain pen on which his name was engraved in gold. He despised modern throwaway biros. Where is it? he asked himself, as he searched his other pockets, as his pen was not in his usual inside jacket pocket.

'Would you like this one?' Celeste volunteered, handing him a fountain pen looking suspiciously like his own—it even had his name engraved on it. This girl had cut her partner's throat; now this bizarre performance from her. Were they safe? Should they call for nurses to remove her?

'Oh, silly me,' said Celeste. 'Somehow, I have got the pens mixed up, this one is yours, I believe. I'm such a duffer, always making mistakes like this, I do. Spend a day with me and who knows what you might lose.'

'Thank you, Miss Lewis, I would be most grateful if you'd remain seated and confine your comments to answers to the questions we put to you.'

'Very good then, Your Honour. You ask away. You can ask me whatever you like and I'll be quiet and answer. No, I can't be quiet and answer, I will have to do one or the other, won't I? Silly me, duffer again. I've got it. I'll be quiet when you are asking like, and then not be so quiet when I'm answering. Got it now. Well come on, ask away. Oh, before you do, I have something important I want to tell you. Would that be okay?'

'Very well, but keep it brief if you wouldn't mind.'

'Sure, 'cos you're busy right. It's…I wanted to say regarding you know what. That is…I'm glad I did it. Yes, I am.'

'Glad you did what, may I ask?'

'Course you can ask, you're in charge. I'm glad I cut his throat. It was a good job. You should have seen his face; lost for words he was. For a moment I thought his head might fall off.' One of the Tribunal, who had been fiddling with his pen jumped, almost knocking over his glass of water. 'Well caught, you must be a cricketer,' said Celeste, before continuing, 'Stupid really, as it was still attached to his spine, by bones, gristle and like. But there was that much blood. Spouting and gurgling like the fountains in Trafalgar Square, but red of course. He asked for it, I should have done it a long time ago. Never mind, better late than never. Now come on, your turns, you ask away.'

The Tribunal ended up asking very few further questions before the Chairman said, 'Miss Lewis that will be all. You will receive a formal letter advising you of our decision within two weeks. A patient representative can explain the details of it to you if you do not understand them. Thank you, you may leave now.'

'And thank you. You are such a nice bunch. I wouldn't want to have to spend my mornings chatting to axe-murderers an' all, like me. Well, I'm not really an axe-murderer, am I? I'd like to have been, but I didn't keep one in the kitchen, so I had to use what was handy, didn't I? So, I can go now? Thanks so much.'

The Tribunal's decision proved no surprise.

21

Winter

Winter wrapped its cold embrace around the abbey. From Christmas through to mid-January Dartmoor delivered one continuous, seemingly never-ending gale with torrential rain, occasionally interrupted by snow, and howling winds that at times blew the monks over, further saturating their sodden habits. Their fields were awash, their crops lay rotting.

After weeks of the gargoyles spewing torrents without rest the wind turned to the north east, granting them relief as the grotesques took to the stage. That night the songs returned in the first major performance since Luke's death.

Frederick lay and listened in his bed. Then he rose, wrapped himself in a blanket over his habit and said to Hubert, 'I need to know more. Don't worry about me, I will take care.'

'Are you sure it is necessary?'

'I am, don't worry.'

Frederick struggled against the wind to close the dormitory door, then walked along the eastern cloister past the Tormented Twins and up the stairwell in the corner of the southern transept. Stepping out onto the gallery an unusual smell of decay struck him. It was surprising that he smelt anything in such a wind. It was not rotten leaves, more animal. Distracted, he slipped on the ice, all but falling and wrenching his aged hips.

Shaken, he chastised himself, telling himself to use more sense, he should have anticipated the ice. He shuddered as the cold penetrated his core, despite his being in a sheltered position south west of the tower.

He shuffled along the gallery around the southern transept, steadying himself by holding onto the balustrade as again the ice tried to trick him. Had the ice tricked Luke? Passing the Yeth Hound with its missing head he heard a soft howling, turning he stared at the hound. 'Was it you?' he asked, not expecting a reply.

Although he did not hear the words, it was almost as if he had, 'You should know better, my concerns lie with the still-born and the unbaptised.' Frederick started to shake. Luke had been here, he knew it, something told him.

He walked on towards the corner where the southern transept met the chancel above the altar. Two large feral cats growled at him—living ones, not stone. He slipped and fell heavily, winding himself and hurting his fragile hip. The cats approached growling and hissing, their tails flared like foxes' brushes. Frederick saw their venom, their anger, their fear, out of all proportion to the threat he posed. Struggling for breath he saw high above him the Pious Lion and the nearby Gloating Priest looking down at him with contempt. He got the message, he did not belong, he should be gone.

What was their secret? What were they guarding, preventing him from discovering? Decay? The smell of Death? Luke's death? Frederick struggled to his feet, trying not to incur further wrath from the cats. As he looked into their eyes they hissed even more until he looked away. Cautiously he backed off, he recalled De Juniac's claim cats were no guardians. De

Juniac was no fool, but perhaps the cats could be guardians when it suited them and on their terms? He reached the end of the southern transept where he turned, escaping their gaze. Descending the stairwell, he was aware of pain not only in his right hip but also in his ribs.

With effort he opened his dormitory door against the wind, went to his bed and sat down with his blanket still wrapped around him.

Hubert asked, 'Are you all right?'

'C-c-cold,' was all he managed. Hubert rose and took the old man's boots off for him and lay him down, pulling his blankets over him.

Dawn broke to the silence of heavy snow falling. Frederick rose as usual and although his hip, his initial concern, appeared not too bad, pain in the side of his chest made breathing difficult.

From mid-January to March snow blanketed the abbey and the fields. On the nights it did not snow, the sky cleared with temperatures dropping to unbearable levels. It became so intolerable that Stephen ordered the lay brothers to move into the ordained dormitory at night and he too slept there, hoping the greater number of bodies, combined with the stove, might generate more warmth for his brethren. The stove was kept burning round the clock, but at night the stars illuminating the heavens sucked the warmth from the Earth.

The crowded dormitory provided little relief from the cold; instead it brought endless coughing and wheezing from the brothers being cooped up together. Their suffering reflected their sinfulness and God's displeasure—they all knew that. At night some of them prayed that their suffering be transferred to the babewyns along with their sins.

Frederick struggled. The cold, ever callous, preys on the old, but there was more. The smell from the tower hounded him. Although he never complained and he hid his concerns from his brothers, his chest continued to pain him and his increasing frailty was apparent to all. He even appeared to be shrinking in height.

James insisted on examining him. Frederick's painful ribs suggested fractures slow to heal and were the likely cause of his breathing problems. However, James also found frostbite on his finger-tips and told Stephen. Abbot Stephen ordered Frederick to cease his scribe duties until James cleared him of frostbite, and instructed him that he was for now confined to the dormitory, the warmest, or least cold room. This caused Frederick more distress than his frostbite, which like his ribs, was a mere inconvenience, whereas confinement involved suspending his work, including his seeking answers to Luke's fall.

James attended him regularly, despite his now extensive commitments in the alms house, where increasing numbers of poor flocked, frozen, sick and starving. One morning, while James was unwinding bandages from Frederick's fingers so that he could inspect their progress, Frederick snapped at him. 'There's nothing wrong with me, let me be and attend to those in need.' But James's familiarity with animals that kicked and bit when suffering rendered him immune to Fredrick's protests.

After a month of wearing fur mittens, avoiding exposure to cold and avoiding most day-to-day use of his fingers, Frederick's fingers had healed to the point they were no longer in danger, although they remained black and painful. The dead skin was peeling as might the skin of a roasted apple. That combined with numbness continued to prevent him from returning to his scribe duties for a further month. In the interim Stephen and James allowed him out of the dormitory, but only with heavy rabbit skin mittens on twenty-four hours a day, further preventing his writing. However, being unable to write left him more time for observing others, and later he would catch up on his writing.

Frederick was not only preoccupied with Luke's death but he was also struck by the decline in morale and tranquility of the abbey. Most of all he was concerned about Hubert and De Juniac. The former had become cold and irritable—even more so than usual—the latter cold and remote.

While the snow lay thick both the grotesques and gargoyles slept, though the gargoyles might half-awaken in the middle of the day to drip water down their growing beards of ice. While a spectacular sight to most of the younger brothers, Frederick saw Hubert openly cursing them as if the icicles were spears that might at any moment be thrown by the gargoyles. He heard Hubert pray the weight of the ice might pull the gargoyles from their perches to hell below and that the ice around the singing grotesques would cause their sound chambers to crack and fall apart, come the eventual thaw. His hate for them now went unchecked.

Where was virtue? Frederick asked himself. This was not what Abbot Stephen meant in relation to transferring ill feelings to the babewyns. Stephen had instructed the brothers to transfer their sins to the babewyns during formal and informal prayer times, not simply by cursing them. When loading a mule with a heavy burden one does so with respect, with due care for the wellbeing of the beast, but Hubert seemed to wish their burdens would break their backs.

Despite occasional strong dry winds, the nights that winter were associated with respite from the grotesques' choral performances as their resonance was stifled by the snow and ice. Yet the brothers did not sleep. The dormitory's peace was interrupted by their coughing and laboured breathing. This combined with the bitter cold, ensured they had little rest. At prayer-time the challenge of getting out of bed to face the cold appeared great for all but Hubert, who was always the first out of bed in the freezing cold. Perhaps it was preferable to the torment in his mind.

Shared adversity may pull brothers together but Frederick saw no signs of this. The brothers' ill feelings towards the grotesques bred suspicion amongst themselves. Their spirit of brotherhood had taken its leave.

Love and suspicion cannot dwell together:
at the door where the latter enters, the former makes its exit.

Alexandre Dumas

22

Cuts

Matilda was livid. Even the grotesques trembled. She felt the closest in years to physically losing control, but strove to honour her pledge of no more of that, telling herself that Torminster at last had hope in the form of Dr Wright.

Jackson had told her a second cleaner must go—Judith, who'd just announced her pregnancy, but that of course was irrelevant, nothing at all to do with the decision, Jackson assured her. Not only was she pregnant but even Matilda acknowledged she was not the hardest of workers and so would struggle to find another job, especially with the current unemployment rates. She had no family in the area and the child's father had nicked off when she announced the good news. What was she to do with her?

But that was only the starter. During her meticulous cleaning of Jackson's office she found the main course, a document about a more disturbing cut—Celeste—getting rid of her. How could he? Judith, in all fairness, was a lazy bitch, who'd blown a few chances, but Celeste was doing so well it made Matilda proud. Celeste deserved a second chance in life; a second chance that her son never had. His life had been a waste. Drugs, booze and his bloody motor-bike. So long ago. Death still held Matilda in his grip.

Jackson knew how the Tribunal members reacted after interviewing Celeste. Not only had he seen their shell-shocked faces as they left, but he had also read their report with copious references to her potential ongoing danger to the community. He wrote to the Board suggesting Celeste's level of dangerousness, as determined by the Tribunal no less, far exceeded Torminster's resources. Torminster had never been designed as a forensic hospital catering for such dangerous 'inmates', who required much more highly trained and staffed wards. Celeste was the most demanding inmate, he argued, and her being the only female, a young one at that, in a ward full of males further complicated matters. If one of the male patients made advances to her who knew what the consequences might be?

Jackson emphasised the hospital's duty of care, not only to Miss Lewis, who clearly needed protection from herself, but also to other patients, the staff, and the general community if she were to escape from her locked ward. Seemingly as an afterthought, he suggested significant savings might result from her being transferred to other more suitable secure facilities in Bristol.

Matilda arranged to meet Celeste on the west gallery where they could watch the sun go down. 'Lovely, isn't it?' said Matilda gesturing with one hand to the sinking sun and with the other offering Celeste a cigarette. "Morning Alfred,' she said to a crow, introducing him to Celeste as one of the regular threesomes of crows. Alfred peered at this newcomer from his perch safely beyond her reach.

'Yes, it is lovely, but I'm not sure God's man down there agrees,' said Celeste, referring to the Demonic Abbot, who appeared to be cursing the sun for preparing its departure.

'Don't you worry about him. He may be a cranky bastard, 'tis the Fisher who runs the place.'

'I don't worry these days. Strange. You know, I feel really safe here. Funny feeling it is, first time ever really. As a small kid I thought things would come right when my father buggered off, but my mother's habit, heroin that is, got worse as did her partners.' Celeste rubbed her scarred forearms. 'She needed their money to pay for her habit. She fleeced them good and proper and not just payment for services rendered. I often saw her going through their wallets, taking what they wouldn't miss. Never slipped me any, mean bitch.' She flicked her barely touched cigarette from the gallery.

'Oi you!'

'Sorry. I remember one in particular. 'Oh baby, you're good, oh baby, I love you,' pound, pound, pound as he rooted her. Next morning, he called her a lazy cow and broke her nose. I tried to protect my Mum, being a dumb kid and all and the bitch let me try and pacify the brute knowing what he'd do to me. He wasn't the only one, they all were like that, but he was the worst as far as I can remember. Worst of all, my mother didn't care. She'd do a convenient disappearing trick. I'll never have kids, I wouldn't want them, I wouldn't trust myself and with blokes I only ever pick losers, so I'm better off on my own.'

Matilda listened sympathetically. Her own childhood was not the best, but it had been better than this. She then recalled her ex- and how they would go five rounds together after leaving the pub, her marital break-up and Simon, her son, dying in a bike accident whilst off his head. She blamed herself for his problems and for his death—she was serving her time. There was no changing the past, Celeste was now her concern.

'Celeste, my love,' Matilda said with unusual gentleness, 'We have a problem. Two really, but with one solution. Now, I don't want you to go getting upset and chucking me off this perch. It's a long way down and ugly witch-bitch though I am, I've left my broom below. I need to tell you the situation, then how we solve it. No getting your knickers in a twist now.'

Celeste gave her a dubious nod.

Matilda started with her staff problem, Judith, as a prelude to the more difficult one involving Celeste. Describing the former she hoped would set Celeste in problem solving mode before she broke the news about her proposed transfer and how they might remedy the situation.

Celeste's clenched knuckles were white but she maintained self-control. 'Yes, I'll do it,' she said through gritted teeth. Then with a smile and a hint of a purr she said, 'You know, you're sort of okay for an old bitch.'

The sun sank on two female faces, plotting like witches sitting around a cauldron—with the Demonic Abbot below, still cursing his congregation six hundred and twenty years on.

On the morning of Celeste's authorised leave she was signed off to the care of her 'brother,' a friend of Tilly's. They'd never met, but he'd oblige for the cost of a case of beer. He'd supposedly take Celeste to a family funeral—whose they'd forgotten and hoped that no one would ask again, in case they got their story wrong.

'My, you are looking pretty special today,' nurse Wayne said to Celeste, who was not wearing her usual black stage make-up.

'A mark of respect,' she said. Instead of black she wore more genteel but fashionable blue eye make-up and had pinned her hair back on both sides with plastic combs. She hated fashion but like a true artist she recognised actors should dress in period. She had even been practicing looking in a mirror smiling and producing inviting looks, with which she was unfamiliar.

'I thought your black might have been appropriate for a funeral. Turn around, let's have a full 360.' Wayne took a good look at Celeste's pert buttocks in her tight jeans, adding, 'I hope your brother is not going to fix you up with one of his ugly mates. Without your war paint you look quite a catch. You take care now.' Wayne was a creep but Celeste knew how to handle him; she knew how to handle all the staff—they were 'child's play.' Favours demanded cultivation—up to a point.

Celeste headed off to the cleaners' tea room with her 'brother'.

'You sit yourself down Robert. Tea's in the pot and there's Woman's Day or the paper,' Matilda told him. 'Celeste and me have got work to do, then you can take her back to the ward and say she wasn't feeling right so wanted to come back early.'

Matilda had chosen Frieda's lunch break. She nodded to the door at one side of Frieda's office. 'He's in. Go for it, girl.' Celeste took a deep breath and knocked on the door.

'Come in,' said the manager, who looked up as Celeste entered, surprised at the sight of an attractive young lady. Since leaving London he had missed young females with an eye for fashion. Here they tended to wear Wellington boots—muddy ones. 'How may I help you?' he asked with a smile and well-practiced charm.

'I am sorry to trouble you but I've been wandering around lost and can't find anyone to show me the way.' There is nothing like a lost young female to evoke male chivalry.

'No problem, no problem at all. Please. Please take a seat. I'm Steve Jackson. I run this show, so I should be able to help you.'

Celeste did not have to make an effort to smile in return, she just needed to take care it was the right type of smile, not the lamb-to-the-slaughter one. Gosh this place smells like a perfume factory, she thought. 'My name is Cathy, Cathy Peacock. My mother is in here, but I don't even know which ward she's in. Even if I did, I wouldn't be able to find it, having not been here before and being a duffer with no direction sense. You know they say men have superior senses of directions to us girls. Thank goodness we have other talents.'

Yes indeed, thought Jackson, checking himself so his eyes did not speak too loudly.

'Amazing hospital you've got here, really cute. Like Dracula's castle a bit, isn't it?'

'Yes, you have nailed it in one,' replied Jackson imagining his teeth chomping down on that gorgeous neck. What was the perfume he smelt? 'I am about to have a coffee; can I offer you one. You are a bit ahead of visiting times—patients will be having lunch until one o'clock.'

'Oh no, what a nuisance. I've got no rush but I don't want to get in your way. But I would like a coffee, if you are sure?' Celeste put on a rare submissive look, face lowered, eyes looking straight ahead.

'No nuisance at all. Even I have to take a break some time. Now is as good as any, Mrs or is it Miss Peacock?'

'Cathy, I am, and it's Miss. I hope I'm not looking that ancient today.'

Jackson gave her a discreet inspection. 'No, not at all. What is it like to be young? Oh, for those days.'

'Come on, you are not so old yourself. You have got a pretty athletic body.'

You noticed, what a shrewd eye you have, he thought. 'I was a champion squash player in London, though I play only socially now, about four or five times a week still. I like to keep myself in condition.'

'A champion. Really? I've never dated a champion. Excuse me, I didn't mean that, dating that is.'

'Champions are like anyone else. We are all human,' even the patients here so I am told, he thought, but resisted saying in deference to Cathy's mother.

Celeste, alias Cathy, stood up and wandered over to the photos on the mantelpiece. 'Are these your kids? Lovely look-ing, they are. Is she your wife?'

'My ex-; they are still with their mother in London, so I don't see them as much as I'd like.'

'Poor you. Life can be so cruel,' said Cathy placing a consol-atory hand on Jackson's shoulder. 'I'm not keen on marrying as it so often brings pain.' Jackson hadn't received such a magical look in a long time. He took her proffered hand in his inspect-ing it, noting the beautiful young skin. Her jacket's sleeves were long enough to cover her scars.

Celeste decided it was now the time to strike. She moved closer as if Jackson was drawing her to him. She placed her other hand on his jacket lapel. 'Lovely cloth. But aren't you hot?'

'I am a bit,' said Jackson sensing a nervous thrill, as he allowed Cathy to remove his jacket. She sat herself back on his desk purring and pulling him towards her. Their thighs met as only thighs can.

'My, you are hard—your fit thighs that is.' Celeste pulled

him tight to her and they kissed, a firm passionate exchange. She undid his tie and unbuttoned his shirt. He stood between her legs as she sat further back on his desk. She let him go and leaned backwards on her outstretched arms. He unbuttoned her blouse and slid his hands inside and around. They kissed again, Celeste making quiet moans of excited passion. As he explored the depths of her blouse, she took the opportunity to lean forward, undo his zip and unbuckle his belt. His trousers fell to the floor.

Celeste then knocked loudly twice on his desk and before Jackson knew it the door opened and in stepped that damn cleaner woman— 'Smile for the camera!' In quick succession she took several shots with flashes. The lens zoomed in on their clothing in all its disarray, while Celeste held on tight, her legs entwined around Jackson's thighs.

He struggled to get away. 'What the bloody hell do you think you are doing?' he shouted at Matilda, before looking imploringly at 'Cathy'.

'I thought you two'd like each other. I hope you introduced yourself Celeste? Don't want any anonymous sex around here, we don't.'

'Celeste?' said Jackson with a growing look of despair.

'Celeste Lewis. I expect you've heard about me, though we've never had the pleasure of meeting till now. But I know you blokes. Tonight, you'll be boasting to your mates you had a grope with Torminster's axe-murderer. Before you know it, you'll be famous, might even make the TV news.' She adjusted her clothing. As Jackson did likewise she brought her knee up into his groin, causing him to bend over, but not to retrieve his pants.

Matilda lowered the camera and employing her sternest look said, 'Listen, and listen good. No transfer of Celeste; no more cleaning staff cuts; and there will be no problems. Simple. Don't you ever forget!'

Celeste looked down at Jackson's crutch. 'And no hard feelings.'

23

Hell

The gargoyles awoke with a start in April, when spring arrived demanding their plumbing skills. The thick ice over the stream surrendered to two days of rain, which in turn yielded to drizzle and fog, which kept them busy while the singing grotesques continued their slumbers.

With spring the other Devon masons returned, including Ralph Scobbahull who was still grieving the loss of Luke, his son, while the others were mostly diffident. Stephen made a point of welcoming them, enquiring after their families.

By the stream, out of earshot, Thomas Pynn, local senior mason, told him, 'Father, it has been a terrible winter for them. Little work was available so their families went hungry and the winter sicknesses were very bad. Matthew and Warren lost little ones to it.' He watched the gurgling stream before looking up again, 'Their wives are still angry that the Alsatians and their families have enjoyed better shelter, wages and provisions than those who have always lived here. I spoke to their wives about the reality. The Alsatians have skills we do not and they had no homes to return to for winter, but the womenfolk, concerned for their children, were deaf to reason. Their husbands have taken the easier option of siding with their wives. They should not be blamed too much for doing so, but now we have a tense situation. I fear they may ill-treat Heinrich's crew. I have little control over them.'

This was not what Stephen wanted to hear, so he carried on as if he hadn't. 'Thomas, I know you will do your best. I will pray to our Lord for his assistance. All will be well.'

As the weeks went by all was not well. In May, Heinrich told De Juniac what he feared. The situation with the Devon masons was intolerable and someone must have taken a hammer to the Sacred Pig, a singing grotesque that Heinrich had carved over winter. It remained on the floor in the cloisters and now cracked, it would never sing and would be unsafe to mount, as ice the next winter might split the crack causing it to disintegrate.

De Juniac met with Heinrich and Thomas, who told them he feared this sort of situation might develop. The three agreed they should meet with the Devon masons immediately. They found them up on the northern transept roof facing the hills and called them down to the cloisters. Thomas accepted responsibility for raising the problems as his men were causing them. 'Our dreadful winter is over, thank God, but some of us want to continue it. Instead of welcoming the return of wages and warmth, some of you want to maintain the cold in your hearts by blaming our Alsatian friends, as if they were free to return to their homeland.'

Gilbert with a deliberately insolent look spat a large glob of spittle onto the cloister floor. 'No friends of ours.'

With a pained look Thomas said, 'Well they should be. We must work as one on this project. You all know the precision required for this church to be a success. Now I want to know who made the crack in this grotesque?'

Gilbert stepped forward, 'Thomas, you have got it wrong. We can't be blamed for sloppy Alsatian work. Point the finger elsewhere, not at us.'

'Here, here,' echoed the others.

Seeing Thomas's hesitation De Juniac intervened. 'Heinrich carved this grotesque.' Heinrich still could not speak much English but he could tell from the interplay of expressions what was going on. 'Heinrich is my most skilled and experienced carver of the singing grotesques, but none of us is immune from cracking them during their making. Over many years both Heinrich and myself have had our share of working for months on single grotesques only to have to consign them to the rubble heap. Usually we know when we have made errors and we bury our flawed creations with sad farewells. On the rare occasions when we have overlooked our errors, we experience far greater embarrassment and disappointment.'

He stared in the eyes of all the Devon masons. None of them could match his gaze. Some shuffled as if about to leave. De Juniac continued, 'It is not so much the mistakes which are embarrassing, it is the failure to detect and admit them. When finished every singing grotesque is blessed or condemned by all us song carvers in a ceremony, in which each of us, except he who carved it, takes a light hammer in turn to the new grotesque. Usually it is the first tap that announces a crack, the rest merely confirm it. If a crack is sounded, unless it is one of my own carvings, I deliver the final blow, then the rubble is cleared away.' He turned to Gilbert. 'Would you like to repeat your accusation about our sloppy work, call every one of us liars, or can we put this unfortunate incident behind us and be friends?'

'All I'm saying is it weren't one of us.' Gilbert and his work-mates shuffled, looking down at the ground. This was not what De Juniac, Heinrich or Thomas wanted, it was what they feared.

De Juniac picked up a heavy iron hammer and the grotesque shattered, slumped to the ground like a beast whose throat had been cut. He nodded to Thomas directing him and his masons to clean its remains away and continue their work, hoping sanity might yet prevail.

Instead of resolving the rift, the meeting merely confirmed it. By July a number of the Alsatians had been threatened phys-ically and a number of their children were injured by rocks thrown at them by the villagers' children.

The unrest reached Stephen's ears, so he met with De Juniac. As he was entering the chapterhouse, he noticed the expression on the faces of the Tormented Twins just outside. He felt their pain and hoped for some sort of resolution, but De Juniac came straight to the point.

'Father, it is with great regret I have to say farewell.'

Stephen looked incredulous and laughed as if De Juniac was mad. 'What do you mean farewell?'

'I mean my masons and I must leave Torminster.'

Stephen gasped, 'You can't leave, you have God's work to do. We have God's work to do.'

'I regret…I wish it were otherwise. My masons, their families, and I, we cannot stay any longer. The situation is intolerable for them; they have been through it before. The lives of their women and children are full of tears. Their chil-dren cry themselves to sleep at night. They want to return to Strasbourg and take their chances. They miss their homes and their kin. Which is worse—the threat of death or the sorrow of one's little ones? I don't know. The standard of our work has declined; their hearts are no longer in it.'

'But our project? No, God's project?'

'Will have to be continued by another master builder. I am weary Father,' De Juniac sighed, 'I have not the strength to be creative in the face of more conflict, so we must leave. You know how much this project meant to us.'

Stephen's arm writhed, 'This is madness. Where would you go? You mustn't go.'

De Juniac stepped forward grasping his friend's hands. 'Go we must, Father Abbot. I beg your forgiveness. I know you will grant it.'

'If it were just myself. What about God? Your commitment to Torminster as you have said has been as great as mine. Are you or am I free to let God down? No, we are not. As your abbot, as your friend, I instruct, I implore you. Give me time to reflect on this so I may find a solution.' Calming himself, Stephen said, 'Please my friend, give me one week to pray to our Lord for an answer to this problem. You can give me one week? One week, one week is all I am asking. God won't desert us at such a time.'

And it transpired Stephen was right.

Following Stephen briefing Hubert and Frederick about the Alsatians' crisis, they joined him in near continuous prayers for a solution. After three days of prayer Stephen met with Hubert in the abbot's cottage, where privacy was guaranteed. Stephen gestured to Hubert to sit. Hubert, suspecting this might be a long meeting, did not resist.

With a look of weariness and fragility, Stephen put on a meek smile. 'God has answered my prayers,' he said. Hubert remained silent, his hands clasped, his gaze lowered. 'The Devon stoneworkers must be brought into line, silenced once and for always.' For once, thought Hubert, he agreed with his abbot.

Stephen continued, 'God instructed me to act. As abbot the responsibility to do so is mine, but I confessed to him while I am devoted to his instructions, I carry the sin of weakness. The Lord replied, 'Who does not?' At first, I thought He was being forgiving, but He was not, He was directing me. Eventually I realised this. God had not made a statement, He had asked the question, 'Who does not carry the sin of weakness?' Hubert—yourself.'

Hubert looked up at his abbot with curiosity.

Stephen continued, 'God has chosen you, Hubert, for this task. I could speak to the Devon masons, threaten them with hell and damnation, but would they heed me? No. But you... They would tremble in their boots. They know if you speak, you mean what you say and you will not be deterred. My faithful prior, God has selected you for this task, without which we will all have failed our Lord.' Stephen paused to give Hubert time to digest his instructions. 'Hubert, we have little time, you must plan your approach and implement it within two days.'

Hubert struggled to hide his emotions before saying, 'Father Abbot, I am honoured to accept your instruction—God's instruction. But I will act now if you please, while I feel the strength of our Lord inside me.'

'Very well, do as you are instructed by Him, but you must succeed.'

Hubert stood up and bowed to his abbot, before leaving. Stephen watched him close the door. Tears fell down his cheeks in a curious blend of emotions, including the sense of failure all too familiar to his youth, mixed with gratitude to his prior for relieving him of his terrible burden and a tentative sense of relief that there was a solution. If he was successful Hubert might save not only Torminster but also Stephen's closest friendship of all, save that with God.

Hubert might have resented his abbot's instructions had they not been from God. That the Lord selected himself for this mission overrode all else and the wrath that dwelt inside Hubert craved release. In his mind the Proud Lion rose up on his hind legs and roared. For the first time Hubert felt as one with a grotesque.

He found the Devon stoneworkers sitting in the interior south gallery. They had not seen the prior venture up there before and the look on his face said more than words. Some expected a berating for their idleness, but when he said 'Follow,' no one doubted they must do so. Hubert led them down the stairs entering the northern cloister via the door adjoining the south transept, past the chapterhouse into the small warming room. It was May but unseasonably hot. The warming room that was a pleasant refuge in winter was intolerable in the heat of summer when the stove was kept running only to supplement the inadequacies of the kitchen. Hubert directed the masons to assemble in a semicircle around him.

He picked up the leather glove used for holding the hot iron handle of the stove lid. He pointedly dropped the glove on the ground, pausing and looking at the masons, fixing their eyes one at a time. He then picked up the iron handle and without haste deposited three more logs into the stove, all the while holding the burning handle, without flinching. He replaced the lid, put his hands together and closed his eyes in prayer.

After some minutes, opening his eyes, Hubert said, 'Brothers, I have been praying for your souls.' He stared at Thomas Pynn, the most senior and loyal of the masons, an unrelenting look, his hands still together in prayer. Thomas started to shake. All his stoneworkers watched. The additional logs, combined with the multitude of bodies in the confined space on a hot day, made the room feel like a hellish furnace. All save Hubert perspired profusely, drips falling from their faces.

'I have prayed for each of you,' continued Hubert, shifting his gaze to Peter Bickle on Thomas's left, where he held it without uttering a murmur. He moved on to stare at Matthew Eglishull, '…each and every one of you.' In silence except for the sounds of the burning stove, the nervous coughing, the shifting of feet, he subjected each of them to penetrating looks that squeezed the air from their lungs. Some of these grown men were gasping, tears mingled with sweat falling from their chins. As he stared at Warren Backvill, Warren fainted to the floor.

'Leave him.,' said Hubert. 'God has deemed him unworthy, an outcast he has become …and will forever be.' He moved on to the next worker whose eyes fell to the floor. After pursuing the same strategy with the final stoneworker, Hubert looked up asking, 'Which of you believes Heinrich—or any other Alsatian—was responsible for the cracked grotesque?' They would have known that one of them must have inflicted the damage, but no one divulged the culprit's identity. Hubert let his question hang for a few long silent minutes. Silence is bliss to a monk who communes with his god, but hell to the guilty who fear they have been abandoned. 'Which of you was responsible?' he repeated in the kiss of whisper. The question went unanswered, until eventually Hubert, barely audible, answered it himself. 'It must have been Warren Backvill, who God has stricken to the floor as an outcast.' Warren excepted, the masons displayed expressions of relief on their faces. That Warren bore the burden of guilt was a price they were happy to pay. They believed their ordeals were reaching a conclusion, but Hubert was just beginning.

'God asks, which of you will not work with His Alsatian masons?' Hubert paused. 'Forgive me Lord. The fires of hell drain my strength.' Then addressing the masons. 'I failed to relay God's question accurately. Which of you will not work joyfully and obediently with God's Alsatian masons?'

Again, no answers were volunteered. 'Do I take it you agree to work obediently and joyfully with the Alsatians?'

'Yes, Father,' was the collective response.

'Think carefully before answering God's next question. Did you and the two masons, one on either side of you, agree to work joyfully and obediently alongside your Alsatian workers? Now take care, for you are answering not just on your own behalf, but also for each brother to the left and right of you—for whose answers you will forever be held responsible. Did you all, including your brothers to the left and to the right agree to God's command you will work obediently and joyfully with his Alsatians, the most skilled stone carvers with whom he blesses this wretched community?'

'Yes, Father.'

Hubert looked each of them in the face, again one at a time.

He then put his hands together again in prayer and looking down with humility said, 'Lord, please give me, thy miserable servant, the strength to complete your commands.' He wiped the sweat that was now pouring from his own brow, and wiped his wet hands on the sides of his habit. With his right hand he picked up the now even hotter iron handle of the stove and stared into the flames flaring from its mouth. He conversed with the flames before replacing the lid. He raised the palm of his right hand for all to see its red blistering streak.

'God in his wisdom advises words come cheap when they come from Satan. There is one last test of your oaths. Each of you must lift the lid that hides us from the fires of hell below, you must look into the fires of hell for what awaits you and your families if you fail to honour your oaths. He who disobeys, does so as he prefers to accept Satan's commands over those of our Lord. Fear not, the flames of hell are powerless against he who is without sin and he who has the fortitude to complete this test will carry the mark of the Lord forever with him on the palm of his hand.' Hubert held up his palm showing it again to each of them in turn before lowering it. 'He who does not carry the blistered mark of our Lord, has been spared by Satan, into whose firmament he will pass and dwell forever.'

The masons shivered, yet perspired even more than before, the flames before them would be as nothing if they failed the test. He who passes the gates of hell finds that hell's furnace is bottomless.

Thomas was directed to go first. As senior mason he rose to the challenge, setting an example to his men. He put his palms together in a brief prayer before bowing to Hubert. He picked up the lid by its iron handle and bent forward to look into the flames. Sparks flew out as the wood crackled. His long hair and beard caught alight but he extinguished them with his left hand without changing his posture, although he closed his eyes to the scorching heat.

'Enough, replace the lid,' instructed Hubert. 'Now show us did God grant you the strength to weather your ordeal, or did Satan spare you the pain? Without looking at his palm, Thomas raised it to his bothers, then to Hubert.

Hubert stepped forward. 'God has blessed you my son, you have redeemed yourself and heaven may yet be your destiny.' Hubert grasped Thomas's upper arms and gave him a lingering kiss on his forehead.

Each of the Devon masons went through similar ordeals, though some came close to faltering, to crying out, or backing away. Without Thomas's lead it might have gone otherwise. While the later of them faced the suffering of those going before and an even hotter fire, they gained strength from those who went before them.

Upon the completion of their ordeals Hubert said, 'God has performed a miracle, sparing you from the eternal flames of hell that deliver suffering without end. All but one of you may now leave and bathe your wounds in the stream.' Looking down at Warren Backvill who remained whimpering on the floor, he said, 'You must stay and cause me further pain.'

Without dwelling for a second on Warren's fate the others rushed out, pushing past the throng of tradesmen congregated outside, and ran straight to the shallow stream leaping into it without fear of stumbling on the slippery rocks below. Even those of them who could not swim lay down underwater bathing their faces, eyes and hands in the cold water. After a while they rose and started splashing each other with joyous abandon.

Thomas stood up drenched, no longer by sweat, but by the cool June stream, a reward from God. He looked at Heinrich and opened his arms, beckoning to him. Heinrich looked at his masons, then back to Thomas before leaping into the stream and hugging Thomas. The two hugged each other like long lost brothers returned from war, while beckoning to the other Alsatian masons, who waded into the stream to hug their new-found friends.

The Devon masons wept with relief that they'd survived their ordeals. The Alsatians, who had guessed what was happening in the warming room, also wept—not with the relief of their acceptance by the Devon masons—they wept that the facial blisters and disfigurations they saw before them were as nothing compared with those they had seen on the Jews of Strasbourg.

And thus I clothe my naked villainy
With odd old ends stol'n out of holy writ;
And seem a saint, when most I play the devil.

William Shakespeare

24

Change

'Tilly.'

'Yes, my lover. What can I be doing for you?'

'I need your help.'

'At last our doctor is learning some sense.'

'How about a cup of tea?'

'Right you are. Let's go upstairs.' Matilda pointed up to the southern external gallery, 'It's a beautiful sunny day except for that cool wind, and up above we'll be sheltered from it. Follow me.'

Wright followed Matilda up the dark spiral stairwell. Up on the gallery he looked through the balustrade down to the garth, where a few patients were trying to find some rays of sunshine to thaw their bones. While the garth was sheltered from the north wind it did not receive the warmth from the sun that bathed the sheltered stone of the southern gallery.

Matilda opened the built-in wooden cupboard in which there were the provisions for tea making.

'My word, you are organised.'

'That we are. Brian installed a power point a few years back. He and I are often up here—closer to the Fisher,' she added with a mischievous grin, pointing to the large grotesque over-looking the cloisters from the west. Its horns and tail remained, but much of what must have been wings had either eroded or fallen off over the years.

'Aside from you and Brian who else are members of your select club?'

'That, you aren't yet ready for my love, but maybe in time.' It was better he not know too much about Horace and Celeste. 'Of course, you can meet some of the permanent residents. Don't ask the Hounds to play fetch, they don't appreciate it. Say hello to Fred and Ginger, those two crows on the pinnacle up there. Servants of Death they are—that's him up there,' she said pointing to a large grotesque in the decayed form of a skeletal monk, missing an arm. 'They keep an eye on what goes on up here, maintaining standards of behaviour. You've been warned now. They know what happened to Luke, but won't tell, not even Brian.'

'Luke?'

'A long story. It'll have to wait for another day.'

'I never realised how many gargoyles there are up here,' Wright said looking at the tower's grotesques.

'Grotesques and gargoyles, don't show your ignorance. Yes, it's their world and they don't like too many of us human trash up here polluting it. Brian got me my membership. The grotesques accept him more than anyone, as he tries to do right by them. Then there's the cats—the live ones, that is. Brian reckons they are servants of the stone cats. 'Oi move over Alfred,' she said to a third crow, which flew down for scraps associated with the tea ceremony. 'Tea's ready. Don't mind Alfred here, and here comes his missus and their young 'un. Alfred stared at the doctor as if demanding to know who he was. The other adult crow was accompanied by a slightly grey and fluffy juvenile. 'Now what was it you needed to ask me?'

Wright told Matilda about his meeting with Jackson. 'The bottom line is I can stand my ground and refuse to change the outpatient figures. But the price will be cuts affecting patient care. The alternative is my selling out, becoming crooked like he is, but I can't bring myself to sink so low. I can't see any satisfactory answer.'

'Quite right, you stand your ground. Tell the bugger to go to hell.'

'But what about the consequences for the patients?'

'You are not the first one to care about them. Me and Brian have had years of practice. I'll see what I can do.'

'But that's it. What can you do? I don't see you or any of us can do anything—no offence.'

'None taken, but there you go again. Have you always been a pessimist? Couldn't be developing a touch of depression, could you?'

'No to both. I consider myself a realist, not a pessimist, and I'm much more content here than I was in London, despite Jackson's best efforts.'

'Leave Jackson to me. But it'll cost you another evening in the Torturers.'

'If you say so. Now how about a tour? Introduce me to some more of your stone friends, if it is allowed.'

'Yes, it's allowed. Now you've been up here twice it's only proper they get to meet you. They'll want to decide whether to leave you be, or to visit you in your dreams.'

Tilly sat in Jackson's office admiring the new furnishings with a cleaner's eye for detail.

'Dr Wright is on his high horse, is he? Pompous ass,' said Jackson.

'Mind your manners, please, he's a friend of mine and don't you forget it,' she said with a snarl, before checking herself. How he got under her skin. 'And remember what I told you before about no cuts.'

'Hang on now. Those cuts we agreed related to your cleaning staff and to Celeste Lewis, nobody else.'

'I'm not sure you are right there.' Matilda did not want to have to play her trump cards, releasing her photos of the amorous administrator.

Jackson noting her hesitation pursued a pre-emptive strike. 'Before this turns into a squabble, let me present the bottom line to you. A lesson in logic. Any business has money coming in and money going out. The hospital's incoming funds cannot be less than outgoing expenditure on wages, bricks and mortar, equipment, etcetera or it goes broke. I can ask for more money; I can ask for a doubling or trebling of our budget. But will I get it? Is Mrs Thatcher a fan of state expenditure? Is she pouring money into state services—education, social security, police, health, the armed services? No. Well maybe the armed services. Think about it. If you've been earning, say one hundred pounds a week, but you are spending one hundred and fifty pounds a week, sooner or later you have to cut back. Unless you can increase the income.'

'I prefer the sound of the second one,' said Matilda. Little did she realise, she'd just lent her support to Jackson's master plan. Change was afoot.

25

Death

If God had delivered a miracle it was no bargain. The Devon masons never harassed the Alsatians again—but at what price? They were left with pain and scars from burns to their faces and eyes. Protective blinking in the heat of the flames lessened the damage to their eye balls, but to the detriment of their eyelids. Warren Backvill, became a permanent scapegoat, outcast and left their community. Some said that he went insane and died soon after.

The masons' bathing in the stream may have reduced the damage to their eyeballs by cooling them, but their eye-lids proved more problematic. The stream was polluted from sheep grazing on the hills above. Its water was boiled before being drunk, if it was drunk at all. Infections of their eyelids developed within a few days. God it seemed had not forgiven them.

James tended the masons daily, bathing their eyes with salt water. Some of the stone workers, already afraid of the pain associated with wound care, were further afraid of having James's disfigured face and his strange sucking noises up so close as he treated their eyes. Their families initially tended to stare at his distorted lips, but after seeing him tend their husbands or fathers, performing delicate tasks they would hate to do themselves, they grew to appreciate him and showed their gratitude.

Thomas was James's fifth burns patient so far that day. 'How are my crew doing from your healer's view?' Thomas asked.

'Badly, in one word badly. This may hurt,' he added as he gently dislodged a pussy adhesion joining Thomas's top and bottom lids. Thomas sat tensely but did not complain or cry out. 'Easy now, let's do the other eye.' 'Some of your men will be left with contractures of their eyelids.'

'Contractures?'

'Tethering of scars causing the lids to no longer sit flush on the surfaces of their eyes, impairing lubrication for keeping the surface healthy. It will feel like a mass of grit in their eyes. Yours, I'm not sure about; it's still early days.' As an afterthought he added, 'What could be a worse occupation? All that stone dust and grit.'

'How long before we can see enough to work?'

'A few months for the lucky ones.'

'A few months! What are we going to do to feed our families?'

'You'd better ask Hubert. If his God has forgiven you, perhaps they both might help out.'

During their protracted convalescence, the Alsatians became their brothers; the persecuted became their deliverers. The Alsatians worked harder to make up for the loss of Devon hands and while some of the locals were unable to work the foreigners and their wives visited them in their homes, helping them as much as they could. Meanwhile, many of the brothers struggled to bring themselves to look at their disfigured faces, finding it easier to retreat into prayers than to bow to practicalities.

Away from his needy patients James did not cope so well.

Passing Hubert outside the sacristy one day he erupted giving him a savage look and abusing him for his cruelty. 'You are meant to be a servant of God. Which side were you working for?'

Hubert did not respond, he did not need to. He had followed God's orders and delivered the miracle that saved the abbey. He also had read that Thomas Aquinas deemed that it was right for even the saints to rejoice in the suffering of the wicked, both as this reflected divine justice and as it enhanced their own blessed relationships with God.

Wilfrid, watching from across the garth witnessed this interaction, though he could not hear the words, he understood the exchange from their faces. Later he delivered an embellished version of it to his brothers, some of whom were less than enamoured with James the Curious—he who bore the mark of Satan.

Stephen thanked God that De Juniac and his masons were staying to continue the project. Stopping in front of De Juniac in the nave he said, 'I feel sad for the suffering of the Devon masons, but it's for their sins they suffer, who am I to suggest God's lesson was too harsh?' His words echoed down the aisle.

'Who are you?' said De Juniac, 'Only the abbot. Where is your virtue? Where is my divinity?' With a sullen look he turned and left.

Stephen was taken aback but soon afterwards, seeing Hubert in the chapterhouse he expressed his gratitude to him for their deliverance. Hubert responded with superficial humility and respect for his abbot who had given him his mission, but as the weeks passed humility and respect evolved into contempt.

Stephen had given him the duty as he was not up to it himself—God knew that.

It became a matter of when, not if, the two would clash and it occurred during a morning community meeting in which Hubert shared with his brothers the results of his research into the rise of Satan. In conclusion he said, 'Brothers, we all have a duty as servants of God to search for signs of Satan and wherever we find those signs we must address them, no matter in whom we find them. Satan has become a threat to Our Lord himself and Our Lord commands our response.'

For once Stephen took strong exception. Rising to his feet, 'Enough! It sounds to me as if our prior has temporarily forgotten his threefold obligations: to God, St Benedict and to his abbot. He speaks as though he is the authority. While many theologians share his views let us not forget that for twelve hundred years after Christ's life on Earth Satan constituted no more than a thorn in the side of Christianity. He was of little consequence. Now, the pursuit of demonology empowers Satan, delivering the terror he so desires. I call on you to exercise moderation, to practice the loving acceptance preached by our Lord and to love thine enemy, for he is still your neighbour.'

Just as Hubert stood up to respond, Stephen announced, 'The meeting is now closed.'

Hubert's face, usually so difficult to read, screamed outrage for all to see, as they were meant to. A multitude of looks was exchanged among the brothers. While many of them sympathised with Hubert's position few were ready to join him in defying their abbot. Nevertheless, it was from this time that some of the brothers switched their allegiances to Hubert. In difficult times the troubled may turn to he who shows strength, in preference to he who champions the path of right.

It was early evening. De Juniac sat on the external gallery feeding his cats, the furry ones. His relief that his men and their families were no longer intimidated and were now secure, was outweighed by his sympathy for the Devon masons who would suffer in the long-term.

He had encountered workers with eye injuries from stone chips, some of whom never worked with stone again and others who suffered long term constant eye irritation from the dust on the damaged surfaces of their eyes. Most of them managed with one good eye, though their fine work was never as precise as before. This was the first time he had encountered workers with both eyes injured, but he could guess the consequences.

He had been stupid to have trusted Stephen. Was he himself responsible for the Devon masons' plight? Had he been serving God—or Satan? Satan the Shapeshifter, Satan the Deceiver, Satan the Tempter. Had Satan used Stephen to lure him into this venture?

James ascended the stairs to the gallery from which Luke was believed to have fallen. On opening the door to the gallery he jumped as he was greeted by screeches of feral cats fleeing from him. James had heard and seen them before but never so near. He found De Juniac sitting in a sheltered spot in virtual darkness surrounded by scattered bits of food. 'So, it is you. You have interrupted my friends' repasts.'

'May I sit with you?'

De Juniac hesitated: 'Jesus too was a healer, so you may.' James sat down next to him. They were both silent listening to faint humming from some of the grotesques. 'It's a night for gentle songs,' said De Juniac.

'Gentleness, what is that?' James replied with venom, surprising De Juniac.

'The brothers lost God's direction long ago,' said De Juniac, 'Hubert is one actor in Satan's play, albeit a key one.'

Looking around him, James asked, 'What do you think happened to Luke?'

'He did not fall, he did not jump and no person pushed him; he was led, that is what I think.' De Juniac stared at the ground in front of him, avoiding James's gaze.

James shuddered. 'Led by who?'

'Not by who, my friend.' De Juniac looked up at the stars.

'Then what?'

'The spirits of the grotesques are not what I designed. I meant them to be part of my celebration of the divine. I had such dreams for them—long ago. Now, I no longer have control over them. The brothers have made sure of that.'

James saw small green eyes reflecting the moonlight, staring at him.

'Come, my friends, he won't eat you,' De Juniac reassured the cats. Returning to James, De Juniac said, 'They are not stupid, they know how treacherous man can be.'

After a few tentative minutes one of the larger cats, probably the dominant male, crept forward low on its haunches. Growling, belly low to the ground, it approached James, who was sitting on the floor, leaning against the wall, with his hands around his knees, pretending not to notice the animal. The other cats looked on as the growling and occasional hisses eased. The cat raised a paw as if about to strike, but James continued to talk to De Juniac as if the cat did not exist. The large male lowered its paw then butted James' hands rubbing the front of its ears against them, while James continued to ignore it.

'It took me months of visiting and feeding them before they would do that to me,' said De Juniac.

'I understand animals and they me. You do better than I with humans,' said James.

'So it may once have been, but that was long ago.'

'Might the cats somehow have played a role in Luke's death?'

'The cats would be the last to do the Devil's bidding. Plenty of others would line up first.'

'What lies ahead for us?'

'That is a question for God.' De Juniac held out a piece of meat to an approaching cat that hissed, then turned away. 'Evil has been allowed to flourish unchecked as I, fool that I am, mistook a man of God for wisdom. I am afraid for the abbey. Our Mother, she is angry.'

De Juniac and Heinrich both regularly carved long into the night, creating their two masterpieces, 'Death, the Skeletal Monk' and the 'Fisher of Souls.' Death came first, and as Death grew it infected De Juniac; the amiable Frenchman was no more.

After months of such work James visited De Juniac and Heinrich one night knowing their creations were nearing completion. He saw two friends working on the Fisher, drained of vitality, finely chiseling its details, as if their spirits had taken flight.

Death, the Skeletal Monk was now complete and De Juniac and Heinrich removed its drape for James' inspection. He saw a skeleton dressed in a monk's habit, with a hood drawn down low over its skull and face, its right hand raised, pointing. Inside the hood was a skull with penetrating but empty eye sockets and an empty cavernous nose. Its ribs protruded from a rent in its habit. James saw Hubert.

De Juniac straightened his back. 'Tomorrow Heinrich and I will position him high on the central tower. He will look to the south west, to farewell the sun.'

James then saw the Fisher of Souls. It towered over them, its massive thighs, long tail, horns and wings of a giant bat almost overpowered him. He had no doubt who or what it represented. James looked into the Fisher's eyes staring down at him. One moment they beckoned him, 'Come with me...' the next they seemed to voice contempt, so much so James could not hold its look, stone though it was, and troubled he looked away. Turning to De Juniac he said, 'You said you were afraid that Our Mother is angry and that the grotesques were beyond your control. If so, why Death and why the Fisher of Souls?'

De Juniac looked at James, still a youngster. 'Could there be life without Death? Death gives life its meaning.'

James mulled this over.

De Juniac continued, 'Also, a candle that illuminates darkness, loses its power when held up to the brilliance of the sun. Too much light may overwhelm its gentler forms. The darkness of Death gives rise to the light of Life. In time all things return to Death, the eternal sleep.'

'And the Fisher?'

'Christ was the light, the Fisher of Men. He gave our lives purpose and meaning. But so does the Fisher of Souls. He puts obstacles in our paths, without which life would be so easy it would be facile. And by offering corruption, he may deliver virtue in those prepared to toil.'

De Juniac paused and wore a perplexed expression. 'The good servants of God have corrupted the grotesques, by instilling evil where evil did not belong and for some reason, I don't understand why, God the Creator allowed this. If He will not help, who else might exert control over them? To whom else can I appeal? If a priest turns his back on a gang of villains attacking an innocent, you might ask the priest to turn around. Alternatively, you might appeal directly to the leader of the gang?' Putting some tools away, he added, 'I hope, the Fisher might make the brothers see the errors of their ways and reverse what they have done. The darkness of the Fisher of Souls may enhance the brilliance of light. Something tells me the end of this folly will be determined by the Fisher. Or perhaps I too have lost my soul.'

James felt panic.

Several days later Hubert, outraged, watched from afar the efforts involved in the mounting of the Fisher, which remained covered until its installation mortar started to set. Death, the Skeletal Monk was already mounted and unveiled in the tower. Death in a monk's habit. An obscenity 'the biggest insult we brothers have ever received,' he protested to his abbot. 'It symbolises the bringer of death, as if we monks are Death's servants. It is too much—it is evil.' Most of the brothers, already unsettled, were to agree with him.

It was another two days before, on emerging from the chapterhouse, that he looked across the garth and for the first time Hubert saw the Fisher unveiled. He coughed as if he was about to choke, then shuddered looking at its evil part goat, part human face. Its eyes were human but so penetrating they saw right through him. He trembled, it was hideous, an abomination. His abbot must take action; he would ensure he did.

Hubert met with Stephen in the abbot's cottage. 'Yes, I know we are being tested,' said Stephen, 'but De Juniac's work has been of the highest standard. God commands him as He commands ourselves. I instructed De Juniac to create babewyns that would be challenging; we should not be surprised now if they are.'

Hubert's nostrils flared with contempt. 'Father Abbot, have you even seen the new devil above the lay dormitory?'

'No, I confess I have not, but I will do so later today.'

'May I suggest we meet again after you have seen it first-hand?'

'I will call you when I am ready.'

Later that afternoon Stephen went to the eastern cloister while it was quiet with the brothers occupied in the fields. He looked up at the Fisher of Souls. It was in a different league to De Juniac's other grotesques, Death excepted. Not only was it by far the largest grotesque, what struck him most was it appeared more alive. Stephen clutched his crucifix while looking into the eyes of the Fisher, and said, 'The powers of love and righteousness will always prevail.' Was it a statement or a prayer?

He startled, thinking he heard a laugh. He looked around but no one was there. He then heard in barely audible words?

'Righteousness. Well-meaning fool, did you think you could deceive me?' Stephen shuddered and uttered a prayer to his Lord. The Fisher's gaze chilled him to his core. 'The Creator and the Destroyer are but two sides of a coin—He is one; I the other; We are the One God; the same.'

'You He? Never. Never!'

'Is everything all right Abbot Stephen?' called Frederick from the other side of the garth. Stephen was taken aback, being caught at such a delicate time, but he was relieved to see it was only Frederick.

'Everything is fine. I have been studying the Fisher.' Stephen struggled to restrain himself from weeping. 'He is a disturbing piece of work; no wonder Hubert is troubled by him.'

'De Juniac told me it is his most important work to date. And we have yet to hear its song.'

Stephen nodded and went on his way.

Later, after time to compose himself, Stephen found Hubert in the chapterhouse. 'I have seen the Fisher. As you said, he is more disturbing than all the others. He appeared almost to speak to me, but of course he could not as he is stone, but stones may stimulate our reflections. Evil must be managed by constant vigilance, humility, self-restraint and honesty. Please, my friend, reflect on those words. That is all.'

Abruptly, Stephen left the chapterhouse.

Hubert stared after him, open mouthed in amazement, ever more outraged.

Still more was in store for Stephen later that day when James knocked on his door. 'May I have a word Father Abbot?'

'By all means James, come in, come in; have a seat. Is it about the Fisher you have come?'

'No, it is about Prior Hubert,' James said, restraining himself from asking whether there was a difference. 'I am struggling Father. Every day for several hours I still tend the burns inflicted by Hubert on the local masons. None of them will ever fully recover. Isaac is in absolute misery with such painful eyes and impaired sight that his children have become afraid to look at their father's face. He struggles to swallow food and water and so I fear he may not survive. We are men of God. Tell me father, how can what Hubert did be justified?'

'The price of correction can be high. Let us not forget the price Christ paid on the cross for our sins. We should be indebted to Hubert for his successful settling of the masons' dispute, for without him the Alsatians would be gone, he possessed the courage to carry out God's instructions.'

'I fear you are wrong Father, I believe Hubert gained satisfaction from his cruelty. The God I serve would not support such actions. If he did, I wouldn't serve him.'

'James! Mind your words. It is not for you to judge the Almighty, nor for you to judge your prior who acted when I was unable and whose actions have saved Torminster from ruin. I will hear no more of this. You have your chores to do, pray do them.'

James left with his face distorted even more than usual; his deformed lip quivered and his deep breaths caused his deformity to hiss. He was in a passion, but he knew his abbot was as kind as any he might hope for; heaven forbid Hubert should ever become the abbot. Stephen should not be the target of his fury, so he took his leave and went to pray in the chapel.

There he found De Juniac, already at prayer. De Juniac looked up at James, finished his prayer and sat up. James had never seen De Juniac on his knees. His designs and creations were his usual ways of communing with God. Curiously, De Juniac looked healthier, more like his former self.

'Lad what on earth has happened to you? Don't tell me the Fisher has scared you too out of your wits?'

'No, it is not the Fisher, it is those of the flesh that scare me.'

De Juniac hesitated. 'It is the spirit of you brothers, or of some of you, that dwells in my creations and it scares me too. In the face of wrath is it good or evil that flourishes? The secret is to remain at peace.'

A few weeks later Stephen heard a knock on his door. Fearing another disgruntled brother, he said, 'Enter.' To his surprise it was De Juniac, who wore a look of serenity, which Stephen had not seen in a long time.

De Juniac hesitated. 'Father, I have come to ask a favour, might I borrow your pony? I need to visit a maker of bells in Sutton and I may be away for a few days. Would you be able to make do without your pony?'

'Yes, of course, by all means. The Frenchman was smiling and did not have the look of someone about to complain. Stephen felt relieved this was all De Juniac wanted.

De Juniac came up to Stephen and took his right hand in both of his own, holding it while looking at the abbot, his old friend. 'We have been through difficult times together. The Fisher will test you Father Abbot; be sure to hear him.'

The days passed with Stephen in a state of contradictions. One friend, his prior accused him of allowing himself to be influenced by Satan, while his other friend, the Frenchman told him to listen to the Fisher. What should he do? He decided to visit the Fisher after dusk when his brothers would not notice him.

Staring up at the Fisher, whose face was illuminated by the almost full moon, Stephen said, 'Are you capable of teaching me, or do you only corrupt?'

Clouds from the south blew across the face of the moon causing the Fisher to appear to turn its head to look down at Stephen—who distinctly heard, 'Could darkness exist if it were not for light? Virtue sits hand in hand with sin, birth with death, joy with sorrow, summer with winter. You have bathed in the bosom of warmth, but now is the time of winter. God is infinite. God is all things.'

'Be sure to hear him.' De Juniac's words, reverberated through Stephen's head. If only it could be otherwise. Stephen craved joy without suffering, but he knew it was not to be. He turned from the Fisher and looked up at the tower where Death should have been. He saw only shadow, emptiness, Death appeared to have taken his leave. It was dark and Stephen was so weary, his walk back to his cottage seemed a journey without end.

Three days later it was a sunny day, but Stephen's mood contrasted with the light. One minute he was pacing the floor of his cottage, the next he would sit down, only to rise seconds later and repeat his pacing. De Juniac was yet to return and he craved his views about the Fisher's words. De Juniac would surely supply the key to understanding—but would it be a key of truth? Were these ideas designed to enlighten or to mislead him? If enlighten, enlighten how? Long ago, De Juniac had spoken of God being infinite and infinity being divine? That God was everything. Infinity and singularity—were they one and the same?

A knock at his door only partly awoke him from these deliberations. 'Enter,' he said. It was James, ashened-faced. Why such a look? With a rude jolt Stephen returned to the present. No not more, please no more, he thought.

'Father Abbot, your pony has been found,' said James,

'down-stream from the stone bridge that crosses the Erme river.' Stephen saw despair in James's eyes. 'And De Juniac nearby.' James laid a familiar but sodden glove on Stephen's table.

Stephen's pony reared before his eyes. He recalled his ride back to St Madern's after he last saw his father. His pony's fear approaching the bridge...

'I forgot to warn him.'

The fearful and the feebleminded divide their worlds into friends and foes.

26

Gratitude

'That is terrible,' said Dr Wright over the phone to Mrs Franks. 'I'm so sorry to hear this. Of course, we will look after everything this end. You take care of yourself and your family. Do call me if there is anything I can help with, anything at all.'

'How shocking,' Wright said to Rosemary Young. 'On the way home from work last night Peter Frank was hit by a drunk driver. He has just died in Freedom Fields Hospital.'

'Oh, no, that's appalling. His poor wife, such a nice lady.'

'Rosemary, may I trouble you to go over to Peter's ward and help his registrar review his patients, look into their needs and break the news if they have not already heard. I can help out myself later if needed.'

'I'd be delighted to. Well not delighted…you know what I mean.'

Wright phoned Jackson, asking, 'Have you heard the news about Peter Frank?' He hadn't, so Wright repeated the little he'd been told.

'What awfully bad luck. You never can tell when your time is up. And Dr Frank has done so much for our hospital over so many years. He's been the longest standing of the medical staff if I remember right.'

'Yes, that is so. I think we should lay on some sort of memorial service or otherwise recognise his contribution in some way.'

'Yes, I agree. Let me know what you decide upon. I'll attend to the necessary.'

A week later a suitable memorial service was held in the hospital chapel. Both Wright and Jackson made the usual speeches. Afterwards over coffee and sandwiches Wright raised with Jackson the issue of advertising for a replacement.

'Oh, there is no point in that. The Board has put a freeze on new positions—pending the transfer of patients to the community.'

'But this is not a new position.'

'New appointments also, just the same. These sandwiches are really rather good. Like another?'

27

Charity

The autumn leaves were falling from the trees and the brothers were under pressure to make up for their farm's bad season. Hubert did not share his abbot's confidence that their Lord would provide for them—the Lord helps those that help themselves. The dark clouds to the west threatened only rain, and snow was unusual in late autumn, but he thought it would be a real threat by December, when their sheep could become stuck in the snow and die. James and Wilfrid arrived with the novice he sent for them and Hubert directed James and Wilfrid to herd the flock down from the higher moorland to lower levels closer to the monastery.

The two brothers trudged up to the high country using the sheep paths where possible even though they were thick with mud. Off the paths the ground was worse; it was waterlogged. Wilfrid grumbled preferring to be in prayer or studying, but James felt invigourated by the harsh conditions and was glad to be away from the abbey.

They reached an area in the high country known as the Meadow. They saw the flock of about thirty sheep with thick heavy coats, bedraggled with mud. The Meadow was crossed by a long line of prehistoric standing stones, which fascinated James. He had not seen them before but he'd heard about them.

They were over a thousand years old and while the stones were small, many only a few feet tall, they seemed to extend forever, about two miles he estimated. How did primitive people move such a vast quantity of heavy stones and why did they erect them in such a remote place? Wilfrid, however, was unimpressed—they were erected and used by pagans, and scarcely warranted a thought.

The sheep were hardy creatures and herding them back initially appeared straightforward to James, but then it started to snow with the snow blowing in their eyes and visibility became poor. Lower down it would be sleet or rain but either way they could become dangerously wet and cold. Three quarters of the way home a group of seven sheep split off from the main flock and bolted back to the high country. James knew Wilfrid did not have the stamina to run after them and it was approaching dusk. He said to Wilfrid, 'I'll retrieve the stray sheep, you continue with the main flock along this sheep track and soon the route home will become obvious. If you don't delay, you'll be home before dark.'

'Shouldn't we stay together? I don't know the country like you do,' said Wilfrid.

'If we do, we lose those sheep. Try explaining that to your prior.'

'Couldn't I wait here with the main flock while you retrieve the strays?'

'It will take me some hours to do so in these conditions and you will freeze standing still. You have a choice, walk back with the main flock now, or you run after the strays and then if you catch them herd them back long after dark—either way alone. You've chosen? Good, go home, without further delay.'

James knew that even he would not return with the sheep before darkness descended, but his years of wandering alone on the moor prepared him well for being out after dark in inclement weather. He veered off the path in the direction he would have taken had he been a sheep. It involved trudging uphill out of the wind and snow. After about an hour of searching in the near darkness he first heard then saw the sheep sheltering behind a small granite tor, though by then the snow and wind had eased. While leading them downhill a thick fog descended obscuring the moonlight and he realised that even he could become lost if he was not careful. He was thankful Wilfrid had set off home before the weather change and was confident that if Wilfrid encountered the mist at all he would already have reached familiar landmarks.

James gently coerced the small flock into obeying his commands. He concentrated on controlling the lead sheep, so the others would follow. The fog grew thicker causing him to rethink his route home. It was too cold to risk a full night lost on the moor so he decided to follow a stream that flowing downhill must grow and enter either a larger stream or the river Erme. He must control the sheep and prevent their panicking which might see them rush back to high ground or worse, run downhill into a deeper stream or river. He called to them soothingly always directing the lead animal.

James arrived home four hours after dark, saturated, cold, but relieved to have reached safety with the errant sheep. He noticed the main flock was nowhere obvious and hoped Wilfrid had secured them for the night, but knowing Wilfrid he may have left them somewhere stupid, leaving James to deal with them. That could wait, for the moment his priority was to warm up and have something to eat. He penned up his sheep before going to the lavatories to wash his hands. He changed into a dry habit and found Brother Graham.

'Has Wilfrid penned the sheep up in suitable shelter?' James asked. He was shivering so much his speech was even more difficult to grasp than usual.

'Wilfrid? Hasn't he come back with you?'

'Didn't he return about a few hours ago?'

'No, he is not back. Why isn't he with you?'

James explained what had happened, adding, 'If he is not back, he may have got into difficulties. There was no fog when I left him but if he dallied the fog may have caused him to go astray.'

'This is serious,' said Graham, 'this fog is getting worse.' 'I'd better organise a search for him. You get something to eat and warm up.'

'I will grab some bread and water while you are organising the others. I'm not tired.'

'You may not be but you look very cold.'

'Not too cold. The decision was my responsibility and if it was the wrong one, I must help correct matters.'

'If you're sure?' Graham agreed with James's reasoning but was concerned about his shivering and appearing half frozen.

They met a few minutes later by which time Graham had informed Hubert and recruited brothers Matthew and Andrew. They set out with unlit torches in hand reserving them for when they were away from familiar territory and for guiding Wilfrid to them.

'How dark it is; more than just fog,' said Matthew.

'There is a full moon behind the clouds,' replied James, 'we should be able to follow the tracks of the sheep I returned with. That will take us part of the way to where I left him. Hopefully we'll find him on that route but if not, we will have to follow the landmarks that I memorised on the way out with Wilfrid.'

They proceeded cautiously. The fog was patchy, and in places visibility improved with the feeble moonlight. It was an hour and a half before they came across signs of a multitude of sheep leaving hoof prints away from their path, heading east away from the trail.

Little flashes of light followed the hoof prints.

'What's that?' asked Andrew, his voice betraying him.

'Fireflies,' said James.

'Unusual,' said Graham, 'I have only ever seen them in summer.'

'I've seen them more often in summer, but I've also seen them in spring and autumn; though never this late in autumn or in such cold as this,' said James.

'Strange, they should be hibernating,' Graham added. They trudged on in silence, at intervals calling, 'Wilfrid,' and waving a lit torch.

'I don't like it, he's been pixie-led,' said Mark.

'That's an old wives' tale, don't be stupid,' said Graham, not wanting to believe in pixies, but many people did believe that pixies led the unwary away from reliable paths, leading them into bogs and the ground was definitely becoming boggier.

'Hush! Listen, what is that? It's a bleating sheep.' They lit the other torches and found a terrified animal making feeble efforts to haul itself out of the bog. With difficulty they hauled it out of the near freezing mire, but it died soon afterwards.

Searching, they found five other sheep—all dead, from

drowning or from the cold bog. After some minutes searching, the light from Mark's torch fell on a human form—Wilfrid, face down in the bog. 'No! Please no! It can't be,' Mark cried. The others rushed over to him. James and Graham struggled to haul out Wilfrid's stiff body. His sodden habit was heavy and the bog was determined not to relinquish its meal.

'Pixie-led,' repeated Mark, gasping. Graham, panting, did not respond. The flashes of light from fire-flies were more numerous around the bog than elsewhere. 'Is Wilfrid dead?' Mark asked.

'He is, lad,' said James. 'How are we going to carry him back?' he asked Graham, aware of the weight of Wilfrid's mud sodden habit and his own exhaustion.

'One each to his shoulders and legs,' said Graham. Within a few minutes of hauling Wilfrid thus, they ground to a halt. The sodden sagging weight suspended from four corners created a strain on the bearers, who were already struggling on difficult slippery ground. James was exhausted, the hours of cold had sapped his strength. Mark and Andrew could never match Graham for strength, and even he was struggling.

'We can't leave him here,' panted Andrew.

Shivering James said, 'T-t-two to each leg. I have managed it with deer on my own.'

'James is right. I wish it were otherwise,' said Graham. They set about hauling the stiff corpse back by its ankles, aware of the disrespect they paid their brother whose back, shoulders and head were dragged through the mud with his habit riding up, adding to his indignity and to their labours. Initially, they were able to drag him for a few hundred yards before resting, but by the time they neared home they were managing only about ten yards. Graham called a halt a quarter of a mile from the abbey. Gasping he instructed, 'We will leave him here and go for help.'

No one complained.

It was past midnight when they found Hubert waiting up for them, having earlier authorised Graham's leading the search party. 'Four of you can't manage?' asked Hubert. 'Very well, how many more will you need?'

'Four—all fresh. The others are exhausted,' said Graham.

'But surely James? He should…' Hubert wanted to finish his sentence, but even to his eyes James looked spent. Hubert arranged for the three brothers to be washed, reclothed and fed, and instructed three other brothers to accompany Graham and himself to retrieve Wilfrid's body, with Graham leading the way.

The following day James was called to visit the prior in the chapterhouse. He presented himself with ominous feelings. Hubert was seated at the table. 'Brother James, come in,' he said with formality. 'I trust you are rested from your unfortunate ordeal. Why did you leave Wilfrid alone to guide the flock home?' Before James could respond Hubert continued, 'May he now be at peace in God's home. You have been brought up to know the countryside, but not so Wilfrid. Aside from our dear brother, we can ill afford to lose that many sheep this winter. You will eat apart from the other brothers for a month to atone for your errors. May God forgive you.' With a nod and glaring eyes, Hubert dismissed him.

James bowed with the respect of a monk, but left with the confused sentiments of a human.

Entering the community meeting after matins Stephen

experienced a sense of misgiving, which was realised when his prior admonished James in front of the brothers oblivious of James' months of diligence tending the masons' eyes daily.

Following Hubert's admonishment of James, Stephen asked Hubert to meet with him. Stephen once more tried to exert his authority, telling Hubert he should have informed him before the meeting if a brother was to be admonished. This might have given him an opportunity to discuss the justice issues involved. 'What were James's instructions to Wilfrid when they parted?' he asked.

'It is enough that James left poor Wilfrid.'

'Enough? How do you know? Did you ask?'

Hubert remained silent, though his eyes spoke revolt.

'Let us not forget James's daily toils with the sick and injured. I take full responsibility for the mason's burns, but in judging James let us not forget he's been dealing with their consequences every day since.'

Hubert interrupted, for the first time losing his grip on humility, respect and self-restraint. 'If I am to be your prior and to be responsible for most of the running of the monastery, I need your support, not your criticism.' Stephen was taken aback, but did not pursue the matter. He would leave it until Hubert was in a more receptive state of mind. In the meantime, they must face the fact the abbey's winter food stores were now further depleted.

The winter that followed, grim for the brothers, was far worse for their congregation.

It was February 29, 1368. An east wind blew that night, not the ideal wind for a performance, but close enough. The grotesques were loath to let the leap year night pass without a chorale.

Around midnight a loud howl was heard. Might it be from the Yeth Hound on the southern transept? Brother Graham asked himself. Sensitive though he was since Luke's death and feeling on edge, he could still appreciate the humour in a beheaded beast singing.

One of the younger brothers, Brother Isaac, was whimpering. Graham then heard a strange grinding noise, as if the hound was breaking free of the stone on which it stood leaving it free to move wherever it would? As the wind grew many other grotesques joined the choir. The discordant noises became unlike anything heard before, much more human. Was it a lament or an expression of outrage?

Isaac implored, 'Please God, preserve my soul. Let them not take it from me; it is for you alone to do with as you please.'

Then the brothers heard a sound immediately outside their dormitory. Was it Death? Was it the Fisher? Was one or the other trying to climb through the wall?

Isaac cried out, 'Lord save us!'

Graham's 'Quiet, lad,' was drowned out by the hysterical furore of the other brothers who were more in tune with Isaac. They froze as they heard the latch of the door click. A tall hooded figure, Death, the Skeletal Monk, stared at them. The brothers screamed defiance at Death, calling upon their Lord to save them. Death raised its arms as if to bring the heavens crashing down on them. The brothers screamed louder. Egbert picked up a small prayer table and threw it at the hooded figure. It was a good throw. Down went the figure with a groan.

At that moment, in stepped another demon who went to Death's aid, cursing the brothers. Graham, for some reason, also bent to assist the demons. The three were oblivious of the other brothers, ignoring their curses. Death did not rise, but his demonic helper did. He drew back his hood, staring at the brothers as if to strike them dead with his look. Slowly they recognised the face of the helper as that of Brother James. 'Hush, hush, hush, it is me, James. Hush, be still now, be calm.'

Graham added, 'Fear not, it is only James. James and Prior Hubert who lies injured from the table.' Lying groaning on the flagstones the brothers saw their prior with blood streaming from his face. The table had broken his nose and dislodged teeth.

Hubert had never been able to sleep during grotesque performances and Luke's death haunted him even more since the loss of Wilfrid. This night, sleepless and with genuine concern, he had risen to check on the wellbeing of his young brothers.

Beware the righteous.

Omen

The cold north wind gnawed at those outside of shelter. Most of the patients were asleep when for the first time in a long while some of the better-preserved grotesques sang. Celeste shivered, as she tried to find shelter from the wind on the south gallery above the Hell Hounds. The song came from the other side of the church but it was unmistakable. Soft though it was, it was like a funeral dirge. Horace had told her about the songs but this was the first time she'd heard one. She was not afraid but tears trickled down her cheeks and she did not know why. Was it the cold or something else?

A small pair of eyes was looking at her. They belonged to one of the wild cats that was sniffing the corpse of a crow.

'You haven't killed Alfred, have you?' She bent down to examine the bird. The crow looked as if it had been dead for some days. It was shriveled up and infested with maggots. 'I hope it's not you Alfred. Poor thing,' she said looking accusingly at the cat. 'I wouldn't eat him if I was you.' She reached out a hand to let it have a sniff. The cat hissed.

'It's okay little fella.'

The end

'Come in Brother Frederick and please be seated,' said Abbot Stephen, guiding Frederick to a seat in his cottage. 'You had something you wanted to discuss?'

'Indeed. Father Abbot. My role at Torminster has been to record our experiment; the transfer of our sins to the grotesques and gargoyles, thereby enhancing our virtue. I have observed, recorded and deliberated. When Torminster started you were as one with De Juniac,' Frederick paused. 'Yourself, Hubert and I were also united, there was harmony and optimism all around. But now, where is the virtue you so dearly sought?'

Stephen's arm became restless; his face appeared weary. 'We cannot stop now. All this will have been for nothing if we do.'

'Are the lost wise to continue wandering? Might they do better to retrace their steps? Our steps.'

Stephen held his fingertips together in deliberation or was it prayer? Where were the signs of tranquility, spirituality, transcendence and virtue? His father had predicted long ago that he would never achieve anything worthwhile. But how he had tried. He trembled, at a loss for what to say. His grand experiment in the service of his Lord, once so joyfully shared with his strange French friend—all gone.

He beckoned through the doorway to a passing novice,

directing him to locate the prior and ask him to come to the cottage. When Hubert arrived, Stephen asked him to sit, then invited Frederick to share his concerns with Hubert.

'Father Abbot, Brother Hubert—we three founding brothers,' Frederick paused. 'I believe our experiment is not working and it may be time we recognised this. Have we a monastery that is more virtuous than St Madern's?'

Hubert sat stiffly erect, his bruised face with its bent nose seemed to voice its agreement with Frederick's sentiment.

'Are we and our brothers any purer than before?' continued Frederick, 'De Juniac was as in touch with our Lord as were we, yet he is gone.'

Hubert grimaced.

'In my miserable opinion we should consider abandoning our experiment.'

'Hubert?' asked Stephen.

Hubert cleared his throat; 'Frederick, I believe, is correct we are failing.' Stephen did not anticipate such a conciliatory response.

'But,' continued Hubert, 'he makes light of De Juniac's role in this. His grotesques more than ever appear to respond to Satan's bidding.'

Stephen felt a wave of finality; if the two of them advocated abandoning the experiment he no longer had the energy to bear the load alone.

To his surprise Hubert continued, 'Do we now surrender handing Satan a victory as Brother Frederick suggests, or do we stand firm, trusting in God?'

Hubert stared at the floor and quietly smiled, confident in his ascendency.

The wind howled that night as if it was afraid. Graham was sweeping up leaves in the north cloister after dinner, as Hubert passed by. 'It is barely dusk and the grotesques are starting to sing, Brother Hubert,' said Graham. 'What does that mean, I wonder?'

Little sleep tonight, thought Hubert.

'God testing us?' Graham added.

God or Satan, Hubert nodded and proceeded to the sacristy.

Vespers followed in the chapel. All the brothers were assembled in neat lines with their habits creating uniformity. No sooner did Abbot Stephen commence the service than loud moaning sounds were heard above. Stephen stopped and waited for the noise to recede, but minute by minute it grew ever louder. Talking over the din was futile—also, like his brothers his sense of foreboding was overwhelming. Tonight was different, discordant plaintive sounds rang out, with Death perched high above them. A strong gust of wind reverberated around the tower.

Stephen asked himself was the Mother Church expressing her displeasure as De Juniac had suggested? What had motivated De Juniac to carve Death, and dress him in a monk's habit? Was Hubert right? Might De Juniac have been corrupted by Satan? Stephen trembled at the thought, for if so what of himself?

From the eastern end of the nave came a deafening reverberation that grew louder threatening to tear off the roof. Stephen feared God had abandoned them for their sins—for his sins? Stephen read fear on his brothers' faces.

Loud howls followed. Were they from the Hell Hounds? No, they could not be, as gargoyles cannot sing. There then was a cacophony of deafening sounds that came from everywhere all at once; discordant reverberations shook the abbey. A large window above the chapel gave way, its glass raining down in pieces on the brothers. Brother Frederick cried out and fell to the ground. James rushed over to him, but his questions went unheard by the old man. He saw blood flowing from Frederick's upper left arm, the sleeve of which bore a rent. He gently tore the rent open and found a shard of glass protruding from the wound. Opening up the two sides of the wound with his fingers he extricated the shard. He tore off a large section of the sleeve and wrapped it around the wound to stem the bleeding. He gestured to his brothers. They helped Frederick to his feet while James used one hand to apply pressure to the wound.

'We shall abandon the service as it is unsafe to continue,' shouted Stephen. 'We will adjourn to the chapterhouse,' he gesticulated and led the way.

Andrew helped James lead Frederick to the infirmary of the alms house for further attention. James lay Frederick on the table while Andrew lit extra candles. James removed the bandage and opened the wound further to explore it for more glass fragments. It appeared that one big shard had lacerated the arm without any pieces breaking off, so he cleansed the wound with clean water. Although it was still bleeding there was no spurting so he proceeded to stitch the wound with 'catgut' thread made from sheep intestines. Frederick appeared frightened but kept still allowing James to do what he must. After stitching the laceration, he put Frederick's arm in a sling. Frederick shook with fear and looked so very old, almost a child again. James reassured him that the wound was clean and that it would heal without problems.

On reaching the chapterhouse Stephen opened the door and

jumped as a magpie standing on the table stared at him, then escaped flying over his shoulder. Inside the chapterhouse where the noise was barely compatible with conversation Stephen told his brethren, 'All is not well. I fear we are receiving a message of displeasure from Our Lord and we must give it due consideration.'

'This is madness,' said a voice. The brothers raised their heads to seek its source. 'This is madness,' repeated Hubert with more authority. 'It is not Our Lord who speaks to us. The calls are from Satan, the Fisher and the other grotesques, his demons.' Further howls seemed to confirm Hubert's statement. Stephen rose. He gestured to his brethren to kneel and pray. They prayed as never before, each voicing his own prayers.

Frederick meanwhile demanded that James and Andrew lead him to join their brothers in the chapterhouse; if he and his brothers were sinners, he was not going to let his frailty excuse him from prayer.

Hour after hour the brothers prayed, kneeling on mats on the stone floor. The considerable pains in their knees and backs were minor compared with their fear. Was it God's displeasure or was it Satan speaking? The former was to be preferred; God might forgive those who repented with sufficient sincerity.

Stephen went to rise shortly before midnight, with the storm continuing its fury. He found himself stuck on his knees. Grasping the nearby table, he hauled himself up to his feet with difficulty. He tried to speak but the howls of the wind were so loud his speech could not be heard so he put his hands together, holding them to his ear, tilting his head in repose to signal they should retire to bed and try to sleep. Even the younger brothers struggled to stand. Frederick was stuck. James rose, stretching his back, then tried to help Frederick, but Frederick remained unable to straighten his knees, so James carried him to his bed with his legs stuck in their flexed position. Laying the old man on the bed James massaged his legs then pulled them straight, while Frederick appeared awake but unresponsive.

Just before dawn the fury of the grotesques subsided and was replaced by blissful silence. As the brothers entered the cloisters, they took care not to slip on the patches of ice on the ground. Small branches lay around blown considerable distances from their trees. Amidst the debris was a dead lark.

Alfred was in the kitchen, to which he had retreated for comfort long before the others rose. To keep his mind busy, he was preparing breakfasts for his brothers, usually reserved for just the abbot and prior. Stephen was last to enter the refectory. Devoid of spirit, few of the brothers ate anything, though they warmed their hands on their hot mugs. It was Graham's turn to read the Bible to them but after a few minutes Stephen gestured to him to stop as he was struggling and no one was listening.

Stephen walked towards the lectern to speak to his brothers. As usual Hubert and Frederick were at the head table and the others were at the two side tables. Stephen said, 'I have prayed to God for our forgiveness.' Mumbling he added, 'We must pray some more.' With this meagre offering he returned to the head table and sat down.

The brothers stared in silence at their mugs. After a few minutes some of them glanced at Hubert sitting next to the abbot. Hubert rose to his feet and said, 'I wish to speak,' directing this at the brothers instead of at his abbot. His nose was crooked, his eyes darkened with bruising and his face distorted with rage. Stephen looked bewildered by Hubert's interruption of the silence, for Hubert was a stickler for rules but Stephen nodded granting Hubert authority to speak.

'I have prayed. I believe my prayer has been answered, pointing out our erroneous ways.' Hubert paused looking around at his brothers, treating Stephen, his abbot, as merely one of them. 'Brothers, may I humbly direct your attention to the Rule 64 of St Benedict, 'On Constituting an Abbot.' ' He paused again to generate more effect. 'The Rule states: 'In the constituting of an Abbot let this plan always be followed, that the office be conferred on the one who is chosen either by the whole community unanimously in the fear of God or else by a part of the community, however small, if its counsel is more wholesome.' Which of you chose Brother Stephen as our abbot?' Hubert again directed his gaze around the room. 'Only Brother Stephen himself.'

Without requesting permission James stood up. 'You know that there were no other brothers when Bishop Grandisson appointed Abbot Stephen.'

'Silence, when your prior is speaking!' Hubert said to James.

Spittle flying from his hare lip James replied, 'We know what you are doing, you seek to generate more dissent. You of all people should know that Rule 64 also says, 'Merit of life and wisdom of doctrine should determine the choice of the one to be constituted' so that eliminates yourself as a potential replacement, if that's what you are angling at.'

Stephen sat in silence, unsure how to respond.

Hubert sneered, and replied, ' 'Rule 69, That Monks Presume Not to Defend One Another: Wisdom and virtue speak for themselves.' You must not stand in collusion with Brother

Stephen. 'Rule 23, On Excommunication for Faults: If a brother is found to be obstinate, or disobedient, or proud, or murmuring, or habitually transgressing the Holy Rule in any point and contemptuous of the orders of his seniors, the latter shall admonish him secretly a first and a second time, as Our Lord commands. If he fails to amend, let him be given a public rebuke in front of the whole community. But if even then he does not reform, let him be placed under excommunication...' I have previously publicly rebuked you, now it is time for your excommunication.'

Stephen interrupted in a voice lacking authority, 'Enough brothers! While I am still abbot, I will have our community treat their brothers with respect.'

Hubert continued, 'Once again you treat Brother James as special as you have from the day of his arrival—as exempt from the Rule of Benedict. He whose face bears the mark of Satan!' Hubert pointed his finger at James with an expression of scorn. James wiped saliva dripping from his mouth. There were gasps of amazement, followed by some murmurings of agreement.

Looking at his brethren Hubert continued, 'None of us can believe what happened last night was not a response to our sinfulness. Stephen,' the abbot's name without title was uttered with derision, 'Stephen believes God was expressing his displeasure. I do not presume to speak for God, but was it God making that dreadful noise? No, the congregation of grotesques the abbot welcomed to our abbey did so and they are Satan's servants.'

Stephen stood up. 'Enough, as your abbot I order you to be seated.'

Hubert stood his ground. 'The Rule of respect for authority may be challenged where there is clear evidence of corruption—as now. Is it not Satan, you Stephen, have been serving all this time?'

All the brothers leapt to their feet with a collective gasp—it was an outrageous assertion, but might it be true? James rushed over to stand by Stephen to lend him support. James shouted, 'How dare you treat our abbot this way? Leave, get out, before I strike you.'

'Does a servant of God strike his prior?' Hubert stepped forwards, 'No but a servant of Satan might.'

There were gasps from some of the keener eyed brothers as Hubert stepped back, a bloody knife in his right hand. The brothers were in uproar.

'What have you done?' Graham shouted. Hubert stood as rigid as a statue. James saw with disbelief that he was bleeding from his side. Graham rushed to assist James, who looked unsteady on his feet. Graham helped him to a bench, and lay him down.

Hubert still stood like a statue with eyes of ice, the knife, a breadknife, still in his hand. Frederick stepped forward, softly saying, 'Brother Hubert, this is a house of God, put the knife down, if you please.'

Hubert stared bewildered at the blood on his knife then snapped at Frederick, 'You bumbling old idiot, I am standing up for God against Satan. Sit down and be quiet!' Hubert pushed Frederick in the chest. The waif like old man staggered back, his right leg catching the corner of the bench causing him to fall, and with his arm in a sling, he was unable to break his fall. His head hit the stone floor with a sickening sound.

Death embraced the old brother.

Abbot Stephen notified the constabulary and volunteered to close the monastery. Within the month, he shut its doors for the last time. Hubert was imprisoned despite being a monk and protesting his intentions were consistent with the Rule of St Benedict and that Frederick's fall was an accident. The judiciary might have accepted that, had Hubert not seconds earlier stabbed Brother James. He was hung a few months later, even though Stephen claimed that he, as abbot, should be held responsible for Hubert's crimes.

Thereafter, Stephen became a hermit, living for some years high up on the moor. James returned to his family farm, but little is known about the fates of the others.

Many years later, one harsh winter's evening, James was bringing his horses into the stables as it was snowing and he expected a bitter night. By the light of the moon he found fresh human tracks in the snow. He traced them and came upon an old man struggling to walk through the snow. 'I am looking for my friend,' mumbled the old man. 'He is a Frenchman and he has been wandering all alone with no one to turn to. He may freeze to death in this weather.' It was Stephen.

'I am your friend,' said James.

'You are? You don't sound French and you look younger than I recall, though your face is familiar.'

With difficulty James persuaded the old man to come to his farm house for some hot food. There, Stephen spent his final months, until the day that Death called. Abbot Stephen had served his penance.

History repeats...

PART II

30

Revelations

Horace Oldham, the once contented history teacher, closed his book. 'Abbot Stephen had served his penance.' With this final remark, his history of Torminster Abbey ended. The old man wore a look of bewilderment. His friends, fellow patients of Ward 9, felt his wretchedness. Mary and Peter stepped forward, gently grasped his elbows and escorted him to his seat, while the others grouped around him muttering their concerns.

Would that we could conclude our tale there.

'Horace Oldham is not so well,' said Dr Young over the phone to her boss. 'It's not urgent but he's the worst I've seen him, I thought you'd want to know. Also, the whole Ward 9 environment appears strangely on edge. Even Fergus seems uptight.'

Later that day, Fergus explained to Dr Wright the events of the previous evening. 'I'd noticed for a week or so he's been a bit different, nothing specific. Then last night his friends became concerned about him. He'd been giving his usual lecture to them. Apparently, he finished reading them his book. Today I can't even get him out of bed. He looks depressed, but I think there's more to it than that.'

'Thanks, Fergus, let's go and see him,' said Dr Wright.

Leaving the office with Fergus and Rosemary, Wright noted the crowd of patients thronging around him. In place of their usual welcoming smiles and greetings, some of them were pacing the floor and others looked at him with an air of expectation.

They entered Horace's room where a patient was sitting with him. She rose respectfully and left. The old man was lying on his back with his eyes closed. He looked frail, almost child-like. 'Horace, old chap, it's Dr Wright. I hear you're not feeling too good.'

Horace opened his eyes and stared at the doctor. 'Are you He?' he said, his face wearing an expression of dread.

'Yes, me, Dr Wright; Dr Young and Fergus are also here.' Despite their endeavours they could not prise another word out of Horace. As Young and Fergus said, he appeared more than depressed, probably psychotic.

Back in Fergus's office they discussed treatment options. 'You say he's not been eating properly for several days, Fergus? What about fluids?'

'We've been managing to get him to drink,' said Fergus. 'His friends have been taking it in turns to sit with him. They have more success with him than we do. Should be a model for the brave new health service; scrap the staff and have patients treat each other. It would give us more time for the pub, though we might not have the money to make the most of it.'

'I suppose we'd better decide what to do about Horace,' Wright said. 'Nothing to date seems to have been particularly effective but we must try something. What do you think Rosemary?'

'It's your call, Sir,' said Rosemary.

'He is not eating, so I think we should try ECT.'

'Two or three times a week? Uni- or bi-lateral?' asked Fergus.

'Let's be generous: bilateral, three times a week.'

Matilda and Brian sat out on the southern gallery shivering in the blustery wind. 'Out with it, Brian. You know you can't hide anything from Tilly. You look like a cat who's found a bowl of cream.' Matilda offered him a cigarette.

'I've given up.'

'Pull the other one. You're not serious, are you? Well I never.' She put the cigarette back in her packet.

'You know that splodge on the north wall with mortar covering the original stone?'

'What splodge? I don't go looking at such things, that's what you do. I do the cleaning and tidying, simple soul that I am. What of it?'

I scraped the mortar off and underneath there seems to be a message carved in the stone:

In regione caecorum rex est luscus

'Come again?'

'Latin: 'In the land of the blind, the one eyed man is king.'

'Oh?' Matilda paused trying to grasp the importance of the message. 'Strange. I wonder why they covered it up.'

'Desiderius Erasmus around 1500 AD, so it can't have been on the original church.'

'One of your friends, was he?'

'He was no fool, but he didn't make a lot of friends when he called for Church reforms. Whoever carved it would have known. The carving's primitive. And there's more splodges mortared over. Applications all looking sloppy and the same age. I thought they were repairs, now I'm wondering what else might be there? Maybe something from De Juniac. How's Horace?'

'Not good, so Fergus says. Poor old chap.'

'I might tell him; it might perk him up.' Brian did so—he was right.

31

Age

Fergus found Horace in his pyjamas in the corridor. 'Horace, old mate, what are you doing out of bed at this time? It's the middle of the night.'

'They are calling. Is it He?'

'You must go back to bed, old chap, it's freezing. Come on I'll take you.'

'But they need me.'

Poor Old Horace, hallucinations bad, thought Fergus. 'You'll be better able to help them in the morning when it's light and not so cold. If you go outside at this time of night you'll catch your death.'

'Death? Death is where the weary lie.'

Fergus took Horace back to the ward. Perhaps the ECT was working, as he was definitely more active, even though he still was obviously hallucinating. Nevertheless, some progress was better than no progress. Having put the old man back to bed he turned out the light and closed the door.

Horace heard a voice from the corner of his room.

'Horace.'

'Is it you, Celeste?'

'Yep. I've missed you.'

'I've missed myself. The border between reason... where has

it gone? I no longer trust my judgement.'

'Poor old fella.' Celeste took the old man's hand in hers.

'Have you heard what Brian found?' asked the old man.

'Yes, is it important?'

'Perhaps, it might be; I think so. The message is not from the time of the abbey, but there may be others and they might be. I've always felt sure De Juniac left clues for those with eyes to see. But I thought they were limited to the babewyns. If there are more messages covered up, who knows?'

Jackson kept his head down following his brush with Celeste and Matilda, but they did not stop his scheming. Sitting at his large antique desk, the coffee brewing he pondered the challenge ahead. He had been appointed to upgrade the administration of Torminster Hospital with a view to the advent of community care and to balance the books. If limits were imposed on his cost-cutting how could he increase Torminster's income? That was simple logic. Since cider production and other produce sales had been curtailed the hospital no longer generated any income.

If farm revenue is a thing of the past, might Torminster's unusual buildings have potential, ghastly though they are? Might they be of interest to history buffs? After all, Buckfast Abbey, not 30 miles away is a roaring success with tourists. Buckfast's origins might have been earlier than Torminster, but the actual church, magnificent though it is, is not even a century old. Alternatively, might Torminster have potential as a museum, or perhaps as a House of Horrors? The grotesques and gargoyles would suit that, particularly if the grotesques could be made to sing on command. Combine them with its asylum legacy, maybe develop some of the inmate horror stories over the last century, even some of the recent ones. No, that might not reflect well on his administration. Maybe it could be developed for weekend stays, have a new plush separate wing for paying guests?

The same blasted problem kept recurring. The patients. Logic dictated if patients were the problem, get rid of them, failing that turn them into something more commercial.

Having thought it through, Jackson called a meeting with Dr Wright and Mabel Willing. 'Three sugars for you Mabel? None for you Dr Wright?'

'Thanks.'

'I've asked to meet with you both today as I have to address the hospital's finances and the staff injuries we've been having. Mabel, Doctor, has three of her nurses off on workers' compensation; two have back injuries, the other has bites on her face that have become infected. Very nasty.'

Miracles never cease; is Jackson considering someone's welfare? Wright asked himself.

'Very expensive, paying for staff to stay at home,' continued Jackson. 'Mabel investigated, Doctor, finding all three injuries were inflicted by demented patients, who Mabel says can be aggressive out of the blue, yet nurses often have to get in close to lift them.'

'Yes, Mr Jackson, we've had a bad run.'

Wright nodded.

'And the nurses' union is kicking up I believe? Now you are the medical expert Dr Wright,' Jackson paused for his flattery to take effect. 'Am I right in thinking dementia has limited prospects for treatment?'

Wright could not bring himself to say Jackson was right, but he nodded again.

'And dementia patients require a lot of nursing attention, Mabel?'

'That, they do.'

'And that is very demanding on my hospital budget. The question has to be asked why do we house so many high cost untreatable patients?'

Where is this leading? Wright wondered, then said, 'Because, their behaviours are so difficult no one else can cope with them.' To himself he acknowledged most doctors wished they did not have to deal with so many dementia patients, as their conditions inspired a sense of therapeutic impotence. In addition, he and many others were considering the possibility that many of them could be housed in the community in well-staffed nursing homes.

As if telepathic, Jackson said, 'Might it be possible many could be housed elsewhere in nursing homes?'

'Yes, if the funds were provided for staffing,' Wright replied with emphasis.

'Mrs Thatcher is advocating the privatisation of some state services, leaving competition to bring costs down. Wonderful way to reduce local unemployment rates. It's surprising Labour governments never thought of that. Also, if they are not admitted to hospital in the first place, they are not our worry, are they?'

'Out of sight, out of mind.'

'Good pun, Doctor, very droll. Now supposing we have a few empty wards as a result of fewer dementia patients. Might that permit us to have some more rewarding ones?'

Wright conceded this sounded an attractive proposition. 'Yes, we could admit more depressed patients, reducing rates of 'suboptimal treatment,' otherwise known as 'community neglect'.'

'And depressed patients don't need as much nursing care in hospital, do they?'

'No, they don't, provided you are happy for them to linger much longer than needed in hospital, risk a few more inpatient suicides and the law-suites going with them.'

Mabel nodded. Jackson was taken aback. 'That would defeat the purpose then. What about a nice civilised type of patient that doesn't need much nursing care? Now my niece, she suffers agoraphobia. Quiet as a lamb she is at home, there she can look after herself fine, makes her own bed, does all the cleaning and cooking so long as her mother does the shopping.'

'Then why put her in hospital?' the doctor interrupted.

'To keep the costs down. That is the point, Doctor.'

'I thought the point of admitting patients to hospital was to treat them; you know, make them better.'

'That is a noble perspective Doctor, but my duty is to contain costs, and I am the one who signs off on the budget. Now, we don't have to make decisions today, but I'd be most grateful if you both will give the issues we've raised some consideration.'

In the following months there was growing talk of change being afoot for Torminster. While the hospital was needed for some years yet, many people—not just the cost-cutting fraternity—were looking forward to the day when this and other large remote psychiatric hospitals would be monstrosities of the past. However, such talk left Brian uneasy. What might this mean for his grotesque friends and the abbey? How would they cope if a new era of oppression were to arrive? He must accelerate his stripping back more of the odd mortar patches to answer some of the riddles.

Horace agreed when Brian mentioned this to him. Lying in bed that night he could not settle. He got up, dressed and took his keys out from under the loose section of skirting. He snuck past the nurses' office and before long, for the first time in months, he visited the external gallery along the church roof. While exhilarated to be out there again, he also felt ill at ease and shivered; the breeze was cold and penetrating.

'Hello,' he said to the Yeth Hound as he passed it, not expecting a reply.

'Do it.'

He turned to face the headless grotesque. 'Do what?'

The stone did not answer.

From the other side of the transept someone called him, 'Sebastian.' Sebastian was De Juniac's Christian name. Were they calling De Juniac or himself?

Walking on, he paused at the Gloating Priest, who looked up from his bible. His eyes pierced Horace like a spear. Horace clutched his chest, gasping. He staggered around to the north east corner of the north transept where he met the Blind Monk. 'Are you He?' Horace asked, trembling. He heard rats scurrying around his feet; where were the cats? He heard the sound of footsteps approaching and turned with alarm.

'Horace, it's me, Celeste. Don't look so worried.'

Horace stood speechless for many seconds. 'He is here.'

'No Horace, I am here. I am real; the other...the other is in

279

your head. Your mind has made it up, it is not real.' Celeste approached him and wrapped both her arms around the old man. 'I'm here, I'll look after you, no harm can come to you while I am with you. Gosh you are cold. Let's go around to the other side, out of this wind.' She led him back to the south gallery where Matilda and Brian's tea cupboard was. 'I'll make us a hot cuppa.' She sat the old man down on a crate. 'I've missed you up here, you know.'

Horace's chest pain slowly subsided. He clutched his hot tea, as yet too hot to drink, but it helped thaw his cold hands, although his shivering caused him to spill some of it. To Celeste he appeared vacant, only half there. All he said was, 'Sebastian.'

32

Time

'Two more large scotches,' Jackson said to the golf club barman. He and Sparks walked from the bar to some easy chairs. 'Bottoms up,' said Sparks, his vast backside sunk deep in a leather chair. He added, 'You need a different bloody pair of eyes to see the solution. Cutting costs is like cutting steak, easy when you know your knives.' Jackson was exploring possible joint ventures with his developer friend, known as Simon Bloody Sparks. Sparks's middle name reflected his use of colloquial language—his every second word being 'bloody'.

'See, your basic idea isn't too bad—getting rid of the demented, packing them off to bloody nursing homes and replacing them with something more profitable. Oh yes, I can see them all lined up waiting at the station. But you have to sell it better. 'The Torminster Centre for Psychological Wellbeing and Enlightenment' has a nice ring to it. That way you'd get a better class of customer —more brass they'd have.' Sparks knocked back his scotch. 'You ask yourself, how much do you make out of your hospital's vending machines. Coca bloody Colas are no bloody use. Scotch and sodas—and all the rest—like this place.' He looked around at the club's plush furnishings and its expensively-dressed members to make his point. 'This is what you need if you are going to make money.'

'Easier said than done; depressed patients don't make the most lavish customers.'

'Marketing. There's depression and depression. I'm bloody depressed. You're bloody depressed, 'n with good reason, but you'd not say no to a good steak and a decent bottle of red. See, your depressed customers need to be the right type. Refined—not wingers; those like the rest of us who are not so much sick, but are suffering the stresses of daily life and might benefit from some time out, away from their families and work. Recruit some new age guru to give the odd seminar. Better still teach your existing staff—cheaper that way. Anyone can be taught to do it: read a few new age counselling books, adopt a funny name, dress weird, smile at the audience with a glazed loving expression and Bob's your uncle. Even the die-hards of the NHS's free health care policy would pay a bloody fortune for such 'enlightenment.''

'I'll think about it,' said Jackson.

Think about it he did. He decided he would try to sell the idea to Dr Wright as an exercise in the prevention of serious mental health problems. Mabel was so obliging she'd be a push-over; if only he could get Wright on side.

'There is no scientific evidence such a venture would be successful,' said Wright following hearing Jackson's proposed plan, explained with as many medical terms and as few financial ones as possible.

'Perhaps, Doctor, but perhaps again because it's too new an idea. Too progressive for research to have caught up with it?'

'Humph. Preventative psychiatry is a nice idea, but you are talking about a major venture based on unproven ideas. Prevention in mental health has had a lousy record—neurosyphilis excepted.'

Typical of the pompous overpaid senior doctor, thought Jackson. 'Look Doctor, given science is so slow on the uptake, let's try common sense. If you give stressed individuals relaxing breaks with all mod-cons laid on, they would have to benefit. They'd go home feeling like new; like they'd had a 50,000 mile service. Arrive in a Ford, home in a Jaguar—or Porsche if you prefer.'

'Not necessarily. Taking such weary folk away from their families might do more harm than good; it might make them crave more pampering and result in permanent separation from their uncaring partners.

'They wouldn't be able to afford it. We'd be charging top dollar. '

'Look I've got patients to attend to and am not going to waste any more time discussing this crazy idea, which I will oppose.' Wright walked out of Jackson's office in disgust—this was becoming a habit.

Jackson explored other possibilities with Sparks.

'You could make something out of Torminster's Gothic heritage. 'Heritage'—beautiful word that. The wife will even watch bloody BBC programs on heritage. And what a heritage Torminster's got? Of course, the patients will have to go—all of them. But that should be easy with the shift to community care under way. 'Community'—another lovely word—makes you appreciate how much we all care about each other. Many asylums up-country have already closed. Even if Torminster's Board was to do nothing, it would be a matter of time before Dr Wright and other pompous bloody idiots get on their soap boxes pleading for more humane community care.'

'I think you're right there.'

'Torminster's days as a hospital are numbered, no doubt about it. You just have to sell the property to the right person.' Sparks gave Jackson a pointed look, smiled, lit another cigar and gave him time to reflect. 'Excuse me,' Sparks said, 'I'm going for a leak.'

In many ways community care sounded like the politicians' dream, thought Jackson, sipping his pint of lager. The left could champion the liberation of oppressed patients from the clutches of their grasping psychiatrists—the 'Some More Flew over the Cuckoo's Nest' notion. Non-lefties, people unafraid of hard work like himself, with the support of the Thatcher government, would understand the economic wisdom of selling the real estate, finding some vacant office space in a cheap part of Plymouth, tarting it up, sticking up signs about excellence in health care and staffing it with Torminster staff who refuse redundancy packages. Rid of patients, the Board could sell the hospital to Sparks. Then Sparks might turn Torminster into a hotel, maybe a golf club, catering for those with historical interests—or for eccentrics.

Sparks's return awakened Jackson from his reverie. Continuing where he'd left off, Sparks said, 'I quite like the idea of a Gothic "House of Horrors", I do. Did you know Jane Eyre and Mr Dorchester were a Gothic story? Everybody loves Jane Eyre, they do. And Torminster as a building has a lot more going for it than bloody Thornfell Hall ever did. I visited that place as a lad; grew up near there I did, an' it were no great shakes. It wouldn't cost much to bring your gargoyles back to life. You could make them in fibreglass or concrete molds—quicker an' cheaper that way. And the golden days of the gargoyles' songs could be better than it ever were if you install an huge bloody sound system. I know my acoustics, I do. You won't have to stuff around waiting for the right bloody wind. Flick a switch instead. Of course, they didn't have electricity in the olden days, but now we bloody well do.'

Jackson agreed to give this new plan consideration. If the worst came to the worst and all these ideas came to nothing the land could be sold for housing development. Everyone wanted to retire to Devon. They couldn't fail.

Matilda knew something was up. Few visitors to Torminster drove Bentleys. Even when Jackson met Sparks elsewhere, locals let her know. There was only one Bentley in the whole region, and Sparks stood out a mile given his bulk and his expensive suits, even before opening his bloody mouth. There was no hiding such talk from Matilda, who passed it on to Dr Wright.

In another meeting, Jackson waxed lyrical to Wright, 'Deinstitutionalization and community care are upon us. The time for our patients—Les Misérables—is here. Rest assured, I will need your expertise to guide me.' How could the doctor argue with this?

The advent of community care could not come soon enough for Wright and for many others, but he did not trust Jackson one iota.

The looming changes were brought to the attention of the patients, the proposed community care recipients. 'Community consultation' was all the rage; invite everyone to contribute ideas—even the care recipients—accept with generous applause those ideas fitting the political agendas and trash the rest.

This talk of change being afoot carried major implications for Horace, Brian and their babewyns; and for Celeste, who might not be welcomed into the local community with her reputation as an axe-murderer, advertised to all via her black attire and war paint.

Brian was concerned. Who knew what might happen to the buildings and the babewyns if Torminster was sold? Aside from his attachment to his stone friends he was now convinced one way or another that De Juniac was communicating something important across the centuries. For years he'd considered this a possibility, but like Horace he thought it would be via the babewyns, but now he realised the inscriptions, hidden by somebody (or bodies) for some reason, might also be involved.

One weekend, while removing another patch of mortar high above the Monkeys and the gallery on the west end, Brian uncovered:

Quem deus vult perdere dementat prius

which Horace later translated as, 'Whom the Gods would destroy, they first make insane.'

'Might have been De Juniac's epitaph?' Brian said, 'Fine line between genius and insanity.'

However, Brian was talking to himself as Horace's mind was elsewhere.

A few days later Brian found an inscription along the gallery on the north side:

Quod in principio est, ad finem

which Horace translated as, 'In the beginning is the end.'

Brian had read that long before quantum theory the ancient Greeks, the Mayans, the Aztecs and some contemporary eastern religions including Hinduism and Buddhism subscribed to the notion of circular time, that over long enough periods the beginning is the end. And when did an end not herald a new beginning?

33

The One God

Horace stood on the external gallery looking out from where he believed Luke might have fallen to his death six centuries ago. It was cold and the smell of log fires was blowing up from the village a few miles away. Amidst the grotesques he usually felt at home, but tonight it was as though they resented his presence. His eyes darted from one to another. He shivered. Was it the cold breeze, was it his 'misery, my friend' as he referred to his depression or was it something else?

'Are you He?' he called to the void beyond. 'You've been lurking around trying to make me do things I don't want to.' Louder he shouted, 'Are you He?'

Silence.

Horace looked at the Banshee standing above him, ever raving with relish about the approach of Death. 'Did you call Luke to his death?' He then looked at the devious Pixie down to her left and from there down to the cloisters and garth below. 'Or perhaps it was you?'

He felt the hag's piercing stare; 'Who are you to question us?' he heard her say.

He looked the Banshee in the eyes. 'Did you push him? Or did you watch and do nothing. Why?'

'Thou shalt follow the Lord, not question his ways. Thou

shalt not question his ways; not question his ways!'

Horace covered his ears from her nagging tirade; the border between reason and insanity, where was it now? Was it the Banshee he was hearing or were they hallucinations from his unreliable mind? He did not know, but to the Banshee he shouted, 'No! I will not give way. No, no, no.' Whispers were all around him but he could not decipher their words.

Behind him across the garth stood the Fisher of Souls, still huge with massive thighs, though stripped of his wings and horns by the passing of the years. 'You are He, the Destroyer,' Horace said with a tremulous voice. 'Why? Why destruction?'

'Spring, a time of birth; summer, of fruition; autumn, of decay; winter, of death.' Was the Fisher talking to him or was it just his mind? God the Creator, God the Destroyer, one and the same—two sides of a coin as the Fisher had told Abbot Stephen. If only it would stop.

'Singularity, infinity, divinity,' he heard as if his friend Brian was repeating the ideas with which he was toying. That singularity was infinite and the beginning was also the end? And De Juniac said—understand infinity and you have glimpsed the mind of God. De Juniac was no more, but was Brian mad like himself? Please not.

'No more!' Horace screamed.

But Brian had found more, another inscription:

Igne natura renovatur integra

(Through fire nature is reborn whole).

Destruction, rebirth. Horace turned and looked up to Death looking down from on high in the main tower. 'Are you too the Destroyer, or just his lackey?'

Death seemed to reply through the icy wind, 'With my

habit open the cold of Death I bring.' Horace stared at the bones, ribs and part of Death's skull, all eroded by time. A realisation spoke in the old man's mind. The Fisher and Death wear the same colours, but the Fisher is the master, Death the servant—the decision maker and his executioner. Death may visit the sick, even the able, but he does not take them without his master's instructions.

Leaving the gallery Horace entered the tower and, for the first time in more than a year he climbed the steps to the top, where he stared at Death standing before him. He never recalled it as being as cold as it now was. He told himself he would soon be out of the cold. His dreams were of hell, perhaps he already was already there? What had once been a short tower, De Juniac had converted to this, which from Horace's vantage point almost reached up to the clouds. The cloister roof, a long way below, beckoned to him. It looked so far away, so far down—in the depths.

He realised the gallery was not where Luke fell from, it was from up here, Death saw to it. The spirit of Death must have predated Death's stone form. It began to make sense; he was sure of it. Had De Juniac been compelled to carve the replica of Death? Did the Fisher make him too do things he didn't want to do? I am not alone, he thought. De Juniac must also have felt cold as he drowned in the icy river. I am not alone, Death has opened his cloak for me.

A voice, a different voice, interrupted his thoughts. 'Horace. It's a coward's way, you are too good for this.' He felt an angel gently enveloping him, wrapping her loving arms around him. He felt her divine warmth, his weary head rested on her breast. If this moment were eternal, he would never tire of it. He tried to shed all other thoughts, to surrender himself entirely to this sensual embrace, but the questions returned. Was this the loving God, God the Creator, the one he had worshipped all these years?

'Horace, love. It's okay, I'll look after you.'

By the light of the full moon he saw streaks of black running down her face. Was it really Celeste? Might she be God? Won't these questions ever end? One thing he knew, at that moment he felt safe and warm with her, with Celeste.

She took him by the hand and guided him to a sheltered spot in the tower, where they sat on the cold stone floor. They wrapped their arms around each other, resting their weary heads together. He felt the icy cold subside, slowly melting into warmth. Divine tranquility suffused him, while Celeste for her first time felt whole. The two drifted asleep in each other's arms floating on a soft cloud close to heaven—wishing they'd never wake.

God the Saviour, God the Redeemer might have taken them that night—turned them to stone while resting in the bosom of tranquility.

34

The Destroyer

Horace paced the floor, lost and agitated. His improvement following his night in the tower with Celeste had lasted only a few days, and now he was more troubled than ever. He had asked Fergus about the talk of the hospital's closure, the end of his home, and worse the talk of Torminster becoming a House of Horrors for tourists.

Now, the grotesques were breaking into song despite it still being daylight. Horace was unsure what it meant, but he was frightened. His internal voices, his inner demons, also would not leave him be. Listening to the gale outside brought him little relief, but it brought some distraction from his inner turmoil.

A few hours after dark Horace used his key to enter the crypt below Ward 6 in the south transept below the tower. He had seen nurses deliver mattresses here for storage, from wards that had been closed. 'Through fire nature is reborn whole,' Dante's words echoed through his head. From across the garth the Fisher beckoned.

'I am not your servant!' Horace shouted to the night. But the Fisher knew better—even the wind obeyed his commands.

Horace felt his self-control slipping, it was as though someone else controlled him; try as he did, he could not resist. 'Only the strong can resist me. You are too weak,' he heard from across the garth. His mind wracked with turmoil, he started stacking mattresses in positions to improve the airflow. Using matches and newspapers, after several unsuccessful attempts, flames finally took hold of a mattress low in the stack. Having cursed his unsuccessful attempts, he cursed even louder when the fire took hold. The flames grew and with their updraught soon became unstoppable. High above stood the tower.

'Why?' Horace cried out.

'Save my clan from ignominy,' came a soft reply.

To his left Horace saw people rushing around screaming in confusion surrounded and trapped by fire. Surely this was not what the Fisher intended? This did not help his babewyns. The people trapped by the fire—were they the Jews of Strasbourg or those of York? Or were they his Torminster friends? Whoever they were, they suddenly disappeared. This was not reality, but it might be a glimpse of what was to come.

'Now who is the Destroyer?' he heard.

No, I'm a creator he told himself, rocking back and forth.

'Destroyer,' he heard again.

Destroyer? he asked himself, his face contorted in anguish. Images in his mind of hundreds of Jews panicking. Images of people running from all directions, coalescing into a Medusa with snakes writhing in all directions from her beautiful head. This transformed into a black-haired person, with imploring eyes, begging him to save her from the fire—Celeste. Reason returned, penetrating the smoke. Celeste, might she be above? Panic stricken, with a sense of dread, he fled the crypt, stumbling up the steps of the tower as fast as his old legs allowed.

He reached the south gallery and ran to where Matilda and Brian drank tea and smoked. Celeste was not there. Breathless, he ran around the southern transept, passing his preferred sanctuary where he saw his two blankets undisturbed. He ran on, becoming more breathless and more distressed. He stopped and looked up at the Pious Lion, appealing to it, 'I didn't want to do it. Destruction was not what I wanted; help, please.' The Lion stared down at him with a look of contempt. He made a similar appeal to the Gloating Priest above the chancel, but quickly despaired of finding any assistance from that quarter. He reached the end of the chancel and looked at See No Evil. His stone friends wouldn't help him that day, for they wanted freedom. I am wasting time, he told himself. Think. His mind was as clear as pea soup.

Perhaps she is up in the tower? Yes, that must be where she is. He entered the tower's northern spiral stairs and started climbing. His legs felt about to give way and his heart was bursting from his chest. He staggered on, cursing his breathlessness and more so his stupidity. The pain in his chest became excruciating, crushing, like a metal band constricting.

'Horace,' he heard his name called. Was it another hallucination? 'Horace, it's me Celeste. What are you doing? You look dreadful.' Celeste stepped into the stairwell from the level above him where she'd been communing with Death.

'Celeste, what have I done?' he implored. He paused to catch his breath as another wave of pain assailed him. 'What have I done? You must run.'

'Horace, what have you done? Tell me.'

'The hospital is on fire. It was He; it was me.'

'What was you?'

'I set fire to it,' he said gasping.

'You set fire to it? To what? Why?' She recognised Horace

couldn't answer, but his face told the story. No, not the time for why? she told herself. 'Where?'

'In the crypt, below Ward 6.'

She looked down from the tower. Although she couldn't see any flames, she saw smoke. 'Oh, Horace, I told you all that shit was in your head. Now look at what you've gone and done. The Fisher, the rest of them, are all stones. They've always been stones, never anything else except what you and the ancients made of them. Why didn't you listen? If even you can be that stupid what hope have the rest of us?' She looked at the frail old man, grabbed him by the hand and said, 'Follow me.' They started descending the tower's narrow uneven spiral steps, but the breathless and exhausted old man was close to falling; he couldn't match her for speed and they were short of time, so she let go of his hand. 'Horace, I've got to hurry. Follow me down as quickly as you can while I get help.'

She ran ahead, slipped out of the tower and into the doctor's office of Ward 13 above Ward 6. She picked up the phone and dialed. 'Come on, fucking answer!' she screamed at the phone, banging it on the desk then putting it back to her ear.

'Matilda's Midnight Massages,' came the answer.

'Fucking hell, Tilly, not you as well!' screamed Celeste.

'Sorry my love, just being my usual silly self. Serious now, what's up?'

'The hospital is on fire. Horace has gone and done it. You've got to call the fire brigade quick. People are going to die if they don't get here quickly. Can you come in and help me? I need your help more than ever, you old cow.'

'Are you sure?'

'Yes, I'm fucking sure. There's smoke billowing up from the

crypt. Stop wasting time, bitch, will you.'

'Celeste, my love, I'll do all you've asked, but the fire brigade has to come from Ivybridge, so it may arrive too late to get all the patients out. You, my love, are in the hot seat. I'm afraid it's up to you. Go to Ward 6 and tell the nurse in charge—Andrew, I think it is tonight—tell him what you have told me about the fire, and that help is on its way, but he must get his patients out immediately and someone must warn the other wards to do likewise. Have you got that, Celeste? Now do it.' Matilda hung up.

Celeste looked into the silent earpiece of the phone as if imploring Matilda to emerge from it. 'Fuucckk! The world's gone bleedin' mad if they have to rely on me.' She threw the phone down and raced towards Ward 6, on the way passing a nurse, shouting to her, 'The tower's on fire, get out, get them out.' She did not stop to explain but rushed down more stairs to Ward 6 above the crypt. Nurse Heather ran behind her, having guessed who Celeste was from her black make up and clothing and that trouble was afoot—fire or no fire. Celeste rushed into the nurses' station in Ward 6 shouting, 'The tower's on fire! Get the patients out and warn the others!'

'What do you mean the tower's on fire?' asked a startled male nurse.

'Just fucking do it or people are going to die!' Celeste dug her nails into her forearms. 'I can't handle this, I really can't,' she protested.

The nurse said, 'How do you know the tower's on fire?'

'Old Horace told me he set a fire in the crypt.'

'You said it was in the tower.'

'Does it matter? You are wasting time! Where's Andrew?

Maybe he'll have more sense.'

'I'm Andrew.'

'Aaaagh, God help us!' she shouted to no one in particular. 'It started in the crypt. It will reach the tower,' Celeste said stamping her foot, kicking a chair and again groaning.

'Well I can't hear any fire alarms and Horace wouldn't hurt a fly.'

'You are wasting time; patients are going to die!' she again spat at him, baring her teeth.

'I want you to go into this room here and stay there while I call your ward nurse to come over and take you back.' Andrew pointed to an open doorway to a seclusion room.

'No!'

'You are to wait in there. If you don't cooperate Heather here will help me put you in there. The choice is yours—the dignified way, or the other way.'

Celeste glanced at the seclusion room. Too much time was being wasted. She didn't matter; it was the others who mattered. She must make Andrew do something. 'Okay, it wasn't Horace, it was me who lit the fire. They keep mattresses in the crypt, I piled them up and whoosh!'

'Oh, you stupid bitch! Heather help me...' With that the two nurses bundled Celeste into the seclusion room. She fell hitting her head on the rear wall. She got back to her feet but not before they had locked the door. She banged on the door shouting, 'Let me out, I can help,' but Andrew and Heather declined her generosity.

'You stay here Heather. I'll go and check nothing is happening in the crypt,' said Andrew.

'No, I'll go with you just in case.' The two nurses left the ward, leaving Celeste.

Celeste took out her master key—but there was no key hole in the door from the inside. She punched and kicked the door screaming, 'Let me out, let me out, there's a fire! Any of you who can hear me there is a fire. You must all get out! Tell everyone there's a fire! Unlock this door, please, I can help.'

Andrew and Heather hurried around to the crypt, hurrying as they did not want to leave their wards for long with their junior nurses. They were confident they'd find no problems but they must be certain, yet long before reaching the crypt they smelt smoke and shortly afterwards saw it. Andrew cautiously opened the door to be greeted by a burst of hot air.

'Shit!' said Andrew recoiling from the blast. They quickly backed away from the furnace. The day's peculiar gale was still blowing and now with the crypt door open it rapidly fueled the blaze, as if the wind delivered petrol to the fire. The flames roared like lions. There was no putting this fire out, it would soon reach Ward 6 and from there it would consume the adjoining wards. Racing back, Andrew told Heather to get her patients out and to warn the other wards. He must look after his own ward which might already be alight.

Matilda arrived before the fire brigade. Standing at the west end, she saw flames curling up the outside of the main tower and smoke rising through the roof of the old nave. All these years of looking after the place, now this. She looked up at Death high above in the tower, looking down at the inferno, welcoming the roaring flames fueled by the gale force updraught. Sparks rode on the backs of flames galloping high above the tower. 'How is this going to help?' Matilda yelled to the Fisher.

She saw many patients huddling well back from the blaze, shivering with fear and cold, with two nurses supervising them. She made her decision and rushed through the main west portal into the wards area of the old church. Wards 1 and 2 just inside appeared already empty so she raced to the floor above to find some of the older patients were coughing and struggling to get down the narrow winding stairs with the help of their few night nurses. One was lying across the steps unable to get back to her feet, blocking those above who were panicking.

'Stop where you are and we'll all get out the quicker,' she commanded. Lifting the arm of the old lady who had fallen and wrapping it around her neck and shoulder, she hauled her down the remaining stairs. She relinquished her burden as a stout male patient came over to help her. 'Thanks love,' she said to him before a burst of coughing.

Thank God they appeared to be getting out in time despite the fire brigade being yet to arrive. But where was Celeste? She asked herself. She'll be okay, she's got a head on her, that one, Matilda tried reassuring herself, as she rushed back in.

Helping other older patients out through the west door she saw the fire brigade arriving. It'll take them a while to get organised, she thought, so again she headed back into the smoke which was now thicker and starting to overwhelm her, causing her to cough and her eyes to run. At times she stood still coughing trying to breathe. She crouched down low trying to get beneath the smoke. The burning heat was such that at times she had to cover her eyes. She crawled up the narrow spiral staircase against the flow of the now thinning human traffic. She headed to Wards 10 and 11, which were on the upper floor closer to the tower. There were fewer patients than she expected, though many of them were in sorry states, coughing in the thick smoke, as they groped their way to the stairs, like the blind leading the blind.

Arriving at Ward 10, the nurse was doing a final check and she waved to Matilda, suggesting all the patients were out. Coughing, unable to speak she pointed Matilda to Ward 11. There, everybody appeared to have left but Matilda found a nurse in trouble, sitting on the floor exhausted, coughing. She hauled the nurse along the ground, unable to tell who she was with the electricity out and the smoke. Flames brought what light there was and the more light they produced, the more she needed to cover her eyes, forcing her to drag the nurse with one hand, like a sack of potatoes.

She lugged her burden to the stairs where she stumbled and the two fell bouncing off the outer wall of the spiral steps. The nurse was spent and Matilda too was on her last legs, when a fireman reached them. A second fireman grabbed Matilda. Before she knew it, she was outside with an oxygen mask over her face. Her eyes and throat felt like she'd smoked several hundred cigarettes the night before. 'I'm giving them up, I promise,' she said before coughing some more.

After five minutes or so she said to the ambulance officer attending her, 'I'm okay now my love, you look after the older ones, they need it more.'

'Take care now,' he said to her as she staggered off, before keeling over without his noticing.

'Wake up, no slacking on the job,' she heard as someone shook her.

'All right, I'm awake,' she snapped, before coughing again interrupted her. Her eyes stung. 'Christ, it's you Brian, where

the hell have you been? Have you seen Celeste or Horace?'
Brian's face was blackened, he had lost his pony tail and his
baggy jeans were burnt through in places.

'No, but while you've been having a kip, I've been looking
for them.'

Matilda felt guilty as she had feared Brian might have been
doing something stupid with his stone friends, who were
beyond any human intervention.

Brian hauled Matilda to her feet. They wandered over to
a fire engine beside which a group was gathered. No more
patients or staff were emerging from the west end but firemen
with breathing apparatus were inside looking for stragglers.
Other firemen were connecting more hoses to hose the old
abbey, which was now well ablaze. She noted Brian was looking
upwards and followed his gaze to find it fixed on the Demonic
Abbot above the main west portal. He was still ranting like an
angry street evangelist warning people of hell and damnation,
while all the time wishing it upon them. He'd be pleased with
this fire and brimstone, but he looked as if he wanted still more.
She saw the flames starting to flicker around the Monkeys
gazing perplexed at mankind's world. Poor little buggers.

'The babewyns,' Matilda said with a look of anguish.

'Perhaps it is better for them this way.' Brian led her over
to the group of firemen and nurses who were assessing patient
counts. Despite the relative success of the evacuation, with a
sense of dread, they heard two were missing. Fergus Anderson
told the station officer one of his ward was missing—Horace
Oldham, a frail old man. Andrew, looking sheepish, said it
was possible a young female dressed in black, answering to the
name of Celeste, might be in the seclusion room of Ward 6.

The fire station officer said, 'Possible you say? I need to know is she, or isn't she in there, before I send my men into the blaze near the tower.'

'I'm not sure,' Andrew replied.

'What is your ward patient count?'

'It is complete, none missing.'

'She is not in there then?'

'She is not from my ward.'

'Then what was she doing in your seclusion room?'

'She started the fire; she told me, so I shut her in the seclusion room. I was going to go back for her but I ran out of time. Here's the key,' he said handing over his keys.

'You idiot!' Matilda said holding her arms tight around herself as if without them she would fall apart. She had told Celeste to go to Andrew.

The fire station officer told two of his crew to follow him. They ran along the burning northern cloister. Debris rained down from above onto the overhead cloister roof, a section of which had already collapsed and was on fire. They intended to access Ward 6 through the north east cloister door but after a token effort the station officer abandoned their efforts, no one could have survived being confined in the thick of it. It was not worth risking his men's lives with an act of heroic stupidity.

The firemen returned to the west end. Matilda asked with a tearful smile of despair, 'Did you find her?'

'No, it was hopeless; anyone in there would have suffocated long ago. Let's hope she got out.'

Brian muttered, 'She would have had her key.'

'Fat lot of good. Seclusion rooms don't have keyholes on the inside.'

Brian stared at Matilda whose face was streaked with black tear-lined soot, a bit like an older Celeste.

'What about Horace? He might be up on the gallery or in the tower,' she said.

'He'd have no chance up there.'

The two snuck away from the fire officers who ordered everyone be evacuated to the Tor Church Alms outside the hospital gates where shelter, water and other assistance could be provided, though accommodating them all might be a squeeze. Matilda and Brian wandered around the hospital administration block to the kitchen from which they entered the southern cloister heading east as the gale was now blowing from the south east, blowing the flames away from them. As roof timbers gave way, sparks and flames greedily consuming the hospital, they looked up at the roof of Ward 15, once the lay brother's dormitory. Amongst the flickering flames stood the Fisher of Souls, perched on high surveying the inferno.

They followed the Fisher's gaze over to the main tower, from which flames appeared to be challenging the stars guarding heaven beyond. There was no hope for Horace if he was up there.

More sparks erupted and then an explosion dazzled them as the main tower gave way. Death, the Skeletal Monk fell from his blazing high perch, crashing to the ground disintegrating into infinite pieces. The Fisher gazed with satisfaction at his handiwork. Over more than six centuries the Fisher and Death had worked in unison, one the decision maker, the other the executioner, but for now Death was dismissed.

35

Last Orders

The Tor Church Alms, a quarter of a mile away from the hospital, escaped the fire but not its legacy. Bereft of its hospital patrons, the pub was now frequented by a trickle of tourists gloating like vultures over the remains of the hospital, devoid of life and resembling a giant spent funeral pyre.

Arthur the landlord reserved a table next to the fire in the lounge bar for his friends Fergus, Tilly, Brian and Dr Wright. Short on friends lately, he'd already responded harshly to a non-local who had protested that there was no one at the reserved table.

Fergus had been almost living at the pub since being stood down, pending an investigation into how Horace, his patient, was wandering that night, and apparently had been doing so for years. Fergus knew his days as a psychiatric nurse were over. Arthur let Fergus help him out behind the bar in exchange for free drinks, but customers were so few this was an act of charity.

Fergus saw Matilda and Brian enter. 'Tilly my dear,' he said kissing her. She reciprocated by giving him a long hug. 'Ooh, you're all wet,' said Fergus.

'Yes, it's pissing down out there,' said Tilly.

'And the gargoyles have been given the night off,' added Brian.

Fergus looked at Brian, noting something was different. Brian was wearing a faded pair of formal black trousers that he last wore at a funeral some decades ago and he appeared to have had a haircut of sorts. 'Brian, what will you have? Same for you Tilly? You go and sit by the fire and dry out.' He ordered three pints.

Soon afterwards Dr Wright arrived, depositing his umbrella in the empty umbrella stand and hanging his damp coat on a nearby peg. He noted something strange. The bar stools stood an orderly three feet apart and were empty of backsides. Also, the pub seemed to have grown and gone were its usual welcoming aroma of spilt beer and cigarette smoke, replaced with unnatural cleanliness and the sterility of disuse. Signs of the times. 'Evening, Arthur,' he said.

'Good evening, Douglas. You are over by the fire. Sit yourself down and I'll bring yours over. The usual?'

'Thanks.'

Over by the warm fire the pub returned to its normal size. Wright shook hands with Fergus as if he was reluctant to let him go. He gave Tilly a peck on the cheek and shook hands with Brian, receiving a limp grip in return.

He sat himself down and Arthur set his pint down on the table. They expressed the usual pleasantries, and exchanged a few humorous remarks before Arthur returned to the bar.

Wright then asked, 'How are you faring, Fergus?'

'Not too bad, have been a lot worse,' said Fergus, though his eyes spoke otherwise.

They all knew, but avoided saying, Fergus would be targeted by the inquest and being a small fry, the regional health administrators would be happy to throw him to the wolves.

Fergus, reading their thoughts said, 'Jackson has been stood down, so I hear.'

'He has indeed,' said Wright. 'We have Brian to thank for that. Come on Brian don't be bashful, tell Fergus how you got the bastard.'

'Watch it, there's a lady present. That's only your first pint you know,' said Tilly.

Brian looked sheepish.

'We're waiting Brian,' said Tilly.

'Few months back, I told him the fire alarms were unreliable, should be replaced. He refused; replace one he'd have to replace the lot and dodgy wiring might be found. Didn't want the expense of replacing all that with the hospital's days numbered. I replaced the ones I knew about, regardless, but didn't know about the store room one and didn't know he'd told nurses to put the mattresses in there. After the fire I told the police, who told coroner.'

Wright added, 'The Board did something useful, stood him down, but as the police were considering charging him with two counts of manslaughter, they didn't have much choice.'

'Of course, the sod denied it,' chipped in Tilly. 'But the Board knew Brian may not say a lot but what he does say is reliable.'

'Here's to you Brian,' Fergus volunteered, raising his glass. 'You must be devastated about Jackson, Douglas,' he said grinning.

'Oh, I am, I don't know how I'm going to cope, now I don't have him to vent my spleen on.' Wright paused then asked, 'Fergus, how are you really travelling?'

'I was pretty cut up earlier, both about the loss of Horace

and Celeste and about being responsible, now they've evidence that Horace started the fire. In truth, I always knew I was taking a bit of a risk with Horace. Not that I thought he'd ever do anything that stupid, but if he did, or even if he fell over and hurt himself... you know. I can't complain; it's the luck of the draw.'

'What will you do now?' asked Tilly.

'My brother has a garage in Plymouth. I've been helping him out. I've always enjoyed tinkering with cars and now it appears cars or the clink will be my future. My brother's a good bloke, so goodbye nursing.' Fergus's voice choked. He ground to a halt, looking down into his glass. 'Don't worry. I'm fine.' He raised his glass.

Wright helped Fergus out, by asking, 'And what about you Brian? Any plans or ideas?'

'Hold on a mo', we are going to need some full glasses for this,' Matilda said standing up. 'My round. Same again everyone?'

Wright stood up, 'No, no, this is on me.'

'Here you; shut up, sit down—or else!' Tilly gave him a commanding look setting him back on his seat with no more ado. As she put the drinks down on the table, she said with pride, 'Go on Brian, tell them.'

'Got a job, permanent now—Exeter Cathedral restoration.'

'Fantastic,' Wright said, 'That was quick. How did you manage that?'

'Tilly knows the boss—surprise. He didn't want anyone from Torminster, but you know what she is.'

'Brian was given a three-week trial and they were so happy with his work they gave him the nod yesterday,' Tilly said with pride.

'What will you be doing?' asked Wright.

'All sorts. Don't have a mason's ticket but the boss said he might be able to use me as a mason with my restoration skills.'

'And how's our Doctor faring?' Tilly asked, turning to Wright.

'I can't complain either. My plans for developing community care have been cranked up. It's been a bit frantic getting the patients rehoused and putting new care systems in place, but it's also very stimulating. The Board is being remarkably helpful and generous with its funds.'

'You are becoming soft, Douglas,' said Fergus. 'Their generosity might have more to do with Simon 'Bloody' Sparks, who's done nicely out of the fire. He's already signed a contract on the remains of Torminster and plans to put a housing estate on it. You're getting tainted money, you are. Word is he got the land at a bargain rate as he agreed to clear it at his own expense and the Board didn't want the trouble.'

Wright looked up with mock surprise tinged with guilt and then changed the subject. 'That leaves you Tilly; what are your plans?'

'I don't know at this stage. It's still a bit early. The hospital was my reason for getting out of bed each day, but it was also my prison. It's almost as though I've done my time and face a new beginning.'

'The Fisher has given her parole.'

'Brian! I really don't know; I'm waiting to be called, you might say. Something will turn up. Change is afoot.'

Fergus raised his glass and said, 'Time for a toast to Horace and Celeste.' He looked about to say more but didn't, so they all raised their glasses.

Wright took a swig from his tankard, before saying,

'Dreadful, all very sad. Does anyone know how young Celeste was away from her ward that night?'

'No,' said Matilda and Fergus in unison.

'I expect you must be feeling it, Tilly. We all liked Horace, but you were the closest to Celeste. And she had done so well with Rosemary's psychotherapy.' Even the doctor sounded a bit choked mentioning their names.

'That I was—oh blast, here I go turning on the taps,' she said mopping her eyes. 'But it's not all bad. I know something which might interest you lot.' Tilly paused, with one of her looks. 'Remember the police investigation said the lock on the seclusion room door was found burnt but in the unlocked position. The bones in the room and the tests suggested Celeste must have suffocated, but the open lock remained a mystery.'

Fergus looked down at the floor, Wright looked at Matilda with interest, Brian looked awkward.

'Well, I have a friend who happens to clean the morgue. Does a good job, she does—thorough like me—or like I used to be. She knows a bit, but maybe I shouldn't divulge it, not being one to gossip.'

'Get on with it, no need to change a habit of a lifetime,' said Fergus.

'Well, she happened to tell me the investigations for the coroner have taken a twist. It turns out those bones they found are those of a male—an elderly male.'

'You don't say,' said Wright, 'Horace?'

'What other elderly male went missing that night?'

'It was Horace. And Celeste?' asked Fergus.

'Only one set of bones.'

'What about Celeste?'

'What about her indeed? No other bones have been found—a mystery—no one knows. Remember, that she told Andrew Horace was behind her, but Andrew told the police he never saw Horace. It looks like dear old Horace may have set Celeste free, but why Horace didn't leave remains anyone's guess.'

'Perhaps he couldn't live with what he'd done,' Fergus suggested.

'More likely, he wanted to go with his friends and the Fisher called him,' said Brian.

'Brian, enough. Well, Celeste wouldn't have just left him there, but those are the facts as we have them.'

'Well I never! Good for Celeste,' said Fergus, with a sad but relieved smile. 'Another toast—to Celeste.' Again, they all raised their glasses, including the doctor who wore a pensive expression.

Wright looked into his beer before looking up and adopting a formal tone. 'It's a good job this is just gossip. If it wasn't, as senior psychiatrist I might have to report Celeste as missing. After all, she's an involuntary patient on a forensic order, who has gone absent without leave.' He took a few long sips of his beer, as if deliberating. 'I was taught as a youngster that resurrections can have complex and enduring consequences.' He again paused. 'The coroner's verdict will be many months away and the investigators will hesitate to pronounce Celeste as risen from the dead, until they have firm evidence she is alive. Maybe we should leave her dead.' He drained his glass. 'I can't see how I can report a dead person as having contravened the conditions of her detention.' Give her time and who knows where she may have flown to, he added with his eyes. 'And of course, professionals don't listen to gossip about patients.'

Brian looked up, 'Not from a bloody cleaner, you'd be daft if you did.'

Death is where the weary lie.
Horace Oldham 1910-1986

Acknowledgements

Special thanks to Ian Mortimer and Jeffrey Burton Russell. Mortimer's 'The Time Traveler's Guide to Medieval England' was particularly helpful for my picturing medieval life and understanding the mentalities. I was especially fortunate that Devon, the setting of my story, features prominently in his work. Russell's Lucifer: the Devil in the Middle Ages was invaluable for my learning about attitudes to Christianity and the Devil at the time.

My thanks to Becky Cantor my wife for her patience and pertinent comments on multiple drafts; to Kathryn Ledson and Regina Acton for their help in the early stages; to Martin Gallagher for his comments in the later stages; Rose Allan for her editing and inspiration and to James Essinger for his final comments prior to publication.